A PLACE OF HOPE

Recent Titles by Anna Jacobs from Severn House

CHANGE OF SEASON
CHESTNUT LANE
THE CORRIGAN LEGACY
FAMILY CONNECTIONS
A FORBIDDEN EMBRACE
AN INDEPENDENT WOMAN
IN FOCUS
KIRSTY'S VINEYARD
LICENCE TO DREAM
MARRYING MISS MARTHA
MISTRESS OF MARYMOOR
MOVING ON
A PLACE OF HOPE
REPLENISH THE EARTH
SAVING WILLOWBROOK
SEASONS OF LOVE
THE WISHING WELL
WINDS OF CHANGE

Short Stories

SHORT AND SWEET

Anna is always delighted to hear from readers and can be contacted:

BY MAIL
PO Box 628
Mandurah
Western Australia 6210

If you'd like a reply, please enclose a self-addressed, business size envelope, stamped (from inside Australia) or an international reply coupon (from outside Australia).

VIA THE INTERNET
Anna has her own web page, with details of her books and excerpts, and invites you to visit it at http://www.annajacobs.com

Anna can be contacted by email at anna@annajacobs.com

If you'd like to receive an email newsletter about Anna and her books every month or two, you are cordially invited to join her announcements list. Just email her and ask to be added to the list, or follow the link from her web page.

A PLACE OF HOPE

Anna Jacobs

This first world edition published 2013
in Great Britain and in the USA by
SEVERN HOUSE PUBLISHERS LTD of
19 Cedar Road, Sutton, Surrey, England, SM2 5DA.

British Library Cataloguing in Publication Data

Jacobs, Anna.
A place of hope.
1. Inheritance and succession--Fiction. 2. Families--Fiction. 3. Lancashire (England)--Fiction. 4. Romantic suspense novels.
I. Title
823.9'14-dc23

ISBN-13: 978-0-7278-8256-1 (cased)
ISBN-13: 978-1-84751-471-4 (trade paper)

Typeset by Palimpsest Book Production Ltd.,
Falkirk, Stirlingshire, Scotland.
Printed and bound in Great Britain by
MPG Books Ltd., Bodmin, Cornwall.

One

Emily Mattison picked up the phone, sighing when she heard her nephew George's voice booming at her. He asked her how she was but didn't listen to her answer. 'My mother's had a bad fall. She's sprained her ankle badly and wrenched her right shoulder. She can't manage on her own, so you'll have to come and help her for a week or two.'

'I'm afraid I'm not free. I've got something important on, something I booked months ago. Aren't you with her?'

'Yes, of course. But that's only by good luck. I was about to fly back to the Middle East to wind things up with my job there. I can't let them down because there's only me with the knowledge and background to hand over properly to the new guy.'

'What about your wife? Can't she look after Liz?'

'Marcia will be needed to pack up our possessions and furniture ready to move back to England. We have to be out of our house there by a certain date. So that leaves only you to look after my mother.'

Emily hesitated. She loved her sister dearly, but didn't enjoy staying with her because they were too different. Emily loved peace and quiet, while Liz was always chattering, and had to have music on in the background all the time, whether she was listening to it or not.

'Surely you're not going to ignore your sister's need, Aunt Emily?'

He was right, the rat. She couldn't leave Liz to cope on her own. Her sister was a weak reed at the best of times. 'Oh, all right. When will you be coming back to England?'

'In a week or two, just before Easter. They're still sorting out a new posting and I have leave they're insisting I take. You know what multinational companies are like.'

No, she didn't, thank goodness. And if they employed people like her bossy nephew in senior roles, she didn't want to know. 'I'll be there this afternoon.'

'Good. Mrs Potter from next door has agreed to stay with Mother till you arrive. Our plane leaves at lunchtime. 'Bye.'

Emily suspected that he could have got time off if he'd asked for it, but for George, the job came first, second and third. He was doing all right for himself, more than all right. He'd always had an eye out for ways of making extra money. She didn't know how his wife put up with him, though. For the money, probably. Like her husband, Marcia had expensive tastes.

Emily went next door to see her friend and neighbour. 'Rach, can you keep an eye on the house for me during the next couple of weeks?'

'I thought you were only going away for one week.'

'I can't go on the course now. Liz has had a fall and needs someone to look after her.'

'Your sister has a son and daughter-in-law. Why should *you* have to give up your course? You've been looking forward to that antiques appreciation course for ages and it won't be run again till the autumn.'

'I know. Six months to wait. But George won't look after Liz whatever I decide, and I couldn't be comfortable, thinking of her on her own. She's quite frail since she had that virus which affected her heart. And anyway, would you want him around if you weren't well?'

Rachel's shudder was eloquent. 'How that man can be a relative of yours, I do not understand.'

'Liz and I don't share the same father, that's how. I always comfort myself with the thought that George gets his arrogance from Mother's first husband, not from my dad.'

Emily was on the road within the hour. She wished she'd bought the new car she was planning for, because this one was very elderly, but she just hadn't got round to it. You felt when you retired you'd have plenty of time to do things, but so far she'd been non-stop busy, getting the house smartened up, ready to sell. She wasn't sure where she was going to move, but she could put her furniture in storage and stay with her friend Rachel while she searched.

She'd retired early, at fifty-seven, as she'd always planned. She didn't miss her work – well, not much – but she still felt herself to be at a loose end, and kept wondering if she'd done the right thing. Leon certainly hadn't wanted to let her go and she missed him, too. They were still good friends. He'd been out of the country on a project but was coming back soon to head the special unit, then they'd catch up.

She went upstairs to pack. She'd been so looking forward to that antiques course. It was well known as a way of helping enthusiastic amateurs to cross into the industry. Of course, all the courses in the world wouldn't give you an eye for a bargain, but she'd done rather well with her buying and selling so far, and she truly believed she had a gift for finding pretty items that people wanted to buy.

When Emily arrived at Liz's house, Mrs Potter from next door gave her the instructions from the doctor and whispered, 'Look, I know it's none of my business, but your sister's upset about the fall and that son of hers is no help. To listen to him, you'd think she was going to be permanently bedridden and will soon need putting into a care home.'

'What? But Liz loves this cottage. She and Nigel bought it for their retirement just before he died.'

'Try telling her son that. If you ask me, George sees only the money she'd get for it, because the area's becoming so popular. And the house might be small, but it has a bigger than average garden, so would be perfect for a development project. It'd be snapped up like that one down the street.'

'Thank you for telling me.' Emily saw Mrs Potter out, then went up to her sister's bedroom. Why was Liz in bed? With a sprained ankle, she'd be perfectly all right on the sofa, watching TV.

Her sister was white and shaken, weeping at the mere sight of her. After a gentle pep talk, Emily persuaded her to come down and sit in the living room.

'George said I should stay in bed.'

'Well, George was wrong. You seem able to limp around OK.'

'I was very shaken by the fall.'

Liz seemed bewildered and dopey. Emily frowned. 'Are they giving you painkillers?'

She nodded. 'George asked the doctor to prescribe some strong ones.'

'Painkillers can make you dopey. Paracetamol might be enough. Shall we try that?'

'But George said—'

'I've told you before that your son is too bossy and you shouldn't give in to him.' But Liz always did give in to stronger personalities. Her husband had done all her thinking for her and when he died, George had taken over.

After making them both a cup of tea, Emily sat chatting to her sister. 'How did you come to fall?'

Her sister shuddered. 'I tripped over a piece of wood in the garden. I'm usually so careful but I was watching two birds at the feeder. Blue tits, they were. So pretty. I couldn't seem to get up again. Luckily Mrs Potter next door heard me calling for help and took me to hospital. I spent the night there under observation. How lucky that George was in England and could bring me home.'

'It sounds to me as if your neighbour's done most of the looking after.' Emily couldn't keep a sharp note out of her voice. 'And George hasn't *stayed* with you, has he?'

But Liz could never see anything wrong in what her son did. 'He can't let the company down. He's such a good son. Since Nigel died, he's taken care of all the business stuff for me. I can't tell you what a load that is off my mind.'

Emily changed the subject as soon as she could. She and Liz would never see eye-to-eye about the way her nephew had taken over his mother's life . . . and her finances. She suspected he was keeping Liz short of money, too, giving her only enough to live on as long as she was careful, yet Nigel had told Emily once that his wife would be extremely comfortable if anything happened to him.

Oh, well. What was the old saying their mother used to trot out? *There are none so blind as those who won't see.*

A few days later George went through his mother's mail, which had been forwarded to him in the Middle East as usual. 'My aunt's neighbour must be forwarding her mail to my mother's house and of course they've come on to me.'

Marcia looked up from doing her nails. 'You'd better phone your aunt and apologize.'

'I might as well check them first to see if there's anything urgent.'

'You can't open her mail!'

He grinned. 'Oh, can't I? I'll only open anything that looks interesting, though. I can say I didn't check the address and thought it was one of my mother's letters.' A moment later he waved an envelope. 'This one is from a law firm in Lancashire. I wonder what they want with my aunt.'

Marcia rolled her eyes and went on filing her nails.

George read the letter, exclaiming, 'Good heavens!' Then he read it again.

By that time his wife had put down the nail file and was waiting to find out what he'd discovered.

'This is from a lawyer in Littleborough. Remember that old cousin of Emily's father? We met her once, Penelope Mattison?'

'Not really.'

'Wizened old thing, rather eccentric, lived in a tumbledown place on the edge of the moors. Anyway, it seems she's died and left everything to my aunt.'

'Lucky Emily. She'll really be able to enjoy her retirement now, won't she?'

He pulled a face. 'I suppose she'll fritter it away on those blasted antiques she loves so much. Wait a minute! There's another letter enclosed.'

A minute later, he exclaimed, 'I don't believe this!'

Marcia waited.

'A local developer wants the land and has made an offer for it.' He whistled. 'And a very juicy offer it is, too.' He sat tapping his fingers on the table for a few moments. 'I must persuade my aunt to let me deal with this. She has no idea of business and she's far too soft to bargain well.'

'I don't think she'll let you handle her affairs, George. She's not like your mother.' Marcia looked at her watch. 'Do you want to ring her now, tell her about her inheritance?'

'No. I'm going to think about it. Time enough to tell her when we get back, anyway. We're going in a few days.'

'George, you really ought to let your aunt know her mail has come here by mistake.'

His voice took on an edge. 'Stay out of this, Marcia. I'm the money person, not you.'

'But it's not your money.'

He smiled. 'It will be one day. I'll make sure of that. After all, who else is there to inherit but me, her only nephew? And if she's paying someone to manage her money, why not keep it in the family? I'm really good with money.'

'You can't be sure her money will come to you, and anyway, she's very young for her age.'

'She hasn't got any other close relatives to leave it to.'

Marcia shook her head but didn't protest any more. When George got that tone in his voice, best to leave him to do whatever he thought right.

She couldn't see Emily agreeing to let him manage the money, though. Emily was very different from her sister. Confident and self-contained.

Two weeks after her accident, Liz was feeling a lot better and Emily was itching to get back home.

When the phone rang, Emily tried to read her book till Liz had finished, but couldn't help overhearing.

'How lovely!' Her sister beamed with delight as she put down the phone. 'George and Marcia will be coming back to England tomorrow and they want to stay here with me for a day or two.'

Too late for me to attend the course, Emily thought. Liz could have paid someone to help her with the housework and let her go to the course, but she'd begged her sister to stay.

'I'll go home first thing tomorrow and leave the spare bedroom ready for them. I have a lot of things to do and you'll be all right for a few hours with Mrs Potter next door.'

'Yes, I will. And George will be living permanently in England from now on, which is such a comfort. I can't tell you how grateful I am for your help, Emily dear. I don't know what I'd have done without you.'

'You're welcome.'

'I'm really looking forward to spending more time with them. Marcia is such a capable woman and always so kind to me, the best of daughters-in-law. Sometimes only women understand how you feel. Dear George thinks everyone enjoys his own robust health. He's *so* like his father.'

For about the hundredth time, Emily held back the words she

really wanted to say: *for goodness' sake, stand on your own feet, Liz Pilby, and stop letting George run your life!*

The following day she was ready to leave by the time her sister got up.

'I don't know how you can do so much this early in the day,' Liz complained. 'Surely you've time to sit down and have a cup of tea with me first?'

Stifling a sigh, Emily joined her at the little table in the kitchen.

As soon as she could, she stood up. 'I'll just go and fetch the rest of my things from the bedroom, then I'll be off. I've changed the sheets for George and Marcia, and put the others on to wash.'

'You're very efficient. Like my George.'

Hah! If she thought she was anything like her nephew, she'd go and see a psychiatrist!

When she came down, Liz was looking worried. 'I think you'd better stay here tonight after all, dear. I just heard on the radio that there's going to be a bad storm later on.'

Emily couldn't bear the thought of spending another night in the small, cluttered cottage, where every sound echoed up the stair well. 'Oh, I'll be home before the storm breaks, I'm sure.'

She set off, feeling happier the minute she turned out of the street. She hadn't told Liz, but she'd arranged to have lunch with an old friend from work who lived half an hour's drive away. Knowing Jan, it'd be late afternoon before she got on the road again, but it'd be lovely to catch up.

It was even later than Emily had expected when she left Jan's house, but it'd only take her an hour or two to get back to Kings Langley.

The sky grew dark rapidly and the storm hit suddenly. Soon rain was beating down on the small car and visibility was poor. A traffic announcement interrupted the radio programme to blare out the information that there was a bad hold-up on the M25 due to a multiple car pile-up. Drivers were urged to avoid that stretch of the motorway until further notice.

Emily groaned as she heard the junction numbers involved. That was the route she'd intended to take. The traffic was always slow there, so the hold-up must be bad to warrant an announcement like that. She stopped at the first lay-by to program her satnav to cut across country by the most direct route.

Bad mistake. She soon realized it wasn't a night to be driving such an elderly vehicle along narrow country roads, but there was nowhere convenient to stop to reprogram the satnav. She should have specified major roads to get her round the problem area. What if she broke down out here in the middle of nowhere?

A loud clap of thunder made her jump, and was it her imagination or was there a roughness to the engine's sound? Perhaps she should try to find a hotel or a bed and breakfast?

Headlights suddenly dazzled her. She looked in the rear view mirror, annoyed to find a car following her closely. Far too closely, especially in this weather! She pressed lightly on the brakes to warn it to stay back, but it drew even closer.

It was raining so hard, she couldn't see clearly what the idiot was doing and cried out in shock as the much bigger car suddenly pulled closer and deliberately nudged her vehicle, sending it dangerously close to the verge. She thumped her horn several times, yelling, 'Get back, you lunatic!'

It came close and nudged her car again.

She braked to let the idiot go past, which was presumably what the driver wanted, but he slowed down to match her speed, horn blaring. Now she was puzzled, as well as angry. What was the driver trying to do? She'd read in the papers of hooligans getting their kicks from nudging other cars, but had never expected to be the target of such an assault.

She braked harder, but not in time to stop the bigger vehicle thumping into hers again. As she struggled to keep control, it bumped into her hard enough to send her car careering right off the road.

She let out an involuntary shriek and braked hard, only just managing to avoid ramming a signpost. Her car came to an abrupt halt at an upwards angle on a muddy slope. For a moment she could only sit there, too shocked to think straight.

When she looked round, she saw the big car slow down ahead, sounding its horn and flashing its headlights on and off.

It was as if it was celebrating running her off the road.

Then it speeded up and vanished.

Her car radio was still playing, so she switched it off, but left the engine running, worried it might not start again. She tried to reverse slowly back on to the road, but her wheels spun in the mud and she couldn't gain any traction.

She pulled out her mobile phone to dial for assistance. Just then another vehicle came into view, slowing down as its headlights caught her car in their beam. It drew up where she'd gone off the road.

A man jumped out of the passenger side, coming to peer through her side window. He was about her own age, but not until a grey-haired woman got out of the driver's side and came to join them did Emily feel it was safe to let down her window. Well, she let it down a few inches, then it stuck.

'You all right, love?'

'Yes. Just a bit shocked.'

'Accidents do that to you.'

'Accidents!' She told him about the lunatic who'd done this to her.

He gaped at her. 'Someone did this on purpose?'

'Yes. Definitely.'

'I've read about it in the papers,' his companion said. She looked at Emily with sympathy. 'Joy riders daring each other to shove people off the road. The police are looking for them, but they steal cars to do it in then vanish.'

'Did you get their number?' he asked.

'What good would that do if the car was stolen? Anyway, I couldn't see the number plate or even tell the make, except that it was a big four-wheel drive.'

'Still, you're not hurt, that's the main thing. Let's see if we can get you back on the road.'

'I think the car's stuck.' She tried again to reverse with the same result.

'Good thing I carry a tow rope.' He turned and saw his companion already holding it out. 'Thanks, love.'

He was very efficient and soon had Emily's car back on the road, by which time they were both soaked.

'There are some bad dents, so you're going to need major work on the body, but the engine sounds all right.'

'I doubt it's worth bothering to repair the car. I was going to get a new one anyway.'

'Have you far to go?'

She sighed. 'Further than I care to drive on a night like this. I'm still shaky. I think I'll look for a hotel. I can't thank you enough for your help.'

He shrugged. 'It's a poor person who passes by when someone's in trouble. I'll follow you for a while to make sure you're all right and that no other lunatics waylay you on these quiet roads.'

Emily drove slowly away and the couple followed her. When they reached a wider road with other traffic, they gave a toot of the horn and passed her.

This was definitely the last time she took a short cut along minor roads in the dark. Last time ever! What was the world coming to when hooligans deliberately tried to cause accidents?

Soon afterwards, she saw a lighted sign indicating a hotel and turned off the road into its car park. There were only a few other vehicles there. She looked round carefully before she unlocked her car door, but they were smaller than the one which had rammed her.

She grabbed her suitcase and ran across to the hotel, getting soaked over even that short distance. The place was small and looked rather run down, but it seemed clean and it'd do for one night. She didn't want to drive on through the storm, which seemed to be getting worse by the minute.

A bored receptionist signed her in and pointed out the lift, then picked up a mobile phone and continued to chat to a friend.

If I was the manager here, Emily thought angrily, I'd soon improve customer service!

She found her room easily enough. It was on the second floor, very basic: bed, TV, chair and the tiniest possible en suite bathroom. Wind gusts shook the window frame and the door rattled in sympathy. It sounded as if someone was trying to get in and she went across to double check that she'd locked the door.

She winced as lightning flashed outside, followed by a clap of thunder so loud it hurt her ears. Thank goodness she hadn't continued driving in such a bad storm. She checked the information folder. First things first. She'd better go downstairs and get something to eat before the café closed.

The lights flickered, then flickered again. She grimaced, praying there wouldn't be a power cut, because her torch was in the car. So was her computer and she wasn't going out to get it now.

She opened the door to check where the stairs were, finding them round the corner from the lift. The stairs were broad and elegant, Edwardian probably, but this corridor had only one light and the carpet was badly frayed in several places. In fact, the whole hotel felt like a set for filming a ghost movie.

She went back into the room, stared at herself in the mirror and sighed. No use trying to do more than tidy her hair. It'd been thoroughly soaked and was a flattened mess. Wrapping a pashmina over her cardigan, she set off for the café.

As she walked out into the corridor, the lights flickered again. She was definitely not taking the lift, didn't want to risk being trapped in it if the power failed.

Just as she got to the top of the stairs, the lights went out completely and she stopped moving. 'Damn!' she muttered under her breath. She stood still, hoping the electricity would come on again. But the seconds ticked slowly past and the lights stayed off.

She could see a faint glow coming from below, so decided to make her way downstairs by feel. After five steps, she turned the corner of the stairs, but caught her shoe heel in a frayed patch of carpet. She fell forward and reached out in the darkness for something to catch hold of.

She lost her balance, scrabbled desperately for the hand rail but her shoe wouldn't come free of the carpet, so she missed it. Everything seemed to happen in slow motion. She continued to fall, her body twisting in the air and thumping into a wall so violently it knocked the breath out of her.

As she tumbled helplessly on, she hit her head on something, crying out involuntarily from the sharp pain. Then darkness swallowed her . . .

Two

George picked up the phone, listened intently then said, 'I'm Emily Mattison's nephew. I'd be the closest relative in that sense. My mother is her sister, but she's too frail to deal with this.'

His wife and mother turned to stare at him in shock.

'Oh, dear!' He shook his head sadly. 'Yes, of course I'll come and see you. Tomorrow. Yes, I'll bring some clothes. Thank you.'

He put the phone down. 'Aunt Emily has been in an accident. She's in hospital in a coma. I think it'll be better if I go to see her first and deal with the formalities, Mother. You can go later, when we're sure she's going to survive.'

His mother gasped for air, then her eyes rolled up and she fell sideways on the couch.

Marcia quickly felt for a pulse. 'Just one of her faints, I think.'

'It's a good thing she has us to look after her. And now Emily is going to need our help, too.' He smiled at his wife. 'It's a good thing I didn't worry her with this property offer and inheritance stuff, isn't it? I'll take care of all that for her . . . if she recovers, she'll be very grateful.'

'*If?* Is she that badly hurt?'

'I'm afraid so.' He smiled again as he said it.

When Emily woke, she had trouble opening her eyes. A machine began beeping and she turned her head slightly to look towards it. She was hooked up to a monitor. Lights were flashing and the beeping hurt her head.

She must be in hospital. What had happened? She couldn't remember.

A face appeared beside her and with a struggle, she focused on it. A woman. A nurse.

'Emily?'

There was something in her throat and she could only manage a faint noise in response.

'Don't try to speak. Blink if you can understand me.'

She did that.

'Blink three times.'

By concentrating hard, she succeeded in doing this.

'Well done. You're in hospital because you had an accident. You fell down some stairs. Blink twice if you understand.'

She managed that.

'Excellent.' The nurse turned to look at the monitor again and spoke to someone nearby. 'Her vitals are improving.'

More discussion which Emily didn't manage to follow, then, 'I reckon she'll be able to breathe on her own soon.'

The words made little sense. The last thing she remembered was saying goodbye to her sister Liz.

She gave up trying to work it out. She was too tired.

The beeping was a comfort now. It proved she was still alive.

The next time she regained consciousness, Emily felt much more comfortable. The tube had gone from her throat, thank goodness.

'Emily? Are you awake?'

She turned her head and saw a young woman in nurse's uniform. 'What . . . happened?' Her voice sounded strange, a monotone, not at all like hers.

'You fell down some stairs and ended up in hospital. You've not broken anything, but you were knocked unconscious. Could you tell me your first name, please?'

'Em'ly.'

'Where do you live?'

'Kings . . . Langl'y.'

She couldn't manage to ask the questions she wanted to. Tears of frustration formed in her eyes and ran down her cheeks. She couldn't even raise her hand to wipe them away.

The nurse did it for her. 'You're going to be all right, Emily. Try to keep calm. Just give it a little time.'

She frowned, trying to remember falling. But she couldn't. She had no memory of it, none whatsoever.

The soothing voice said quietly, 'Try to rest now, Emily. You've done really well today. We're very pleased with your progress.'

Jane watched her patient for a moment or two, feeling hopeful now of at least a partial recovery. You could never be sure with coma patients, though. Making a quick note on Emily's records of what had just happened, she went back to the nurses' station.

When the phone rang, she sighed, hoping it wasn't another admission.

'Intensive Care Unit.'

'Reception. We have someone here who says he's Emily Mattison's nephew. He's insisting on seeing her straight away. Can I send him up?'

'I suppose so. She's asleep, though.'

A couple of minutes later Jane heard the lift ping as it stopped. A burly man with close-shaven receding hair and what looked like expensive clothes stopped for a moment to look round, then strode towards the desk as if he owned the place.

'May I help you?'

'George Pilby. I gather you have my aunt here – Emily Mattison. I'm her closest relative. I was told she's regained consciousness.'

'I thought her closest relative was her sister?'

'That's my mother, who's rather frail, so I came to see my aunt instead.'

Not *can I see her?* Jane noted. 'You can only see her for a moment. She's not fully conscious yet.'

'Is she in her right mind?'

What a way to put it! 'Your aunt answered to her name and asked what happened, so we're very hopeful.'

'Did she remember the accident?'

'No. But that means nothing. It's quite common with head injuries and comas.'

'At her age, the memory loss can't be good. And anyway, she was showing signs of becoming forgetful before it happened. Growing old is so sad.'

Old! The woman was fifty-eight, according to her driving licence. Jane didn't consider that to be old and anyway, Miss Mattison didn't look anything like her age. Her face was quite pretty, even with the bruises, and her dark brown hair was only lightly greying at the temples.

She accompanied Mr Pilby to the cubicle where Emily was being cared for, her vital signs still monitored night and day.

He stood looking down at his aunt, showing no signs of being upset, merely studying her carefully. 'Will she regain her senses?'

Jane hurried him away from the bed. Who knew what coma patients could and could not hear? 'We can't tell yet, but it's likely she'll recover completely.'

'Hmm.' He stared round. 'How long will she be here?'

'A few more days perhaps, then she'll be taken to a rehab unit for a week or two.'

'It might be kinder if she died than if she recovered to face Alzheimer's.'

'We try to help all our patients to recover. And I've already told you that means nothing at this stage.'

'But you'll put on her records about my poor aunt Emily already having some problems. I don't want anyone nagging her and upsetting her with questions she doesn't understand.'

'Yes, I'll put it on her records.'

'I'll phone every day. It's not worth coming again until she's properly conscious.'

Jane watched him leave, glad she wasn't dependent on help from such an unfeeling person.

When George got back to his mother's house, he took her into the living room and sat next to her, taking her hand and patting it.

She looked at him apprehensively. 'Emily's not . . . dead?'

'No. She may even recover, though in what condition they're not sure. The accident is quite likely to trigger dementia, I'm afraid.'

Liz gasped and put one hand across her mouth. 'Oh, no! Not Emily! She's always been so clever. I *must* go and see her for myself.'

'Not yet. She isn't fully conscious. I don't want you exhausting yourself unnecessarily. I think I'd better go and check her house, see that everything is all right there. Oh, and I need to get her car back. It's apparently still in the hotel car park, so the key must be there. It wasn't in her handbag with her house keys. Marcia and I will pick the car up on the way to Kings Langley.'

'That's very kind of you, George dear. Don't forget to tell her neighbour who you are. She's called Rachel Fenwick and she has a key to the house as well.'

'I'll do that.'

The following day George and Marcia set off after breakfast for Kings Langley.

'We should be house hunting on our own behalf today,' she grumbled. 'I've had to cancel today's appointments.'

'We might not need to go house hunting. Someone has to keep an eye on my aunt's place, so if it's at all decent, we can move in. It'll save paying rent for a few weeks, if nothing else. It's quite easy to get to London from there. I looked it up on line. About twenty miles, with a station nearby.'

'But how can we? Your aunt's in no condition to give permission.'

'Exactly. So she can't refuse us. Besides, we'll be doing her a favour, taking care of her house. You're a wonderful manager. I'm sure you'll be able to bring it up to scratch. Old people never keep their houses nice.'

'I don't regard your aunt as old. She's very young for her age.'

'You didn't see her in hospital. She looks dreadful, as if she's aged ten years. We'll make a detour to pick up her car. Which do you want to drive? This one or hers?'

'This one.'

Later, when they both drew up outside Emily's house, he got out of his aunt's car and studied the place.

Marcia joined him. 'It's quite pretty.'

'Bigger than I'd expected, too,' George said. 'Much bigger than Mother's house. My aunt probably has some decent retirement money. She's never been a big spender. Let's hope it's not old-fashioned inside. We'd better go and get the key from this neighbour.'

'I thought you had a key.'

'I do. But I don't want the neighbour coming in to poke around our things while we're out, so I'll pretend I haven't got a key.' He strode down the path of the house next door, ignoring his wife's sigh.

The woman who opened the door to him seemed to be around his aunt's age. She needed to lose a few pounds and dress to suit her years, he thought disapprovingly. He'd not let his wife get so porky.

'You must be Rachel. I'm George Pilby, Emily's nephew. I believe you have a key to her house.'

'Yes. Is Emily worse? I've been worrying about her since Liz phoned to say she'd been in an accident. Your aunt usually keeps in touch.'

'My aunt has been in a coma, and it's not certain she'll recover.'

Tears filled Rachel's eyes. 'Oh, no! Where is she? I must go and see her.'

He shook his head. 'I'm afraid not. It's only close family at the moment and anyway, she's still not fully conscious. They've yet to find out whether there's been any brain damage.'

She looked at him in horror. 'Emily? I can't believe it.'

'We'll have to hope for the best. Whatever the outcome, she'll be in rehab for some weeks.'

'Please tell me as soon as she's able to have visitors. Where is she exactly? I'll send a get well card and flowers.'

'I'll let you know when it's worth making contact. In the meantime, my wife and I will be staying here to keep an eye on her house, so if you can let me have the key . . .'

'Of course.' Rachel went inside and came back with the key. 'The mail is on the hall table. Emily asked me to forward her mail to her sister's for a couple of weeks then keep it here.'

He took the key and walked away quickly. What a busybody! He hated neighbours who tried to live in your pocket.

The less this one knew about his aunt, the less she could interfere with his plans. He'd tell the hospital to allow no visitors except for him.

George smiled at Marcia and waggled the key, then went to open the front door of his aunt's house. He'd not visited it before, because she'd always come to his mother's, so he'd seen no point in going to her place as well during his brief visits to the UK.

They walked round in silence, then stood in the kitchen.

'Perfect,' he said. 'Smaller than I'd like, but nicely laid out and the furniture's good. She has some nice-looking antiques. I must check them out on line.'

'The house has a nice feel to it.'

'Yes. We'll move in tomorrow. I'm getting a little tired of sleeping in that uncomfortable bed at my mother's and sharing a bathroom with her.'

'Will your mother be all right on her own? Perhaps we should bring her here with us?'

'And perhaps we shouldn't. She'll be fine. She's coped perfectly well on her own while I've been overseas, after all.'

He picked up the mail from the hall table and started going through it. 'Ah! Another letter from that lawyer chappie.' He slit it open and read it, smiling. 'I'll have to let him know that I'll be taking charge of negotiating with the property developer.'

'But what if your aunt doesn't want to sell her new house? Anyway, you don't have power of attorney over her affairs.'

He scowled at her. 'I can still negotiate the sale and once it's clear that she's not going to recover, I'll get a power of attorney.'

'I'm always amazed at how directly you go for something when you want it.'

'It's the best way.'

'What if your aunt recovers?'

'I don't think she will. We shall have to wait and see.'

He stared out across the gardens. He'd planted a few seeds about his aunt's mental health being doubtful. He'd find a way to plant more. She was bound to be confused when she came out of the coma. Maybe he could ask for her to be sedated.

It'd solve a lot of problems if she didn't recover. His mother would inherit, surely? If she didn't, she could contest the will.

There was always a way to get something if you wanted it badly enough. You just had to find it and pay people, if necessary, to help you bend the rules.

He'd look after his aunt, of course. And his mother. Make sure they had everything they needed. But older people were best living simply and quietly. Everyone knew that.

The next day George went to the hospital again. On his own. He made his way to intensive care. 'How is my aunt?'

'Still drifting in and out of consciousness, I'm afraid, Mr Pilby.'

'I'll go and see her.'

By the time the nurse had caught up with him, he was standing next to his aunt. 'She looks worse than last time.'

The sister gaped at him. 'She's recovering well.'

'She doesn't look well to me.'

'Please don't say such negative things in front of her, Mr Pilby. We never know how much coma patients hear and understand, especially those who are recovering.' She slipped round to the other side and spoke to the patient, as he should have done. 'Your nephew's here, Emily.'

'I'm here to look after you, Auntie dear,' he boomed. 'Don't worry. They think they can help you.'

The patient opened her eyes with a start, focused on him and frowned. 'Go 'way, George.'

Jane didn't allow herself to smile. From the patient's expression, it was clear that George wasn't a favourite relative. As for what he was saying, well, she had to wonder if he was deliberately trying to scare his aunt.

She'd seen everything in her job, from loving families to ones who couldn't wait for their elderly relative to die. The latter weren't always averse to nudging them along a bit, either. This guy definitely wasn't the loving type. Was he one of the dangerous ones? She'd have to keep her eye on Ms Mattison whenever he visited.

'Mother's asked Marcia and me to move into your house, Auntie, to keep an eye on it until you're able to go home. It's very convenient, because we've not found anywhere to buy in England yet.'

Jane could see her patient getting agitated and struggling to respond, so moved to his side. 'You'd better leave now, Mr Pilby. You're upsetting her.'

He shrugged and allowed himself to be led away, not attempting a word of farewell or encouragement to his aunt. 'I need to speak to her doctor now. See how disabled she's going to be. This might make the dementia worse.'

'I think Dr Spenser is still on the ward. Yes, there he is.'

Jane handed Mr Pilby over with relief, but could hear him haranguing poor Dr Spenser in the interview room right from the other end of the corridor.

That man was definitely hoping his aunt would not recover, she decided, presumably because he expected to inherit.

He seemed to have taken over his aunt's house without anyone's permission! It wasn't Jane's business to interfere, but she felt sorry for Emily Mattison, she really did.

The next time Emily woke, she felt more herself. There was no beeping apparatus beside the bed and she was hungry. She eyed the tube and stand, wondering what was being dripped into her arm, because she felt very dopey.

The nurse she'd seen before came in.

'Good morning. How are you feeling today, Emily?'

'Better. Hungry.'

'That's good. I'll get you a light breakfast.'

'How long . . . here?' To her dismay, Emily could only speak in short bursts.

'You've been here for two weeks.'

'Two!' Emily swallowed hard. 'What's wrong . . . with me?'

'You fell down some stairs and hit your head. You were in a coma for a few days, but you're recovering well.'

'Can't . . . speak prop'ly.'

'That's normal. Your brain's still getting used to being awake. Your speech will gradually improve.'

'How long . . . stay here?'

'The doctor will discuss that after he's examined you. Let me make you more comfortable then we'll get some food into you.'

Emily let them help her, obediently swallowing some sloppy porridge. When she was on her own, she tried to practise speaking and moving parts of her body, even if it was only a little bit. She was terrified of remaining like this. Her voice was a toneless monotone, not sounding at all like her, and she couldn't think clearly.

But she could remember George's visit. Oh, yes. And was furious every time she thought of him living in her house. Only she was helpless at the moment to get him out. He might have taken over his mother's life – and finances – but he wasn't going to take over hers.

A doctor came in, looking tired. He asked some simple questions and assured her she was making a good recovery, so she repeated the important question.

'How long . . . stay here?'

'Not long. We'll transfer you to a rehabilitation unit soon.'

'How long . . . there?'

'With head injuries, there are no hard and fast rules, so I can't be specific. A few weeks, probably.'

The thought of that horrified her. 'No. Go home. Go *home*.'

'You couldn't cope, Miss Mattison.'

'Ms.' She hated being called Miss. It reminded her of school and spinster teachers. She always made a point of being addressed as Ms.

His voice was impatient. 'Does that matter now?' He glanced down at her notes. 'Your nephew is looking after things for you, so you have nothing to worry about. Just concentrate on getting better.'

'Don't want George . . . in my house.' But the words came out garbled and the doctor was already turning away.

She wished her sister would come to see her. She knew Liz

cared about her. George didn't seem to care about anyone except himself, and to a lesser extent, his wife. He'd always been money-hungry and would have pounced on the opportunity to get free accommodation at Emily's house, she was sure. He'd probably poke through her things, but at least he wouldn't damage her possessions.

She sighed and closed her eyes. It was so hard to think clearly and she got tired very quickly. She loathed feeling helpless, wanted her mind to be sharp and active again.

One thing she was determined about. She wasn't going to stay in hospital for one day longer than necessary. She'd always been independent and that wasn't going to change now.

The doctor went on to see the sister. 'I think we ought to send Miss Mattison to the geriatric rehabilitation unit.'

'She's not all that old,' Jane protested.

'No, but the nephew said she was showing signs of early dementia before this happened.'

'Ms Mattison seems to me to be thinking as clearly as can be expected at this stage of her recovery.'

'She's got you calling her Ms as well, has she?' he said sourly.

'She certainly has. It's what she prefers.' She scowled at him. 'And it's what I prefer too, actually.'

He sighed and ignored that, his eyes challenging her to protest again as he continued, 'But we don't know Miss Mattison, do we, and the nephew does? Besides, the rehab unit is overflowing. She's the second patient I've had to send to geriatric care this month. There was a fellow beaten up so badly he's lost his memory.'

You didn't argue with a busy doctor, not unless you were stupid. And this one wasn't the most communicative of men at the best of times, especially with women.

Jane sighed, but began to make arrangements as instructed. Once patients left your care, you were not responsible for them. And it was unprofessional to care for some more than others.

But she wasn't happy about the situation, or the way they were treating Emily Mattison. And she knew the sister of the geriatric unit, didn't envy Emily being in care there. Pauline had a 'keep them quiet at all costs' attitude.

* * *

You read about it in books, but you never expected to lose your memory. He was way out of it with painkillers when he first regained consciousness. He seemed to have been in an accident. All he could mutter when they asked his name was that he couldn't remember.

He woke up a couple of mornings later and they asked him if he'd remembered anything more. He *knew* somehow that he was called Chad, and told them that, but could give them no reason for this, let alone his surname. 'What's wrong with me?'

'Post-traumatic amnesia,' the nurse said briskly. 'They're trying to find out who you are, but no one of your age has been reported missing.'

'Will my memories come back?'

'No one can tell, I'm afraid.'

The next day he was more alert and they doled out some more information about his case. Apparently he'd been featured in the local paper but no one had come forward to identify him. They couldn't use a photo, because his face had been too battered and bruised.

He couldn't stop thinking about it, desperate to find himself. Did he have no family at all? And where were his possessions?

'Your pockets were empty,' the nurse named Jackson told him.

'Had I been robbed?'

Jackson could only shrug. 'Who knows? Concentrate on getting better and worry about the rest later.'

All right for someone else to say that. It was terrifying to lose your memory, your very identity. And you felt so helpless.

Three days later they told Emily they were transferring her to the rehab unit, taking her by ambulance because it was in a separate building on the far side of the campus. She was still not speaking normally but she was thinking more clearly each day, and thank goodness she was starting to walk, or rather, shuffle along.

They wouldn't let her walk without someone in attendance, though, and it still took a conscious effort to keep putting one foot in front of the other.

It was hugely frustrating and she felt as if she was going mad from boredom.

In the new unit, she found herself sharing a room with an old woman who'd suffered a major stroke, and wondered why they'd sent the poor thing here for rehab, when it seemed clear even to Emily that her companion was not likely to recover.

The room was depressing, looking out on to a blank wall. And sharing with someone who wasn't really conscious made Emily want to run for her life – only she couldn't even walk properly.

The nurse in charge of the unit introduced herself as Sister Pauline. She was brisk and efficient but not given to chatting with patients, as Jane had done, or even listening to them properly. She talked loudly and slowly, treating all her patients like halfwits.

When Emily was alone – well, as alone as you could be in a hospital – she felt tears trickling down her face.

'Emily? Is something wrong?'

She turned to see another nurse, a man this time, dark-skinned, with a lovely smile. Then something she'd seen from the ambulance came back to her, something which had puzzled her. 'What is this place called, please?'

'The Geriatric Care Unit.'

'I'm not a geriatric! I'm not even sixty.'

'But you do need rehabilitation and as they were short of beds in the main rehab unit, they sent you here. You're not the only one.' He gestured towards a man sitting slumped in a wheelchair in the day room, which was just opposite Emily's room.

'Still not right,' she grumbled.

'Then we'll have to work hard and get you home quickly. My name's Jackson, by the way. That's my first name. I'm a specialist rehab nurse. Do you feel up to trying a few things now, so that I can start to assess your needs?'

'Yes. Please, yes. Work hard.'

'That's the right attitude.' His voice softened. 'You're already doing well, Emily, and I promise you, I'm not making that up. Someone wrote on your notes that you're speaking better and in less of a monotone, and starting to move more naturally.'

'Am I . . . sedated?'

He hesitated. 'Just a little.'

'Don't want it. Hate feeling dopey.'

'Only for a day or two longer, hmm?'

Not if she could help it. If they didn't pull that drip out soon, she was going to rip it out herself.

But she was tired again, dammit, so when Jackson had finished with her, she gave in and closed her eyes for a little rest.

Three

George came to visit Emily at the new unit the next day. She'd just finished her exercises and been looking forward to a rest when he marched up to the bed. He began talking to her loudly and slowly, in the same patronizing tone as Sister Pauline.

Oh, how she hated that tone of voice! Being older didn't automatically equate to losing your wits.

'Don't worry about your house, Auntie dear. Marcia and I are keeping things going. She loves gardening and she'll soon get the place in order.'

Auntie dear! He'd hardly been near her for years, had just sent printed Christmas cards with a scrawl for a signature and no message.

'Don't want you . . . in my house . . . George.'

He laughed as if she were a silly child. 'You're not thinking straight, Auntie. Only to be expected. You needed someone to look after the place. It was very run down, and too much for you to manage at your age, anyway.'

'Not necessary. My neighbour can . . . keep an eye on things . . . till I get back.'

'Mrs Fenwick? She's had to go away. An illness in the family. I forget who, but someone close to her. No, you definitely need our help and we're happy to give it.'

She stared at him. He'd just told her an outright lie. Rachel next door didn't have any close family in England because her only son had emigrated to Australia a couple of years ago. She was very upset about that.

But Emily couldn't think how to get George out of her house at the moment, because the sister in charge of this unit refused even to discuss it. She kept insisting that Emily wasn't thinking clearly yet and should be glad there was someone willing to look after her house.

Sister Pauline's motto seemed to be to keep the patients under firm control and above all quiet. And physically Emily was reasonably well looked after, she had to admit. But she was going mad from boredom.

She didn't have much to watch, except for the man in the day room.

He was watching her, too. He waved at her every morning and smiled sometimes. But when the nurses came round, he slumped in his wheelchair and said very little. This puzzled Emily.

Once they took the drip out, she asked what the tablet they gave her morning and evening was.

'It's necessary for your recovery. If you don't take it, we'll have to put the drip back.'

Emily looked at the sister's determined face and put the tablet in her mouth, swallowing some water but keeping the tablet in the side of her mouth.

As soon as she was alone, she spat it out. As she did this, she looked up and saw the man raise one thumb to her, a signal that said he approved of what she was doing. Strange.

She started feeling less dopey as the day passed, but was getting angry now. How dare they continue to sedate her like this?

The following day she asked if anyone had seen her handbag.

'I'll release it to you tomorrow, if you maintain progress,' Sister said.

The following day Emily got it back, minus her purse and mobile phone, so asked about them.

'Oh, your nephew took those, to keep them safe. Very wise, too.'

So Emily asked George to return them and he refused point blank. She wanted to throw a tantrum – oh, she'd have loved to do that – but kept her emotions tightly bottled up. She wasn't going to give them any excuse for assuming she was hysterical and sedating her more strongly.

If it hadn't been for Jackson, she didn't know what she'd have done. He came and chatted to her, switched on the TV, and went through some gentle exercises with her several times a day.

The man in the day room was now starting to get up and walk around, but only when the nurses weren't in the vicinity. When he saw Emily watching him, he put one finger to his lips and she nodded to show she understood.

One day Jackson brought a magazine for her to read, but that made her weep, because the words might have been gibberish, for all the black squiggles meant.

He took Emily's hand. 'It's normal to have trouble reading for a while after a coma. I did warn you just to let your eyes get used to looking at pictures. Why don't you watch TV instead? Your nephew has paid for it for you.'

Reluctantly. Only when she'd threatened to create a fuss. It was her money, not his.

After George left her, she'd seen his reflection in the glass windows of the day room. He'd stopped to talk to Pauline in the corridor, then had gone into her office and they'd shut the door. Why? What had they been saying about her?

She realized her mind had wandered off and turned back to Jackson. 'Sorry. I was just remembering something.'

'I was saying that your body is still recovering, which includes your eyesight and neural connections. Give it time. You're doing really well, I promise you, unlike your poor roommate.'

They wheeled the barely conscious woman away that very evening, murmuring about 'intensive care'. But Emily had seen the look of death before. She wasn't frightened of it, but she damned well wasn't going down that track herself. She had a lot of things she wanted to do with her life now that she'd taken early retirement. She'd more than earned it.

And why wouldn't they let her go beyond this stretch of corridor in her short walks? She wanted to go and sit in the day room, at least, where she could talk to other patients. There weren't many people in there, but the man who waved to her was about her age. He looked alert yet frustrated. He had the yellowing remains of bruises on his face and hands, so perhaps he too had been in an accident. It must have been a bad one if the bruises had lasted so long.

She couldn't understand the lack of people moving around till she realized this was a locked unit, with nurses keying in a code to get in and out. Patients weren't allowed out on their own at all.

Why not?

Well, at least the fog in her brain had cleared now she'd stopped taking the tablets, though she still pretended to be a bit dopey, so as not to make them suspicious.

It took her a few more days to realize there was something wrong about this unit. She didn't say this to anyone. Until she was able to function independently, until she had more idea what was going on here, she felt safer keeping her thoughts to herself. She'd learned that sort of caution in a strange situation in her former job.

The man in the day room must have felt the same. He pretended to be dopey whenever nurses were around, even Jackson, so Emily did the same.

She was beginning to worry about her future. They were still refusing to give her a date to go home, not even a vague estimate.

Something was very wrong here. And she was helpless to do anything about it.

When Chad was feeling more himself – as normal as you could feel when you were unable to walk properly – a pair of young police officers came to interview him. They didn't seem hopeful of finding out who he was, not unless someone came forward to report him missing. And they seemed only mildly surprised that he remembered nothing whatsoever about the incident.

'I've seen it happen before,' one said. 'Just be glad you're alive, sir. Some people are beaten to death.'

'But why would anyone want to beat me so badly?'

'We'll try to find out, but it's a bit difficult when you don't remember anything about yourself, sir.'

'You're in good hands here,' the other one said before they left.

But was he?

Whatever the sister in charge of this so-called rehabilitation unit said, he *would not believe* that he'd never walk more quickly than a shuffle again. He and Pauline had had quite an argument about that. In the end she said he was getting too agitated and she'd have to give him something to keep him calm. She produced some tablets. When he refused to take them, she said they'd put a drip in.

He decided this was not the time to pick a fight and pretended to take the pills, holding them in his cheek and spitting them out the minute she left his room. It didn't seem to occur to her that he might be disobeying her and two pills instead of one turned up again the following morning.

This was clearly her kingdom and she felt herself to be in total control of it. Well, she wasn't going to control him for a minute longer than necessary.

Chad decided his first priority was to get better. If he hadn't been a patient man before, he was now. It was no use trying to do anything until he could move about properly, after all.

The sister scolded him for trying to exercise more. 'It's too risky, Chad. You must take things slowly and use the wheelchair most of the time.'

Since he didn't need much nursing now, they dumped him and that damned wheelchair in the day room in front of the television. They dumped other semi-comatose people there too for hours at a time.

He tried getting into conversation with the others, but it wasn't a very rewarding activity as some of them clearly had dementia.

So he watched the newcomer in the room opposite. She was about his own age and looked more alert than most of the patients here. He could tell she was frustrated and she too had stopped taking the tablets – wise woman.

Join the club, lady! I'm doing the same thing.

He edged his wheelchair forward slightly so that he could see more of the inside of her room. It gave him something to watch other than the television. A real-life drama. That nephew of hers was a loud-mouthed boor. And why did he keep going to see Pauline in her office, with the door closed? They didn't realize how clearly that was reflected in the big glass doors of the day room.

When Jackson, by far the most communicative of the nurses, came to check on him, Chad asked what the newcomer's name was.

'She's called Emily Mattison. Why?'

'No real reason except I like to know people's names. Sometimes I feel like a number here. No one should feel like a number.' He bit back more hasty words and told himself to calm down.

Jackson waited, not rushing him. 'You holding together all right, Chad?'

'I'm feeling a lot better.'

'Don't let them know you're not taking the pills. And try not to look too lively.'

'Why the hell do they want to dope me?'

Jackson shrugged. 'Mine not to reason why, not if I value my job.'

'Could you tell me more about the accident that put me in here?' Chad looked down at his body. 'I need to know the details.'

Jackson sighed. 'Are you sure? OK, I'll go and ask Sister.'

He came back a few minutes later. 'She'll see you in her office. I'll just wheel you there.'

'No. I'll wheel myself.' It was slower, but any exercise was helpful, he'd decided.

Pauline was unsmiling, as usual. He rolled to a halt in front of her desk and she made no attempt to come out from behind it.

'You wanted to know how you ended up here, Mr – er, Chad,' she began. 'According to the police report, you were attacked and beaten senseless. Left for dead, in fact. You now have post-traumatic amnesia as a result of the beating as well as the physical problems.'

'I'm sure I'll gradually recover the full use of my legs.'

'I'm afraid that's wishful thinking, Chad. The tests were very thorough. You'd be better facing facts. You won't walk properly again, just shuffle along.'

'So I'll need to strengthen the upper part of my body, I presume. When are they moving me to a proper rehabilitation unit?'

'They'll be moving you to a care facility once a place becomes available. You'll make friends there and be looked after. And of course you'll get some physio to keep your body as healthy as possible. Unfortunately there isn't anywhere permanent available for a few weeks, so you'll have to stay here until then.'

He didn't protest. What good would that do with a woman like her?

When Jackson escorted him back, Chad said quietly, 'I *shall* walk properly again! But I won't do that if I don't exercise.'

His nurse avoided looking at him. 'Sister is very experienced in this area. But I'll test your reflexes this afternoon, just to be sure.'

His legs weren't working as well as they should and even Jackson seemed convinced that he'd never walk freely again. So after that Chad kept quiet.

He knew enough about sport and fitness to devise some exercises for himself – though he didn't understand why he felt so sure of what he was doing. He checked out the CCTV cameras, but there didn't seem to be any in this end area of the square of corridor, just near the reception desk and lifts. So he was able to exercise when he was on his own. And he did.

He could see Emily in the room opposite watching him, her head on one side, so he put one finger to his lips and she nodded.

The next day she stood up herself, watching what he was doing to strengthen his legs and imitating him.

They heard voices and he moved quickly back into his wheelchair. Emily sank into the armchair beside her bed, slumping a little.

They brought round some tea and biscuits then went away. He wouldn't start exercising again until they'd cleared away the empty cups and plates.

He pretended to watch the television, but had a lot to think about, so had no idea what programme was on. Why would anyone want to beat him up? Who was he? Had it just been a robbery? Or had someone wanted to hurt him, kill him even?

Why, why, why?

He continued to exercise and his legs began to improve. Strange, that, after what he'd been told.

It was very strange that they were so lackadaisical here about actual rehabilitation. It was more like a storage facility for the elderly, and few relatives visited.

Emily didn't look to be either elderly or suffering from dementia, not with that alert expression. In other circumstances he'd have found her very attractive.

He didn't even know how old he was. His hair was silver, but he didn't feel elderly and his body, as far as he could tell, was in fairly decent shape now that the bruises and swellings were mostly gone.

Did you ever feel old? Who knew?

He suddenly remembered someone telling him that as you grew older, people treated the age, not the individual. They were certainly doing that here. Now, who had told him that? And why had he remembered it when he couldn't even remember who he was?

He sighed. Until he could see his way more clearly, he would have to pretend to be docile, because he had nowhere else to go.

But one day, he'd get out of their clutches, whatever it took. And he wasn't going to wait too long to do it, either.

Emily asked Jackson again if she could go and sit in the day room.

'Sister doesn't like people going anywhere on their own till they're independently mobile.'

'Then could I have a wheelchair like the man over there? I'd be all right in a wheelchair, surely? I'm not likely to fall out of one, am I?'

'I'll see what I can do.'

'And I need access to a phone. How do I arrange that? I want to call my friend and neighbour, to ask her to bring me some more clothes. I'm surprised Rachel hasn't called me.'

He hesitated. 'Maybe later.'

'What? Why ever not?'

'Sister thinks it upsets people till they've settled in.'

She looked at him and he avoided her eyes, which Jackson only did when relaying instructions he didn't approve of, or so she'd guessed.

'Has Rachel already phoned?'

'I can't discuss that.'

'She has, hasn't she? And they won't let her speak to me. Do you know why? She's my closest friend, for heaven's sake.'

'Ask your nephew about it. Though I'll deny telling you to do that.'

So she asked George about Rachel. He smiled and said her neighbour was still away. 'I'll speak to her about getting in touch when she returns, but you should rely on family first, Auntie dear. They're the only ones you can really trust.'

'If so, why haven't you brought my sister to see me?'

'I will do once you're stable.'

'Then let me have my mobile phone so that I can phone people up to chat. I'm going mad from boredom.'

'You need time to adjust to your . . . incapacity. It really isn't a good idea yet to see or talk to other people.'

'*Incapacity?* As I understand it, I hit my head and went into a coma. I came out of the coma and I'm feeling better by the day. I have slight post-traumatic amnesia, in that I don't remember the accident itself, but apart from that, my mind is fine, thank you very much.'

'You're not as well as you think. But don't worry. I'll look after you, as I do my mother.'

Over my dead body you will!

No way was Emily letting George take over her life as he'd taken over her sister's. And as soon as she could get to a lawyer, she was changing her will. George wasn't going to benefit from her years of hard work, not after the way he was treating her now.

Chad woke during the night to hear a muffled sound. He listened carefully. Someone was weeping.

He got up and went to the door. The sound was coming from the direction of Emily's room. There was no one around at this hour, so he'd go and see her. She'd been looking very depressed since her nephew's visit.

She had her face buried in the pillow, but her shoulders were shaking and she was weeping hard.

He knelt by the bed, needing to steady himself on it.

The movement made her raise her head and stare at him.

'I heard you crying.'

She wiped her eyes with the edge of the sheet and pulled herself into a sitting position. Tears were sparkling on her eyelashes and the pillow had a damp patch. 'I can't . . . bear it. I think I'm going mad, seeing conspiracies to keep me here. What's going *on*?'

He couldn't help it. He sat on the bed and put his arm round her shoulders, ready to move away if she seemed to object.

But she didn't object. She buried her face in his chest and let him hold her close, seeming to need that human contact as much as he did.

When her tears stopped, he said gently, 'Hold on. We'll get out of here somehow.'

'How? We might not be called prisoners, but we are.'

'I don't know yet how we'll escape, but with two of us watching for opportunities, we'll manage it.'

She smiled at him then. 'Thank you.'

'Thank you too. I need someone as much as you do.' He stuck out one hand. 'Partners in crime?'

She shook it. 'Jackson says you've got amnesia.'

'Yeah.'

'Must be terrible not knowing who you are.'

'Not the best.' He glanced at the clock on the wall. 'I'd better get back to bed. If they find us together, there'll be the mother of all fusses.'

At the door, he turned to smile. 'How about a date tomorrow night?'

Her smile was even brighter, lighting up her whole face. 'You're on.'

The following morning Emily asked Jackson, 'Could you please add some extra exercises to my routine? Perhaps there are some I can do safely on my own?'

He looked at her, biting his lip. 'Sister wants me to take things slowly. Your nephew has been reading up on comas, it seems, and is afraid of a relapse. He keeps questioning her about your treatment. She thinks he's the sort to sue if there's the slightest hint of trouble.'

'My welfare has nothing whatsoever to do with George. Why will they not believe that? I'm in charge of my own life. Well, I will be once I recover.'

Jackson shrugged. 'I'm not the person in power here. Not for me to judge.' He looked bitter as he said that.

'But I'm feeling better every day, surely you can see that? You spend more time with me than anyone else here does.'

'You're definitely getting better.'

'Jackson, I need to get away from here. *She* seems to be blocking my recovery.'

He was still hesitating and avoiding her eyes, so she said very firmly, 'I'm used to keeping myself fit. If you don't give me more exercises, I'll work some out for myself.'

He lowered his voice. 'Well, do this in secret, then. And don't, for goodness' sake, go anywhere near the reception area if you start walking about, which I'd recommend you to do. They've got CCTV there and *she* checks it regularly in case anything has happened during the night. Talk about a control freak.'

He let her know when Sister was off to her lunch, then Emily paced three sides of the square of corridor that ran round their floor. She saw no one moving about, because they put the patients to bed for a nap at that time. Some of the patients clearly had dementia. Why was she still in a geriatric rehabilitation unit? Surely they had a bed free now in the proper rehab unit?

She stopped in the doorway of the day room to chat to Chad. He was looking depressed. 'Is something wrong?'

'I felt as if I was remembering something, then it slipped away. I can't even remember my surname, only that it's not Chadderton. Chad must be short for something, though.' He gave her a sad smile and a half-shrug. 'You're doing better with the walking.'

'Don't tell anyone I'm moving about. I'm not supposed to walk round on my own. But how can I get stronger without exercise?'

'I won't say a word. Who would I talk to? They're all afraid of Sister Hitler.' He covered his mouth, his eyes dancing with laughter now.

'I don't have to ask who you mean by that! How are you getting on?'

'They're still saying I'm never going to walk properly again, let alone run, but I won't accept that.' He glanced quickly round. 'Don't tell anyone, not even Jackson, how much better you're feeling. They might . . . give you some happy pills.'

She nodded. 'I've worked out that something is wrong here. We have to escape.'

'We need to work on our strength and endurance if we're to do that. Only . . . where am I going to go? I don't have any money or ID. Whoever attacked me cleaned out my pockets.'

'We'll think about that when we get out.'

'Yes. Who's the bossy young guy visiting you?'

'My nephew.' She scowled at the mere thought of George.

'Don't trust him. He's in cahoots with dear Sister Pauline about something. I've seen him pass her an envelope.'

'What?'

He put one finger to his lips. 'I'm getting very good at faking a doze.'

'George passed her an envelope?'

'Yes. I saw it reflected in the glass doors. She was in a hurry to attend the heads of wards meeting, or she'd have gone into her office to take it, I'm sure. She didn't open it, but put it straight into her pocket, so she must have known what was in it.'

George was definitely up to something, Emily thought angrily. He'd always been sneaky.

She began to work even harder at the exercises. Chad was right. Something was very wrong here. And it wasn't too fanciful that they'd need to escape, because no one would give her a date for being discharged and they were talking about care homes now.

How could this be happening in the twenty-first century? She'd heard of occasional health facilities that weren't performing well, or ones where someone was abusing elderly patients, but had never expected to be trapped in a place like that herself.

'You'd think people would want me to get better as quickly as possible to free up a bed,' she fumed to Jackson after another nurse had warned her not to overdo things.

'Pauline's terrified of pushing patients too hard. She'll do anything to avoid having an incident that needs investigating – she had one before, you see, and it put a stop to her efforts to get a promotion. But if you quote me on that, I'll deny telling you. And having the dementia patients here gives her an excuse to keep the outer doors locked. All visitors have to report to reception downstairs first, so she gets warning of who's coming up. She does so like to be in complete charge.'

He scowled in the direction of Sister's office, his expression showing how he really felt about her.

Emily was quite sure her own dislike more than matched his.

When Jackson had left and all was quiet, Chad pushed his blanket aside and stood up. 'Time for my next exercise session,' he whispered to Emily, who was sitting in her wheelchair next to his.

He walked round the day room then began to move up and down the corridor.

She joined him, able to move faster than he could, but matching her pace to his so as not to emphasize this.

Once they'd both had enough, they sat and chatted. Chad might not be able to remember who he was, but he could remember films, books, things he liked doing, so they always seemed to have something to say. He was into antiques and seemed to know a lot about them. So was she.

It was such a comfort to have him there. In other circumstances, she'd have hoped he'd become a good friend. Possibly more.

In the present circumstances, neither of them knew what the future might hold. Either of them might be dragged away without a moment's notice.

They had to escape. And soon.

She didn't want to lose her chance of help in escaping, and, to her surprise, she didn't want to lose Chad, either. She didn't know whether anything might come of their friendship, and it was certainly the strangest way to make a friend . . . but she really did like him.

'I shall come and visit you twice a week from now on,' George declared on his next visit. 'Tuesdays and Fridays.'

'Then you can bring my mail.'

'Auntie dear, you're not ready for any hassles. *I* can deal with the mail for you. And anyway, there haven't been any personal letters, only bills and circulars. Marcia and I will be paying the gas and electricity bills as our contribution for use of your house.'

'They're on automatic deduction.'

'Then when you come home, you must let us have a bill for what we've cost you.'

'What about my emails, then? You could bring in my laptop. If I can go down to the public areas here, I can get on line.'

'Too upsetting yet to let you leave the rehab unit. They want to keep you calm, in order to maintain progress. Why, you can't even walk properly yet. If you'll give me your computer password, I'll check your emails for you.'

'No, thank you. They're private.'

He shrugged.

When she complained about him refusing to bring her mail in, Pauline stared at her as if she was stupid. 'What do you think I can do about that? You should be grateful to your nephew for his help. Of course he's dealing with your mail. *You* can't do it, after all. Some of our patients have no one to care for their homes and possessions. You're one of the lucky ones.'

Emily told Chad what was going on and he shook his head.

'You aren't going to win with those two.'

'I hate the thought of George opening my mail, but you're probably right.'

'Let's step up the exercising, and do more at night.'

'Good idea. I can't sleep because I'm not really tired.' And because she was worrying and feeling trapped. If only she could get in touch with her former boss, Leon. He'd have her out of here in a trice.

Come to think of it, why hadn't he been in contact, asking if she was all right? She could guess why. They'd told him she had come out of the coma with mental impairment.

Dare she invite him to come and visit her once they escaped? She'd have to think about that. But she did trust him. And like him.

So why not?

The next time her nephew visited, Emily couldn't face seeing him and pretended to be dozing in her wheelchair in the day room. Chad was away being supervised in having a shower.

George stood in the doorway with Pauline. 'My poor aunt doesn't always make sense when I talk to her. I fear the dementia is progressing.'

Through her fractionally open eyes, Emily saw him slip an envelope to the sister.

'Perhaps you should apply for a power of attorney over her affairs,' Sister said. 'We at the unit can't always tell if your aunt's being accurate when she speaks about her former life. Did you say dementia runs in the family?'

'I'm afraid so.'

Liar! thought Emily, digging her fingernails into the palm of one hand to stop herself shouting out at him. It was exactly the opposite. Many of her ancestors on either side had lived past ninety, enjoying their old age as they'd enjoyed the rest of their lives.

Her sister was one of the exceptions. Liz now had to live quietly. Though that life was quieter than it need be, Emily was sure, because of her lack of money.

Emily was beginning to feel more like her old self but still lacked her usual strength and stamina. She'd rarely had a day's illness in her life and had always tried to keep herself fit, without going overboard. This was her first stay in hospital and she prayed fervently that it would be her last.

She was sure she'd have recovered far more rapidly if they'd let her go home. She could easily have afforded to get help around the house and Rachel would be next door.

Of course, George and Marcia would have to move out then. No wonder he was keeping her here!

How could she let her friend know she wanted to see her, and needed help escaping? Even Jackson said it was as much as his job was worth to pass on a message.

The only solution Emily could see was to leave the unit without permission and somehow get home under her own steam, then get Rachel to help her. She could deal with any trouble from a position of more strength, or she would be able to if she got George out of her house and found a lawyer to help her.

There had to be a way to escape.

The day following George's visit, Emily had a serious talk with Chad about escaping.

'I've racked my brain how to do it,' he admitted. 'The trouble is we'll need some money.'

She glanced around and leaned even closer. 'I have some.'

'You do?'

'Yes. Sewn into the lining of my handbag. George may have taken my purse and credit card but he doesn't know about this.'

'Do you always do that?'

'Definitely. I travelled round Europe quite a bit and was mugged once. My purse and credit card were stolen. Such a nuisance getting that sorted out! Afterwards, I always made sure I had money elsewhere among my belongings.' She didn't tell Chad that although she kept one credit card in her purse, and of course George had that now, she also had a second one hidden at home.

'You're sure the money is still in your bag?'

'Trust me. The stitching hasn't been touched and I recognize my own handiwork. I won't unpick it till we're ready to go. I think there will be enough to get a taxi back home again. I'll go straight to Rachel's and she'll help me find a lawyer.'

She looked at him. 'Um . . . would you like to stay with me after we escape?'

He looked at her very steadily. 'You're sure about that?'

'Very sure.'

He clasped her hand briefly. 'Thank you. I'm grateful for your offer. One day I'll make it up to you.'

They sat smiling at one another.

He looked at the clock. 'They'll be round with the tea soon. I'd better pretend to doze. I do that better than you. You read your book.'

At least she could read properly now. Books were a life saver here, and even Pauline approved of the patients sitting quietly reading.

Once the nurses had made their round, Chad opened his eyes again and grinned at her.

She tried out her thoughts on him. 'You know, we're able to walk so much better, wouldn't it be easier to show them how well we are, then take some tests or whatever you do to get out?'

Chad was very definite. 'Don't say a word! Whatever you do, don't tell them anything.'

'But surely they'll have to listen to me if they know I'm fully in control of myself again.'

'Not necessarily. There's something going on here and I don't trust Sister Hitler. Who knows what she might inject you with to keep you quiet and dopey?'

Emily sighed. 'She isn't the only person here.'

'She's the one in charge of this unit. We'd have to get past her and I don't fancy our chances.'

'I suppose you're right.'

'This isn't the normal way the health system treats patients, for all its faults. And even here, we've been well cared for physically. No, she's running some sort of scam and she won't thank us for trying to upset a lucrative apple cart.'

He reached out to give her hand a quick squeeze and the warmth of his smile was of immense comfort.

They sent a different doctor in to speak to Emily the following day and it didn't take her long to realize he was checking her mental capacity.

'I don't have dementia, you know,' she said impatiently.

'What made you say that?'

'The sorts of questions you were asking me. I saw a programme on TV about it last year.'

'And yet your nephew is worried because you're getting your facts wrong.'

'I'm not getting them wrong.' She realized protesting wouldn't prove anything. 'George has been overseas for the past few years and doesn't know me or my life very well at all. I'm still furious that he's moved into my house. Look, can't you—'

'Your nephew is very fond of you and is only trying to help.'

'He's very fond of my possessions, you mean, and is hoping to inherit.' She leaned back, tired of playing games. 'I'm not answering any more of your questions. There's no need. I want to contact my former employer, please.'

'He's not your employer now.'

'I know that. I took early retirement. But he's a close friend.'

'You want to contact him for medical reasons?'

She looked at him in astonishment. 'Not at all. For help in sorting out my life. He knows me far better than George does. So does my next door neighbour who is my closest friend. I'm not answering any more of your questions till either Leon or Rachel comes to see me.'

'Sister says your friend is away from home. You keep forgetting that, apparently. And I don't think this is something a former employer will want to deal with.'

'Someone could ask him! Leon has been a close friend for years.'

His expression said he didn't believe her. What had George been saying, for heaven's sake?

When Jackson came in later, he scolded her. 'You'd have done better to co-operate, you know.'

'That man was asking me totally stupid questions, like what day of the week it is.'

'And you gave him the wrong day.'

'I didn't!'

'You did.'

She'd been so sure of that, because Sister Pauline had corrected her about what day of the week it was only that morning. Had that woman been setting her up for the interview, trying to put her in the wrong? 'Well, it's hard to keep track of the days in here with nothing happening. Look, now that I can read again, can I order a newspaper to be delivered?'

'You can get one sent up from the shop if your nephew will pay for it.'

Fat chance there was of that. George wouldn't even give her spending money.

Jackson hesitated then said quietly, 'I'm going on leave next week. Someone else will be taking my place. Tracey's a bit of a stickler for the rules, so don't tell her about the extra exercises or your night-time chats with Chad, hmm?'

'How long are you going for?'

'Three weeks.'

That settled it. They would have to escape before then. 'Which day is your last?' She kept her voice low, remembering how clearly she'd overheard George one day.

'Friday of next week.'

A sharp voice interrupted them. 'Excuse me, Jackson, but you have another patient waiting.'

'Sorry. See you later, Emily. You did very well today.' He walked away.

'The staff are not here to gossip,' Pauline told her severely. 'We're short-handed and struggling to cope. How would you like it if you had no help in getting washed because someone was wasting staff time by gossiping?'

Emily didn't argue that she was taking full care of herself now. What was the use?

On their next walk round the unit at night, she and Chad saw a mobile phone lying on the ground in a corner underneath some of the nurses' outer clothing. Usually coats and shopping bags were locked in the cupboard, to which only Pauline had a key, but someone must be wanting to get away quickly.

They looked at one another, then he picked it up. 'Our need is greater than theirs.' He passed it to her. 'I have no one I can call, but you do. Be careful when you use this.'

She ought to have handed it in, didn't like to steal anything, but he was right. Her need was too great to waste what might be her only opportunity. She slipped the phone into the pocket of her dressing gown then hid it at the back of her bedside drawer, for lack of anywhere better.

When one of the staff came to take her obs the following morning, she said firmly, 'I'd like the rest of my day clothes back, please. I don't like being told what to wear. They gave me someone else's clothes the other day.'

'They can't have done.' The nurse's voice grew gentle. 'You'd probably forgotten they were yours.'

Emily stared at her in shock. 'Of course I hadn't!'

Sister popped in later. 'Why do you say we gave you someone else's clothes?'

'Because you did.'

'Miss Mattison, we did not. We are scrupulously careful about our patients' possessions.'

'*Ms* Mattison.'

But Pauline wasn't listening, was already walking away.

Emily told Chad about the incident later.

'Next time, don't say anything. You're only giving them fodder to prove you're developing dementia.'

'I'm not good at being deceitful, at thinking about the impact of every word I say.'

'No. It's one of the many things I like about you.'

She looked at him, swallowing hard. 'I can't believe this is happening. Sometimes I think it's a nightmare and I'll wake up suddenly.'

'Well, whatever they do, don't protest from now on. They'll only blame it on your supposed dementia.'

Jackson popped in to see her on his way home that evening. 'Don't push them about clothes. I'll get you some of your things, enough for your purpose, anyway.'

She looked at him in shock.

'I overheard you and Chad talking one day. You need to be more careful about that.'

'Thanks for not giving us away.'

'I can only take so much.' As he wrote on the clipboard, he added in a whisper, 'I'll even show you where to hide the clothes.'

Why was he suddenly agreeing to help her? Was this a trap? She looked at him suspiciously.

He put one finger to his lips. 'It's not a trick. I'm about to give in my notice, so I won't be coming back after my leave. I've found another job, thank goodness. I don't like what's happening here. How they've escaped being caught for so long, I can't figure. But I'm not going to be the one to blow the whistle on them. I don't want to ruin my career.'

He was gone before she could comment on that.

Thank goodness they'd found the phone.

The following day, as she sat chatting to Chad, she told him Jackson was leaving.

'Yes, he told me too. I think we have to escape this Friday, after he's gone on holiday. The relief nurse might clamp down on us and make it impossible to get away, or even to see much of one another.'

'I'd hate that.'

'So would I.'

She sat frowning into space, wondering how to do it.

He was silent for a long time and when she turned sideways she saw he was looking sad again.

'Are you sure you still want me to go with you, Emily? I can't walk as quickly as you can yet. I might hold you up.'

'But you can walk steadily. How far do you think you'll be able to go?'

'However far it takes. I'll crawl on my hands and knees, if necessary.'

She laid one hand on his, understanding his frustration. 'Then help me plan it.'

'It has to be at night, when *she* isn't around.'

Emily nodded. 'I have the mobile phone. I had a look at it and the battery's quite low, so I've been saving it to ring Rachel once we have a definite escape time sorted out. Jackson's even got me some of my own clothes.'

Chad gestured to himself. 'I have only the clothes they provide and no outdoor ones.' He sat lost in thought. 'We'll stand a lot more chance of success if your friend's there to help us get away. Will she come for us?'

'Yes. She's a very good friend. I'll phone her tonight.'

She couldn't imagine Rachel refusing.

* * *

She took out the mobile phone in the middle of the night and listened to it ringing. *Please answer, Rachel*, she prayed.

'Ah, Rachel. Emily here. Sorry to disturb you at this hour, but they won't let me use a phone so I had to sneak this call.'

'Emily? But George said you were—'

'He's telling people I'm losing my marbles. I'm not. Rachel, could you please get my mail and keep it till I come home? He won't bring it in and I bet he's reading it.'

'Look, just to check that this is bona fide, what did we do on your fifty-fifth birthday?'

Emily knew this was a way for her to let Rachel know if this was a trick, but told the truth, smiling at the memory. 'Went out for a curry then got drunk together. You sang Happy Birthday to me three times, none of them in tune.'

'I'm ahead of you on the letters. I know how you feel about George. I've been getting your mail when I can. They aren't always around when the post arrives. I've got one letter that looks quite important. I've been worrying what to do with it.'

'You're an angel. Do not give it to George under any circumstances. Couldn't you bring it in to me? We can't escape yet.'

'Your nephew says you can't have visitors and they haven't let me speak to you when I've phoned up.'

'Just turn up, come to the Geriatric Care Unit and come at five past ten precisely. Sister will be on her break then. Make a big fuss. I'll hear you because it's a very quiet area. There are a lot of stroke and advanced dementia patients.'

Rachel gasped. 'What on earth are *you* doing in a unit like that, then?'

'George has made them think I'm developing dementia. The trouble is, I don't even have my purse and credit card because he took them away. Could you lend me some money, do you think? And help me get a lawyer? And can I stay with you at first?'

'Yes, to all those.'

The phone beeped and she looked at it in dismay. 'Look, I can't chat any more. The battery's running low.'

She sat and wept after she'd hidden the phone. Then she got annoyed at herself for being so weak. To prove she was getting her old spirit back, she went on the prowl to try to find a way of getting out of the hospital at night. She needed a code for the keypad to the stairs door, was going to watch for someone going out that way, which the nurses did sometimes on their breaks. She might be lucky and see what number they keyed in.

She waited for over an hour, sleepy but determined.

In the end, she was indeed lucky. A yawning nurse keyed in the number that opened that door to the stairs, doing it very slowly.

They would need a lot more luck than this if they were going to escape, but Emily felt it was a good start.

The following day she told Chad what she'd found out and he clinked his teacup against hers in a toast to her success.

'Well done! You're an enterprising woman.'

'I'm feeling much more like my old self. How about you? No more memory flashes?'

'Nothing useful. I could see a garden, and a huge building with a sign on it. Only it faded before I could read the sign. Apart from that, I see oddments of furniture, old things. I must have liked antiques.'

'I love them – well, not all periods, but I have a few nice pieces. I always watch antiques programmes on TV.' She took his hand. 'Don't worry. You *will* remember more. I'm sure of it.'

He raised her hand to his lips and kissed it gently. Desire speared through her and she gazed at him in shock.

He smiled knowingly. 'It's hitting me, too.'

She didn't try to deny it. 'Of all the places to meet someone!'

'Fate's been kind to us. What would I have done without you to keep my spirits up?'

She kept hold of his hand. 'You've done the same for me. And we *will* escape.'

'And be together.'

Two days later, while Sister was on her tea break, Rachel came to visit, sneaking up in the lift with some other people.

'I'm afraid Miss Mattison's nephew has requested no visitors and . . .' the nurse at the reception desk was saying.

Emily walked along towards them, calling out, 'Rachel! How lovely to see you!'

Her friend immediately hurried towards her.

'We'll just be in my room!' Emily told the nurse.

The woman looked worried, opened her mouth then shut it again.

Chad gave them the thumbs up as they passed him.

'Who's the dishy man?' Rachel asked. 'Surely *he* hasn't got dementia?'

'Keep your voice down. Chad's a friend. And if you've got any mail, give it me now, in case they send you away. And the money too, please.'

'I just brought the important looking one, in case it's urgent.' Rachel passed over an envelope and two hundred pounds. 'It seems to be from a lawyer in Lancashire. Isn't that where your family comes from?'

'Yes. But I daren't open it now.' She tucked the envelope under her mattress.

'How are you, Emily? Really?'

'Better than I let them know. There's a conspiracy to keep me in here.'

'George said you weren't as well as you thought.'

'My nephew is a liar. He said *you* had gone away to sort out a family crisis. And he's told them I had dementia before the accident.'

Rachel's shocked expression showed Emily's guess had been correct: her being away had been a lie.

'Don't you have a lawyer I can contact?'

'No. I've never needed one, except for buying my house.'

'Well, you need one now, Emily.'

Sister arrived just then. 'I'm afraid we decided on no visitors except family,' she said with one of her tight smiles.

'Then I'm afraid I'll have to make a formal complaint,' Emily said. '*I* wasn't consulted about that. Or my friend can do it on my behalf. I've asked you before to stop George coming to visit and you haven't done it, and now I find you're stopping the people I do want to see from visiting me, like my best friend. This is outrageous. How do I make a formal complaint? Rachel, will *you* find out for me?'

'It'll be my pleasure.'

There was a pregnant silence, then, 'Five minutes only.'

'See what I mean,' Emily whispered. Then she pointed. Outside there was a shadow across the corridor. Someone was eavesdropping. She nudged Rachel and put one finger to her lips, mouthing, 'I'll phone you.'

The five minutes went all too quickly and Emily felt near tears as she saw her friend firmly escorted to the lift by Sister.

She waited a while, sitting by her bed, pretending to read, then as lunchtime approached, she went to sit with Chad and bring him up to date on what Rachel had said.

He looked at her very solemnly. 'You're sure you don't mind me coming along with you now you've got Rachel to help?'

'I told you: I'd prefer to have your company for the Great Escape, and you're welcome to stay with me as long as you need to.'

He closed his eyes in sheer relief and when he looked at her again, his eyes were bright with tears. She knew how desperate he felt, because she did too, so covered his hand with hers. They sat there quietly for a while.

What would she have done if she hadn't had Chad to talk to and keep her sane?

Footsteps came towards them and they moved slightly apart, bending over the crossword puzzle they'd been pretending to solve.

When they were alone again, she sighed. 'We still have to work out how to get away once we leave hospital. I wish I'd dared discuss that with Rachel, but I knew someone was standing outside my room, eavesdropping.'

'We'll play it by ear, if necessary.'

How could this be happening to her in England? Emily thought as she was escorted firmly back to her room to rest after her meal, in spite of her protests that she wasn't tired.

As she lay fuming on her bed, she suddenly remembered recent media reports on TV about how older patients had been badly treated for years in one poorly run institution, some beaten regularly, and she grew depressed about her chances of escaping. Those people hadn't, had they?

No, she mustn't let the situation get her down. She must think positively.

Emily didn't dare read the letter Rachel had brought till the middle of the night, and what she found astonished her.

A distant cousin of her father's had died suddenly and had left everything to Emily, a house in Lancashire *and* some money. Penelope's lawyer, a Mr Jeremy Tapton, had contacted her before but her nephew had said she was ill. Mr Tapton hoped she was now better, because he was unwilling to let her nephew finalize the sale of her inheritance until the lawyer had seen her in person, or George had obtained a power of attorney.

He'd be happy to come south to visit his client.

Emily hadn't known Penelope Mattison very well, but this couldn't have come at a better time. She needed a refuge and now one had turned up. 'Thank you, Penelope,' she murmured. George might be in her house, but she could stay in Penelope's until she'd dealt with him once and for all.

He might know where to find her, because he must have opened the earlier correspondence, but it'd be inconveniently far away for him and she'd have this lawyer nearby.

When George came to visit her, she heard his loud voice, exchanged glances with Chad and hovered near the door of the day room, unashamedly eavesdropping on what he was saying at reception.

'I'm going away tomorrow, Sister, so I won't be here again until Tuesday of next week. I couldn't leave without visiting my poor aunt, though.'

Pauline said something, but not loud enough for Emily to hear. It soon became obvious what she'd said.

'Well, in future I'd be grateful if you'd keep your part of the bargain and keep that meddling neighbour away from my aunt. Rachel isn't as good a friend as she pretends.'

'I'll certainly do that, but I'll need you to sign an authorization for it. Are you going somewhere nice for your holiday, Mr Pilby?'

'I'm spending a long weekend in Brighton. A reward from my employer for good sales figures. I haven't been able to take it until now, because I've been too busy.'

'How marvellous. Come into my office and I'll find you a piece of paper for the authorization.'

The other rehab assistant came along the corridor just then. 'Have you lost your way, Miss Mattison?'

'*Ms* Mattison.' She wasn't going to give up correcting them on this. 'Of course I've not lost my way. I'm avoiding my nephew.'

She realized from the way Chad rolled his eyes that it was probably the wrong thing to say and added hastily, 'He's such a bore.'

George came to see her shortly afterwards and insisted on going into her room to talk privately. She endured a scold about Rachel's visit, then ten minutes of him boasting about being top salesman. He didn't sound to be looking forward to the holiday he'd won, in fact, she'd guess he'd been postponing it. He wasn't the sort to go on holiday to Brighton.

In the end, desperate to get rid of him, she said she had to use the bathroom.

'I'll say goodbye then, Auntie dear. I don't want to tire you out. You're looking rather pale. You should have a nice nap now. I'll see you next Tuesday. Oh, and by the way, Rachel won't be coming to see you again. I'm not having her upsetting you.'

'Mind your own business, George, and don't you dare tell Rachel not to come.'

'You *are* my business now.' He leaned forward, grabbing her wrist and holding it tightly, as he slammed her against the wall. He spoke in a whisper but his words were no less threatening for that. 'And you'd be wise, *dear . . . Auntie* . . . to do as I suggest. As my mother does. If it comes to a struggle, you really are no match for me, physically or mentally.'

She was still staring at him in shock as he let go of her and left the room with a loud, cheerful farewell.

He'd just been threatening her. And he was such a big man, she'd felt extremely intimidated. Whatever happened, she didn't intend to follow her sister's example and let George get his hands on her life and money.

But why was he so certain he could continue to control her? What else was he planning?

And why did she think he couldn't carry out his threat? He'd been controlling her against her wishes for the past few weeks, hadn't he?

She and Chad were certainly seeing the dark side of the health system here. How was Pauline getting away with it? And why was she doing it?

She remembered the envelope that George had given Pauline. A bribe?

How much money would it take to persuade a trained nurse

to behave so badly? Had Pauline been doing it for a while? Was she going to take off into the wide blue yonder when she had enough saved?

So many things to worry about.

But Emily wasn't going to give up. And she wasn't going to leave Chad behind. He had been such a comfort to her. She felt as if she'd known him for years.

Afterwards, she hoped . . . She could feel herself blushing at what she hoped for from Chad.

Emily waited until the middle of the night then rang Rachel, praying the battery on the mobile phone would last long enough. 'Look, George is going away this weekend. Could you come and pick me and a friend up on Friday night? Well, Saturday really by then. About one o'clock in the morning.'

'Of course I can.'

'Wait for me in the northern car park.' Chad had found a map of the campus near the lift and had figured that was the nearest car park.

'Yes, I can do that and—' There was a burst of static then nothing more from Rachel. Emily tried to dial again, but the phone was dead. Its battery must have run out completely.

She could only trust that her friend would be waiting for her outside the hospital the next night.

Four

There was a knock on the door on the Thursday morning and when Rachel opened it, she found Emily's nephew George standing there. She didn't like her temporary neighbour, especially after what her friend had told her about him, and tended to avoid him. 'Yes?'

'Don't try to visit my aunt again. Your visit upset her.'

'No, it didn't. She was glad to see me.'

'I'm asking you *very politely* not to go to the hospital again.'

'I shall definitely keep going to see my friend.'

He leaned forward, thrusting his face very close to hers. 'I don't want to have to get more forceful about this.'

She took a step backwards, suddenly afraid of the look on his face.

He smiled. 'You're beginning to understand how deeply I care about my family. *I* will look after them. *You* will mind your own business.' He turned to leave, but stopped to toss back at her, 'I hope you decide to be sensible. I wouldn't want you to get hurt. You'll see what I mean.'

Then he turned and walked away, whistling cheerfully, stopping to talk to the neighbour across the street, with whom he'd struck up an acquaintance.

Rachel watched him chat for a while, then go back inside Emily's house. She'd seen him look reasonably suave, in an expensive business suit, but today he had a swaggering bully's walk, and his meaty hands were swinging free instead of clutching a briefcase. In fact, he looked like a caricature of a gangster. Emily said he was something in sales and was doing well. Amazing, that. Rachel would never buy anything from a man like him. No, he was connected to engineering, industrial pumps, perhaps. It wasn't like shop sales. But still . . . he wasn't a likeable man.

She shut the front door and locked it, her thoughts going back to her friend. She and Emily hadn't had time to plan the escape in detail before they'd been cut off. She could only hope she'd heard enough to know she was supposed to pick Emily up from the northern car park of the hospital at one o'clock on Saturday morning.

When Rachel went outside the following afternoon, intending to go to the shops, she found that all four of her tyres had been slashed. She'd heard nothing, seen nothing.

She felt so threatened by this, she went inside and locked all the doors and windows. She was quite sure who'd done it, not at all sure how best to deal with it.

In fact, she felt out of her depth about the whole business of getting Emily free.

George's car had gone, and she didn't know when he'd be coming back, but that didn't stop her feeling nervous.

If she got the tyres repaired before closing time, he might slash them again during the night. She didn't have a garage to keep her car in, so it stood on the drive. And the drive was sheltered by bushes and trees, so anyone could creep up to the car without the neighbours seeing.

How was she going to help Emily now? They'd only have one chance for this escape, Rachel was sure.

After some consideration of the problem over a cup of strong coffee, she came to the conclusion that she had to find help. She simply couldn't do this on her own.

As she prepared to escape, the most difficult thing for Emily was staying awake until after the late shift came on duty. Several times she found herself nodding off.

By midnight the bustle of changeover had died down. She waited until the night nurse had finished her first ward round, then got up and dressed quickly, shaping what she hoped looked like a sleeping figure under the bedding.

She put her dressing gown on over her outdoor clothing, in case anyone was monitoring the CCTV system. Maybe if someone saw her, they'd think she was just walking round the floor.

She saw a shadow on the floor of the corridor, approaching her room slowly, and stiffened. Please let it be Chad! She couldn't bear to fail before she even started.

The shadow jerked and moved along the floor, coming closer and closer.

Not until the figure stopped outside her door could she tell that it was him. She let out a sigh of relief and went to join him, holding out her hand.

He took hers and gave it a slight squeeze. She felt better for the touch, so very much better knowing she wasn't trying to escape on her own.

'All right?' he mouthed.

She could only nod, because her throat was suddenly dry.

They got outside the unit without any hassles, taking the stairs and using the code she'd memorized for the lock. To her huge relief the same code opened the outer door as well.

Suddenly Chad tugged her back into the shadows behind some bushes and put his forefinger across her lips. She didn't know why, but stayed silent.

A security guard appeared, checking the outer doors and flashing his torch around.

When the man had moved past, Chad grinned, his teeth shining white in the moonlight. 'I always did have excellent hearing.'

'Thank goodness!'

Moving as quickly as they could, they made their way across the first car park, meeting no one.

'I can't see any security cameras,' she whispered.

'Neither can I. There must be some, though. I wish I knew where, so that we could avoid them.'

As they turned the corner into the small overflow parking area where they were to meet Rachel, Emily looked round eagerly. But to her dismay, her friend's car wasn't there.

'What shall we do if Rachel doesn't come?' she whispered.

'We press on regardless. You have enough money to get a taxi to her house.'

They found a sheltered spot against the wall of an outbuilding and waited, because it was a little before the agreed time still.

'How are you feeling?' she asked.

'I'm fine. And you?'

'Nervous.' She reached for his hand.

Once she thought she heard the sound of footsteps in the distance, and glanced at Chad. He was listening, but after a minute or two, he relaxed and smiled at her, so whoever it was must have passed by.

She figured about ten minutes had passed. It felt like ten hundred!

Chad spoke quietly. 'If your friend doesn't come in a few minutes, we should set off walking. If we can find a phone box, maybe we can call a taxi. They often have a free call service.'

It might be late May, but it was a cold night and Emily shivered. She didn't have anything warm to wear.

Chad was shivering, too. He put an arm round her shoulders and leaned against her. 'Who's supporting who?' he muttered.

'Whom.'

He chuckled. 'Good at grammar, are you?'

'Very.'

'More than ten minutes have passed, surely?'

'Yes.'

'The map showed an exit at that corner.' He pointed. 'Let's use it.'

When they got there, they found a barrier in place, with a strong metal pole shutting off the entrance.

'No wonder Rachel wasn't waiting in the car park. Maybe she's parked down the road.' Emily didn't really believe that. If Rachel were here, she'd have come looking for her.

As Emily squeezed past the barrier, a man stepped out from the shadows. 'May I ask what you're doing here, madam, sir? You were seen on CCTV wandering round the car parks.'

She gasped in shock and for a moment couldn't form any words. The guard was standing between her and Chad. 'None of your business what I'm doing here. This is a public area.'

'Oh, I think it is my business. Two people answering your descriptions have been reported missing from a locked ward.' His voice took on a patronizing tone, as if he were speaking to an idiot. 'You shouldn't be wandering about like this, madam. The hospital won't want you getting hurt while you're in their care.'

'We've removed ourselves from their care.' Chad pushed past the guard to join her.

She knew they couldn't run away from this man. Neither of them was in any condition to outdistance anyone, and he was much younger and fitter than they were. But when Chad's arm round her back urged her on, she moved forward again.

They had to try.

The guard was already speaking on the phone. 'Frank? I've got them. The woman sounds perfectly normal, I must admit, and he's walking pretty well. I thought he was supposed to have difficulty moving around.'

'I don't have dementia!' she exclaimed indignantly.

'No, of course not,' he said soothingly. 'But you're not well and you shouldn't be out here alone at night. Nor should you, sir. You still need caring for. Let's be sensible and go back. It's a cold night and it looks like rain.'

He moved to bar the way again, and when they tried to go round him, he shoved them back, not bothering to be so polite now. 'I said: we're going back to the hospital.'

Chad stumbled and as she steadied him, despair filled her. George had won, damn him.

At that moment she heard footsteps, more than one person running towards them along the road outside the hospital. Her captor turned round, grabbing each of them by the arm.

'Let my client go immediately!' A man's crisp, educated voice rang out loudly.

She didn't recognize the voice. Who was this?

She didn't care. Whoever he was, she'd go along with being his client.

The security guard's grasp tightened, if anything. 'This lady is a patient at the hospital, sir, and a power of attorney has been applied for by her nephew, because she's not fit to take care of herself.'

'In that case, I can save the hospital a lot of trouble. I'm Oliver Tapton, Ms Mattison's lawyer, and I shall be taking care of her from now on.'

Oliver Tapton, not Jeremy? Emily wondered.

'I'm afraid I can't release her without authorization, sir.'

'Didn't I hear you say a power of attorney hadn't yet been granted? If that's true, she has every right to leave the hospital whenever she chooses. She doesn't need any authorization.'

Emily could feel tears of relief welling in her eyes. She tried to pull away but the guard kept hold of her arm.

'People in their right senses don't run away in the middle of the night, sir. They walk out of the front door in the daytime.'

'Not if it's locked,' Emily said bitterly. She watched the guard turn his head, as if listening for someone coming to join him.

'They have a right to get out any way they can if their freedom has been taken away.' Mr Tapton turned to Emily. 'I do apologize for not getting in touch sooner, Ms Mattison. My son and I hadn't realized how badly you were being treated. I think I got here in time tonight to help you, though.'

'I'd given you up.' She couldn't stop her voice wobbling. 'And can you please tell this man to let my friend go, too? They've been keeping Chad here against his will as well.'

'Certainly.' The lawyer's tone was sharp and icy. 'Will you let go of my clients *now*.'

The security guard hesitated. Emily was puzzled by this. Surely it couldn't matter to him whether she stayed or left? She recognized him now. He'd visited the unit a few times. Another person who seemed on excellent terms with Pauline.

No, she was seeing conspiracies everywhere. If she told anyone about such suspicions, they would have a very good excuse for locking her up again.

Perhaps the guard would be the one the authorities would blame if she escaped. Yes, that was more likely the reason for him keeping hold of her. Too bad. They'd had no right to detain her in the first place.

Mr Tapton took a step forward. 'Ms Mattison, do you wish to leave now?'

'I most certainly do.'

'What about you, Mr – um, Chad?'

'I wish to leave, too, and I'm very happy that you've agreed to act on my behalf.' Chad tugged away from the guard.

The man let him go, but still kept hold of Emily, jerking her backwards. 'I really can't allow you to—'

'*Let go of her this minute or we'll sue you for deprivation of liberty!*'

All hung in the balance for a few seconds, then the hand on Emily's arm slackened and she hurried across to stand beside Rachel – a few yards in distance, but a huge step towards freedom.

Her friend gave her a quick hug. 'I'm so glad you got out of that place tonight.'

Tapton gestured in the direction from which he'd come. 'We'll return to my car now. You must both be chilled through.'

As Chad started moving, he stumbled. 'Sorry. I haven't walked this far for a while.'

The lawyer steadied him. 'My car's not far. Since we couldn't get into this parking area, we had to leave the car where the verge widens. Didn't want to cause an accident by blocking such a narrow, twisting road.'

The security guard continued to walk beside them. 'I'll need your name, sir. And your address.'

'Oh, I can do better than that. Here's my business card.' He thrust it at the man. 'Oliver Tapton at your service. Any further enquiries should be made to my rooms during working hours.'

He clicked a remote and ahead of them a car's lights flashed twice. 'Come and sit in the back with your friend, Ms Mattison. I'll put the heater on and we'll soon have you both warmed up.'

Chad got in slowly, then leaned back with a groan. 'I thought I'd be able to walk better than this.'

'You managed well enough. We got away, didn't we?' Emily said.

Oliver glanced in the rear view mirror. 'Everyone strapped in? Right, let's get out of here. Another fellow's joined that guard and they're on the phone again. Before we know it, they'll be bringing in reinforcements.'

As he drove away, he added, 'It was my son Jeremy who wrote to you in the first place about your inheritance, Ms Mattison. When Rachel phoned, it sounded urgent, so since he couldn't get away because of another important case, he asked me to investigate. I'm retired, but I still help out now and then. I'm sorry we're a bit late, but the traffic was heavy and I had to drive down from Lancashire.'

'I've never been as glad to see someone in my whole life, Mr Tapton. Only I'm afraid they might try to get us back by legal means, given that my nephew wants to keep me locked away and is claiming I have dementia. Do you think they have any chance of succeeding?'

'By the time I've phoned the hospital in the morning and told them I'm initiating a formal complaint on behalf of both of you, they'll let the matter drop, I promise you. Or maybe I'll get my son to do that. He can sound far more ferocious than me.' He frowned. 'What I don't understand is *why* they were keeping you both locked up. Surely we're trying to use beds efficiently in the hospitals, not clog them up with long-term patients – especially ones who don't want to be there, and don't need to be, either.'

'The sister in charge seemed to be on extremely good terms with Emily's nephew,' Chad said. 'I've seen him give her envelopes. I don't know why they were keeping me there, though.'

Oliver let out a low whistle of surprise. 'How is she getting away with it? And why is he doing it? The usual reason? Money?'

'Yes. He already manages his mother's affairs and he must be keeping her a bit short, because my sister said her investments aren't paying as well because of the recession. It might be true, but she had such a generous income before, I can't understand why she has to be so careful with money.'

'We'll make sure your case is looked into, believe me,' Oliver said. 'Oh, and I don't know your full name, Chad.'

He sighed. 'I don't know it, either. I have amnesia after being beaten up. But I'm pretty sure people used to call me Chad. Only I can't remember anything specific about my identity.'

'Haven't your family reported you missing?'

'That's what's puzzling me. If I have any family, they've definitely not reported me missing, let alone come to see me. Apparently a "Can you help?" notice was put out in the local newspapers and on regional TV, with my photo. Well, that's what they told me had been done. But they said no one came forward. That still shouldn't mean me being locked away, though. I don't have dementia.'

'No. It definitely shouldn't.'

'Perhaps someone is after my money too, Mr Tapton. If I have any. But how are they getting away with it? Surely I have friends and family?' Chad shook his head helplessly.

'Well, we can discuss what to do about your situation in more detail later. Let's use first names, shall we? So much more friendly. I'm Oliver.'

'Fine by me.' Emily tapped her friend's shoulder. 'Where are we going, Rachel?'

'Home.'

'Is that safe?'

'George is away at the moment,' her friend said. 'He left late yesterday afternoon.'

'Oh yes, I overheard him telling Sister he'd be away for the weekend. I know it's out of your way, Oliver, given that you've already driven down from Lancashire, but I do need clothes and other things. Only, I don't want to stay there and confront George. I confess, he makes me nervous.'

Rachel made a sympathetic noise. 'Me, too. He came round to warn me to stay away from you. Then someone slashed my tyres. I think it was your nephew. He probably did it during the night.'

'George did that?'

'I've no proof, but who else could it have been just after he'd threatened me?'

'Then I definitely need somewhere else to go till this is all sorted out,' Emily said.

'You should report him to the police for what he's done to you!' Rachel said indignantly.

Emily sighed. 'I'd like to report him, but the trouble is, I don't want to make too much fuss about what he's been doing, however unlawful it is, because his mother is my only sister and Liz is quite frail. And anyway, how would I prove that he's trying to take my money? He'd just say he was trying to look after me.'

'I can't prove Pauline was deliberately keeping me there, either,' Chad said. 'But I can't see why I was locked up like that and told I'd never walk properly again. It doesn't make sense.'

'Why don't you come up to Lancashire and live in Penelope's house, Emily?' Oliver suggested. 'It's a bit dilapidated but it's habitable. She lived there until she died, and that was only a couple of months ago.'

'I was thinking of doing that.'

'And if you have to get back quickly, Oliver, I can bring Emily up to Lancashire after she's packed,' Rachel said.

'I don't have to get back,' Oliver said. 'There's no one waiting for me because I lost my wife two years ago.' He fell silent for a moment, then took a deep breath and continued in a more cheerful tone, 'Besides, I must confess that I'm intrigued by this situation. I definitely want to see it through. My son's far too busy to give you all the help you're going to need.' Oliver's deep voice was calm and reassuring. 'You can take your time at your home and sort out everything you're likely to need. I'll wait with you, if you can put me up.'

'I definitely can.'

'I'll volunteer to feed you all,' Rachel put in. 'I've got plenty of food and I don't want to be left out of the excitement. Heaven knows, my life's been all too quiet lately.'

Emily leaned forward to clasp her friend's shoulder for a moment in unspoken sympathy. 'Chad will be staying with me, too. He doesn't know who he is or where he lives, and he has no money. When they beat him up, they took everything that might identify him.'

Rachel whistled softly. 'Wow! Sounds like a gangster movie. Who's got it in for you, Chad?'

'I only wish I knew.'

'Must be hellishly difficult,' Oliver said. 'We'll get you on social security payments once you're settled in Lancashire. That'll at least give you something to live on till you come into your own again.'

Emily glanced sideways and saw that Chad was looking at her.

'Are you sure about me staying now that you've got friends to help you?' he asked in a low voice.

'I'm very sure. I don't want to live alone at the moment, even if I'm nowhere near George.'

'Your nephew's really frightened you, hasn't he?' Oliver said.

'He's frightened me too,' Rachel put in. 'Wait till you meet him. Great big bully is a perfect description for Georgie boy, even when he's dressed in an expensive business suit.'

'But what can he actually *do* to you now you're out of hospital, Emily?' Oliver asked.

'Who knows? He's cunning enough to think something up. I need a lawyer *and* a bodyguard.'

'You've got a lawyer,' Oliver pointed out.

She turned to Chad. 'Since you're not a lawyer, how about applying to be my bodyguard?'

He smiled. 'All right.'

'I'm worried about what he'll do next, too,' Rachel said.

'Why don't you come up to Lancashire as well, Rach?'

'Do you mean it?'

'Of course I do.'

'You're on!'

Emily felt desperately tired all of a sudden, so snuggled down, resting her head against Chad's shoulder as she added, 'One for all and all for one. The Three Musketeers have nothing on us.'

Chad didn't say anything. His head had fallen against hers and he was breathing deeply and slowly.

'Maybe I can become an honorary musketeer, since I live just down the road,' Oliver said. There was no answer from the back. He lowered his voice. 'Are they asleep, Rachel?'

'Yes. Cuddled up like a pair of lovers.'

He gave her a boy's grin on an older man's face. 'You can feed me tea and cakes and sympathy.'

'What do you need sympathy for? Aren't all lawyers rich and comfortable?'

His voice grew harsher. 'Money isn't enough. I've been unable to settle into retirement. It was an earlier retirement than I'd planned, too, because I gave up work to nurse my wife through cancer. But Trish died anyway. I feel lost in that house. She used to . . . brighten it up.'

'I'm sorry for your loss.'

'You get used to it. You can't change things, after all. What happened to your husband?'

'Divorce. I don't talk about it. Ever. Tell me why you can't go back to work.'

'I'd spoil things for my son. Jeremy loves heading up the rooms, and he's good at it, too. Fortunately, he does toss me the odd case now and then to keep me from dying of boredom. Like this one.'

'Emily and Chad certainly need your help.'

'Yes. It's a strange situation, isn't it? I've never heard of anything like it. I intend to have a word with one or two people about what happened to Emily. Such a situation can't be allowed to continue.'

'Friends in high places?' she teased.

'Moderately high. But investigations into bureaucracies take time, so don't hold your breath.'

'I hope they get George, but somehow I doubt it, Oliver.'

Emily woke when the car stopped outside her house. It was still dark, but the sky was starting to lighten to grey. She felt so disoriented, it was only when she gazed into Chad's eyes, so close to hers and looking blurry with sleep, that she remembered what had happened. Then she sat up with a jerk, terrified something was wrong.

'We're here, love,' Rachel said from the front seat.

'Oh . . . yes . . . Goodness, I was sound asleep.'

Beside her Chad had come fully awake, doing it as gently as he seemed to do everything else. His eyes were brighter now, very blue, seeming to see the world so much more clearly than most other people she knew. And yet he was one of the quietest people she'd ever met. Even his voice was low and soothing. Had he been like that before his accident? She hoped so. She found the calm strength that emanated from him very attractive.

'Is this your house, Emily?' he asked.

'Yes, it is.'

'Pretty garden.'

'I love flowers.' She frowned. 'They've put in new bedding plants. I'd not have chosen those colours, but they're making a good show, aren't they?'

Oliver opened the driver's door, letting in some fresh air, and came round to open the rear door. 'Are you all right, Emily?'

'I'm fine, thanks.' She wriggled her shoulders, trying to stretch some life into her body, and smiled as she realized Chad was doing the same.

Rachel came to stand beside Oliver and study the other two. 'Do you want to start packing your things or do you need more rest? You could lie down for a bit. It's not really morning yet, is it? Oliver and I'll be here in case George the Horrible turns up.'

As Emily looked at the house, she felt strangely reluctant to go inside. It seemed to belong to a stranger, someone she'd known years ago. It wasn't hers any longer.

She shivered as a terrible thought struck her. 'Um, I know it's cowardly but I don't want to go inside at all if my nephew is there. I'm not in the best state to face him.'

'I'll go and check for you, shall I?' Oliver turned towards the house.

'George's car isn't there,' Rachel said. 'Only yours. It's rather battered. George drove it back from the hotel where you had your fall. It looks as if you'd been in a car accident as well as the later fall. Maybe that's why you were staying there.'

Emily spread her hands in a gesture of puzzlement, wondering why she didn't remember a car accident or a hotel. 'They told me I fell down a flight of stairs at the hotel, but I don't remember it. Post-traumatic amnesia, they call it. Minor. Just the accident and fall missing from my memories. Well, I think it was just the accident, and I don't care if I never remember that.'

'Do you have a house key?' Oliver asked.

'No. George took it out of my handbag, together with my purse.' Anger surged up in her yet again at the high-handed behaviour of her nephew. 'Rachel has a spare key, though.'

'Not now, I don't. George conned it out of me the first time he came here and refused to return it.'

'I hid one behind the water butt as well, under a brick. When you live alone you become paranoid about getting locked out.'

'I'll get it.' Rachel slipped out of the car and vanished round the back, returning almost immediately brandishing a key. 'I know my way round the house, so I'll help you check that no one's there, Oliver. Though they'd surely have come out to confront us if they were.'

'It won't hurt to set Emily's mind at rest,' he murmured.

They went into the house and after a short time, Rachel came back to the front door and beckoned. 'All clear.'

Chad looked exhausted, but his smile was warm as he looked at her. 'I'd better sit down. Sorry I'm not much use. Pushed myself a bit far last night.'

'But we did escape.'

His smile became a gleeful grin. 'Yes, we did. Sister Pauline must be furious.'

'Let's go into the kitchen first. I'm dying for a cup of tea.' Automatically, Emily went to put the kettle on.

Rachel took it out of her hand. 'I'll do that. You go round the place again with Oliver and check that everything's all right. I think they've moved some of your furniture.'

Emily went into the sitting room first and stared round indignantly. Rachel was right. They'd rearranged her furniture quite drastically.

'I can see by the marks in the carpet that they've moved things,' Oliver said quietly.

'Yes. If I were staying here, I'd move them straight back.'

Upstairs in the main bedroom there was no sign of Emily's clothes or other possessions. The wardrobe was full of someone else's garments, a man's and a woman's, graded neatly according to size and type. Presumably these were George and Marcia's.

'They've certainly made themselves at home,' Oliver commented.

'What have they done with *my* clothes?'

They found them piled anyhow on the bed in one of the smaller bedrooms. Since the hangers were still attached to the clothes, it appeared George had simply dumped the wardrobe's contents here.

It was as if he hadn't expected her to return at all.

'Tea's ready!' Rachel called from the kitchen.

They joined Chad at the breakfast bar and Emily sipped her tea, grateful for its warmth and fresh taste after the hospital's offering, which always tasted stewed.

'Are you sure you don't want to call the police in about George taking over your house?' Oliver asked.

'No. For my sister's sake I won't do that. I'll be content to keep him out of my house and life permanently. Maybe I could take out a restraining order or something to keep him away from me.' She looked round, grimacing at the changes. 'I wonder if I shall ever feel comfortable here again.'

After another mouthful of tea, anger took over. 'Can I throw their possessions out into the street, Oliver? Until I get rid of their things, it's as if George and Marcia are still here. They must have got some of their stuff out of storage because there's more than they could have brought on the plane.'

'I don't think you should do anything that might damage their possessions, like leaving them outside in the rain.'

'Pity.'

Chad set his cup down. 'How about putting your nephew's stuff into another storage facility and changing the locks so that he can't get inside the house again?'

Three people stared at him and began to smile.

'What a brilliant idea!' Emily said.

Oliver nodded. 'It's very tempting. And that wouldn't be against the law.'

'Let's do it, then.' But before Emily could stand up, a yawn overtook her suddenly.

'Why don't you and Chad have a nap? Oliver and I can make a start on clearing their clothes and other things out,' Rachel suggested. 'When you wake, you can check everything.'

'I'd like to shower and change my clothes first,' Emily said.

Chad looked down at himself ruefully. 'I don't have anything to change into.'

Oliver studied him. 'We're about the same height, though you're a bit thinner than me. I brought an overnight case, so I'll lend you some clothes till you can buy more. If you don't mind wearing them, that is. I wonder what's happened to your money?'

'I don't know. I presume my wallet was stolen when I was beaten up. Unlike Emily, I'm definitely going to contact the police.'

'I'd advise you not to do that until you've consulted a doctor.'

'Why do I need to see another doctor?'

'You both do, to prove that you're in your right mind, should the need arise. You seem fine to me, but I'm a lawyer. If anyone tries to get you back into hospital, it's a doctor's opinion that will keep you out.'

'Oh. I suppose you're right, but I feel as if I've seen enough doctors to last me a lifetime. Only . . . now I come to think of it, it was mainly nurses I saw, except for that doctor with the nervous twitch.'

'I couldn't stand him,' Emily said. 'He treated me like an idiot.'

'Yes. And he didn't seem to hear what I said.'

'Perhaps he's in it with Pauline.'

'Or just jaded and turning a blind eye.' Chad looked across the room. 'We'll do as you suggest, Oliver. No way are they getting me back inside.'

'Better safe than sorry,' Emily agreed. 'We're giving you a lot of trouble, Oliver.'

He shrugged. 'Look. Truth to tell, I was bored and feeling sorry for myself till I got involved with you folk. I think this is going to be a rather interesting series of events.'

'The more the merrier,' Emily said. But she was looking at Chad as she spoke.

'Are you really, truly sure?' he asked in a low voice. 'I don't want to be a burden.'

'Very sure. I'll feel much safer if I have someone living with me.'

Rachel nudged Oliver and winked. The other two didn't notice, so after giving them a moment or two, she spoke loudly enough to catch their attention. 'That's settled, then. Come and lie down in the sitting room. I'll fetch you some blankets.'

'We can't sleep all the time,' Emily protested, fed up of wasting her life doing nothing.

'It's your choice what you do from now on, but you've had a very stressful night and you're not fully recovered yet.'

Oh, how blissful it was to be in charge of her own life again! Emily thought as she settled down on the sofa. Then she sat up again, on a sudden idea. Should she ring her former boss and tell him what had happened? Leon would help her clear up this mess, she was sure. No. She'd told him she could manage her own life. She didn't want to admit that she'd landed in trouble.

She had no idea what the place in Lancashire was like, because she'd not been close to her much older relative, apart from meeting at an occasional family function.

She wriggled down into a comfortable position. She was too tired to ask any more questions. The answers would still be waiting when she woke up. The sofa was so comfortable . . . she'd often fallen asleep on it watching TV. She closed her eyes and let her worries slip away . . . just for a little while.

Five

Emily was woken a couple of hours later by the front door bell. She could see through the living-room window that it was her neighbour from across the road, a man she'd never got on with. *He* wouldn't be here to wish her well, she was sure. He only usually came across to ask her to join him in complaining about something to the council.

Rachel answered the door, but Emily wasn't having anyone else dealing with Mr Teddington for her, so got up and straightened her clothes.

There was no sign of Chad on the other sofa, but she could hear water running upstairs in the bathroom.

'George asked me to keep an eye on the place,' her neighbour was saying. 'He told me no one had permission to come into his house. So what are *you* doing here, Mrs Fenwick?'

Emily went out into the hall and pulled the front door wide open. 'Rachel's helping me settle in. I suppose *I* am allowed to move back into my own house, Mr Teddington?'

He gaped at her, his mouth opening and shutting like a stranded fish's. 'George said you'd not be able to come home again, that you'd need . . . looking after.' He was staring at her suspiciously.

So he was on first name terms with her nephew. She'd never attempted to get friendly with Teddington or his wife, who were a pair of snobs. 'George was wrong. I don't have dementia, if that's what he told you, and I'm perfectly capable of looking after myself now that I've recovered from my accident. You can tell him that when you ring him up to let him know we're here.'

He flushed, which told her that her guess about what he was going to do was correct.

Oliver moved Rachel gently to one side and joined Emily on the doorstep. 'I'm Ms Mattison's lawyer and I'd advise you not to interfere at all, Mr— er?' He glanced at Emily.

'Teddington.'

'Mr Teddington,' he repeated. 'You don't want to find yourself involved in legal action later on. Mr Pilby had no right to move in here. It isn't his house and his aunt didn't give him permission. Did you even check that he was her nephew?'

There was silence as the man stared from one to the other then backed away. 'None of my business.' He walked across the road, shoulders hunched, hands thrust deep in his pockets.

'How dare he poke his nose into my affairs?' Emily muttered. 'I might have known *he* would get friendly with George. They both think they're better than anyone else.'

Oliver laid one hand on her shoulder. 'Ignore him. I've got some good news, for a change. I've found a company which will pick up and store your nephew's possessions today! Rachel and I have got most of them sorted out. We dumped them in the dining room. We just need you to check a few things.'

Emily felt instantly better. 'Wow, you must have worked quickly. Thank you so much.'

'It was a pleasure.'

Chad came downstairs to join them, hair damp from a shower. He looked younger, even though Oliver's clothes hung rather loosely on him, and his colour was much better for even that couple of hours' rest.

She smiled at him. 'Are you all right?'

'I'm fine, though my muscles are protesting a bit about the extra exercise yesterday. How about you?'

'I'm better than I've been for a long time. But like you, I'm out of practice at being active.' Emily turned as the noise of an electric drill started up from the back of the house. 'What's happening?'

It was Oliver who answered. 'We took your consent for granted and hired a security company to do a rush job on this place.' He gestured as a man came into the hall and opened the fuse box under the stairs. 'This is Terry. Terry, meet the owner, Emily Mattison.'

The man raised one hand in a quick salute and turned back to deal with some extra wiring.

'Terry and his staff are not only changing the door locks,' Oliver went on, 'but setting up a basic security system on the ground floor. Your nephew won't get in again unless he breaks a window, and if he does, the police will be called automatically, because the place will be monitored 24/7.'

She clapped her hands together at that news. 'Oh, I do wish I could see George's face when he finds out his key doesn't work.'

'I think you'd be wise to avoid a confrontation for the time being.'

'Yes. I know. I'll just have to imagine the scene. George will go bright red and swell up with anger.'

'I can pay the security company for you and then take it out of the estate later.'

'No need. At least, there won't be a need if my second credit card is still in its hiding place. I'm hoping George didn't find it.' She went to the bookcase, which had a false panel behind some of the smaller books on a lower shelf. As she opened it, she sighed in relief. 'He hasn't discovered this lot, thank goodness.'

Both men looked at her in surprise.

'I'm a bit paranoid about losing my credit card and not having access to my money. It happened to me once when I was overseas. So I keep two cards.'

'Where's the other credit card?'

'You'll have to ask George. It was in my purse, which is also missing. I'll cancel that card on Monday.'

'We found your purse. At least he didn't take the money out of it, but you're right: there's no credit card.'

'He'll claim he was keeping it safe, I suppose.'

'Never mind George the Horrible. Am I still coming with you to Lancashire?' Rachel asked.

'I hope so.' Emily turned to her lawyer. 'I have no idea what Penelope's house is like. I've never visited her there.'

'It's old and rather run down, with a rather strange set of outbuildings. It used to be a pub called The Drover's Hope – the name dates from the days when people brought their animals to market on foot, so some parts are quite old. I think it's structurally sound, at least the main building is.'

'A pub!'

'Hasn't been licensed for a decade or so. I did a quick walk through with my son after Penelope died. Her flat on the ground floor is the most modern part. Everything's very old-fashioned, though. Some of the outhouses at the rear need attention. We didn't feel it right to do any renovations without your permission. After all, you may want to knock the whole place down and build a modern house, or sell it.'

'How many bedrooms does it have?'

'Apart from the flat, six at least, perhaps more.'

She looked at him in surprise. 'Goodness! It sounds far bigger than I'd expected.' She turned to her friend. 'Plenty of room for you to stay . . . unless you want to stay here and confront George?'

'No way. He'll be furious and he'll guess I was involved in your escape from hospital. I won't want my tyres slashing again. Or worse. How about I follow you up to Lancashire? I can't pack and load my car until they've finished changing the tyres, and they can't start the job till later today.'

Oliver turned to Emily. 'Right then. We can leave as soon as you and Chad have had something to eat. I'm sure the security firm can be trusted to finish their work and lock up behind themselves. I'll instruct them not to let George in if he comes back early, whatever he claims.'

'I'd like to leave him a message.' She smiled. 'I'll stick a note on the inside of the window and leave details of what we've done with his things at Mr Teddington's.'

'Good idea. And since there's a good doctor in the village near The Drover's Hope, I can ring and make an appointment for you both for tomorrow morning.'

'I agree.' Chad frowned. 'Why do I keep thinking about the legal side of things? There's something hovering.' He tapped his head. 'I wish I could remember it.'

Emily reached across to give his hand a squeeze. 'Don't try to force things. I'm sure you'll gradually start to remember.'

'I feel as if I'm on the verge of it.' He made a little growling noise in his throat, shaking his head in exasperation. He kept hold of her hand for a minute, then shot her a quick smile, before letting go.

She turned back to Oliver. 'Does Penelope's house have internet access? I'll want to take my computer.'

'I'm pretty certain it doesn't, so we'll have to get it connected. Penelope wasn't one for modern technology. Even the cooker and fridge are ancient. But she did buy a lot of books, so you won't be short of reading material. I think reading was her main form of entertainment as she grew older. She had very eclectic tastes.'

He pulled out a notebook, muttering 'Internet connection' as he added it to his list. 'Now, if you'll get something to eat, I'll dismantle your computer. Do you want to check it before I do that?'

'No. It can wait till later. I've no doubt George has already had a good look at my files, but I doubt he's seen the important ones. I have a double system set up, with one hidden behind a security wall. A computer expert would find it, but I doubt George has that much expertise.'

'You're into computers?' he asked.

'Into using them. And into security for my private files. I'm not good enough technically to set up a system like that myself, so I paid someone I used to work with to do it for me.'

As soon as they'd eaten, Oliver ushered them out to the car and set off. 'I'm glad George didn't come back. Everything will go much more smoothly if we can avoid any confrontations with your nephew.'

She didn't share his confidence. George was still a threat, as far as she was concerned.

George wasn't enjoying himself in Brighton. He'd only come because it'd look bad to turn down a prize from his company and he'd put it off longer than was tactful.

He took an instant dislike to the room they'd been given and insisted on paying extra for a suite. They could well afford it these days, after all. It was very economical living at his aunt's. And now, there was the prospect of more money coming in when he took over her affairs.

He scowled as he watched his wife unpack on the Friday evening.

'Smile, dear. You're supposed to be enjoying yourself,' Marcia teased.

'I'd rather be at home.'

'Well, I wouldn't. Anyway, we don't actually have a home now, not even a rented one.'

'At my aunt's house, then, if you must be pedantic. I like living there.' He looked at his watch. 'Time to get a meal. Let's see what's on the menu here. We can go out and explore tomorrow.'

She pulled a face, but went down with him to the bar.

The following day after breakfast, she said, 'Come on. Let's go out and explore the centre of Brighton. I don't really know it.'

He wandered along the Lanes with her, disgusted by the high prices being asked for the antiques and trinkets. 'Most of this is rubbish.'

'No, it isn't. And no one's forcing you to buy anything. Just let me enjoy looking. You know how good I am at spotting bargains in jewellery. We'll go to the Pavilion next.'

'Do we have to? I'm not into stately homes.'

'You know I've always wanted to see it.'

He shrugged and went with her. He had nothing else to do, after all. But he couldn't see what all the fuss was about. The place was garish and ridiculously fussy, Indian in style outside, Chinese inside. The man who designed it must have been crazy.

At least they found a good Indian restaurant near the hotel.

The next morning they went for a drive, which was marginally more interesting to him, because they were studying the area with a view to retiring there eventually.

At lunchtime they found a country house hotel where they had a superb meal. He enjoyed fine living. One day, he'd live like this all the time.

Since Marcia never drank more than one glass of wine, he finished off a bottle of rather good Australian merlot and let her drive them back.

He took a short nap on their return, but once he woke up, he grew restless again. She had her head in a book, one of her damned romances probably, and he'd finished reading the financial pages. When his mobile sounded, he fumbled for it eagerly, hoping it was something that would take him away from here and let him get back to his computer, which Marcia had insisted he leave behind.

'It's Phil Teddington from across the road, George. You asked me to keep an eye on your house. Did you know your aunt had come back?'

'*What?*'

George listened in growing anger. How the hell had Emily got out of hospital? That damned sister wasn't keeping her end of the bargain.

When he broke the connection, he told Marcia what had happened, then rang the hospital.

He was unable to speak to the ward sister. Pauline had a rostered day off, it seemed. Did these people never do a full week's work?

'Why the hell has my aunt been discharged? She's not fit to turn loose on the world.'

'Ah! I'll need to put you through to Central Admin. They're dealing with this case.'

Which only confirmed that he was right to be uneasy.

'Can I help you?' A man's voice this time.

'George Pilby here. I want to know why my aunt – Emily Mattison – has been discharged. And why couldn't the geriatric unit sister tell me about her just now? *What's been going on?*'

'Give me a minute.'

Some inane music began playing in his ear. He glared at the handpiece and held it further away.

'Mr Pilby? Right. Your aunt has discharged herself from the hospital and is no longer our concern. I thought she'd have let you know, since you were listed as her next of kin and have been visiting her.'

'She was in no fit state to look after herself. And how did she manage to leave, anyway? She didn't have a car or money. And surely *I* should have been consulted. After all, *I* was looking after her.'

'Her lawyer came to collect her and—'

'Lawyer! What lawyer?'

'Um . . . I'll find his name if you'll hold for a minute.'

More of that inane, tinkling music.

'You there, Mr Pilby?'

'Of course I am!'

'Your aunt's lawyer is a Mr Oliver Tapton.'

'Tapton . . .' George remembered the lawyer's letter about the legacy and offer to buy, but that had been from a Jeremy Tapton, not an Oliver. 'Why did this Tapton take her away from the hospital?'

'I don't know. It's none of our business now she's left. Further enquiries should be directed to Mr Tapton's business premises, it says in the notes.'

'And where are they?'

'In Lancashire, near a place called Littleborough.'

George frowned. That was the address he had, even if it was another Tapton who'd written to inform her of the legacy. But his aunt lived in Hertfordshire, so why would she go to Lancashire? Was it to escape him? Or had she found out about the legacy and was going to check it out? But she'd gone back to her own home first. Typical of her crazy thinking. It just showed he had been right to have her looked after.

'Mr Pilby?'

He focused on the phone again. 'It seems to me that you've let her out before she was ready and if she falls ill again, I'll damn well sue you.' He ended the call and dumped his mobile phone on the table. After thinking furiously, he picked it up again and rang his mother.

'Have you heard from Aunt Emily? I've just found out she's discharged herself.'

'Without telling you, after all you've done for her? That's very ungrateful, but at least it must mean she's a lot better, which is good news. How is your holiday going, George dear?'

'It's as boring as holidays usually are. Marcia and I are going home again today.'

'You mean to Emily's house? Will she want you there now?'

'I won't know till I see her.'

'You can always come back here.'

'I'll let you know. Call me if you hear from Emily.'

He sat drumming his fingers on the bedside table. His long-term plans did not include his aunt coming out of care again. And Pauline had assured him that could be arranged.

When his wife came out of the bathroom, he told her what he'd found out. 'You'd better start packing. I need to look into this.'

Marcia looked at him anxiously. 'Have they discovered what you were doing?'

'I was only ensuring that my aunt was cared for properly. Make sure you remember that at all times.'

She gave him one of her worried looks, half-opened her mouth, then clamped her lips together and started packing without a word.

He left her to it and went down to tell the hotel staff he was leaving, checking every detail of the bill before he paid it. Then he asked for his car to be brought round.

Back in their room, Marcia was finishing off the packing with her usual efficiency. She looked at him anxiously. 'Where will we go? We won't be able to stay at your aunt's house now.'

'Whether we can stay there or not, we have to go back, if only to collect our things. We'll no doubt pick up some useful information while we're there. She doesn't know about . . . anything.'

'She must guess.'

'Not for certain. She was in a coma for days, dammit! She shouldn't even have recovered from that. And it must have affected her.'

He paced up and down the room, then stopped to say slowly, 'I bet she hasn't really recovered, and someone's taking advantage of her. It'll be that interfering bitch next door who brought in the lawyer. I thought I'd made sure she wouldn't interfere again.'

'You shouldn't have done that. You go too far sometimes.'

'I go as far as is needed when I want something. *You* should remember that.'

She shook her head slightly but didn't argue, bending over to zip up their suitcases.

He smiled grimly. He could always keep Marcia in order, if he needed to. His dear wife enjoyed her comfortable lifestyle as much as he did.

And he could keep his mother in order, too.

His aunt had better watch out. He wasn't finished with her yet. She'd come to heel before he was through.

By early afternoon, Rachel had cleared out her fridge, packing the fresh stuff as well as her clothes and computer, and was ready to follow the others. When she heard a vehicle draw up next door, she peeped out of the window and exclaimed in dismay as George and Marcia got out of it. 'Oh, hell!'

What had brought them back early? Thank goodness he hadn't caught her outside packing her car.

After locking all the outer doors, she went up to her bedroom to watch what George was doing. As an afterthought she got out her camera. If he touched her car again, she'd get proof of him damaging it.

But she wasn't leaving the house till she was sure she wouldn't run into him. She didn't dare.

What was there about him that made her feel so nervous? She was usually able to stand up for herself.

George followed his wife to the front door of his aunt's house, dragging one of their cases. 'Doesn't look as if she's here. All the windows are shut. I'll go over and see Teddington while you put the kettle on. I'm parched.'

Marcia had her key in her hand and was looking at it in puzzlement. 'It doesn't fit, George. But it's the right key, I know it is.'

He snatched it from her hand and tried it, with the same result, then peered at the lock 'The bitch! She's had this lock changed.'

'Oh, no! Most of our clothes are inside. And our other things, including your computer. Do you think she's here?'

'No. We'll have to break a window and— Look at that!' He pointed to the new security system, silver lines edging all the windows. 'She *has* been busy!'

Marcia walked along the front of the house. 'There's a note for you stuck to the inside of this window, George. Didn't you see it?'

'No, I damned well didn't.' He went to stare at the piece of paper, which said in large letters:

To George Pilby

Information about your possessions has been left at Number Five.
O. Tapton, lawyer.

He cursed and hurled the useless front door key into the flower bed, red rage filling him.

'George, calm down. *George!*'

It took him a few minutes to do that. It always did on the rare occasions when he got into one of his rages.

'What do you think your aunt's going to do now?' Marcia asked once he was breathing steadily again.

'I don't know. But I intend to find out. Damnation! Of all the times for us to be away on a stupid holiday. And now they've locked up my computer somewhere! I told you I should have taken it with me.'

'You'd never have stopped playing with it, if you had. I wanted a real holiday for once.'

He didn't answer, was staring in through the front window.

After a while, Marcia ventured, 'We should go across to see Phil Teddington, George. The note says information has been left with him. We need to find out what they've done with our things.'

'I'll do that. You wait for me in the car.' He marched across the street and came back a few minutes later brandishing an envelope.

After getting into the car, he opened it with his usual meticulous care, unpeeling the stick-down flap bit by bit and easing the letter out carefully. After reading the single page, he passed it to his wife, then sat scowling into space.

She read it quickly and waited for him to speak. But he didn't. After a few minutes, she said, 'George?' She had to repeat it before he turned to look at her.

'What?'

'We need to find somewhere to stay tonight before we do anything else. I don't want to go back to your mother's. Her spare room is far too small.'

'We're definitely not going there. I don't want her involved in this. We'll find a hotel for tonight and think about what to do.' He looked at his watch. 'It's too late to get our things out of storage today.'

'Where shall we go?'

'What does it matter? We just need to find somewhere nearby for tonight.'

She knew then that he was seriously upset. He was usually very attentive to his own comfort when staying in a hotel. And to hers.

She continued to wait. There were times when it was best just to let George get things out of his system.

He didn't drive away immediately. 'I'm not letting this go, Marcia. It's got too much . . . potential.'

'Are you sure?'

'Of course I'm bloody sure.'

He still didn't start the car and sat drumming his fingers on the steering wheel. 'What I don't understand is why she's got herself a lawyer from Lancashire, of all places. I know she's inherited that old house, but why not get a lawyer from near where she lives to look after things for her? Or perhaps this guy has taken over and is telling her what to do. Yes, that'll be it. He intends to feather his own nest. Him and that bitch next door.'

Marcia looked across at the house. 'It's such a waste. It doesn't look as if Emily's going to be staying here at all.'

'No. I bet she's gone up north with him.'

He glared at the house next door. 'If that bitch's car is still there tonight, I'll make her sorry.'

'What for?'

'She's the only one who could have arranged all this. That's why she went to see my aunt in hospital.'

As they pulled up at a hotel, he said grimly, 'At least we know where my aunt's lawyer is. And where that place she's inherited is. We'll find him easily enough. And her, too.'

She looked at him in alarm. 'You're not going after her? George, no. Leave her in peace now.'

'I shall leave her in peace after I've taken charge of the land she's inherited. That's the important thing, to maximize the profit from selling it.'

'It's not our land!'

He gave one of his sneering smiles. 'No. But I'm going to look after her business matters, as I do for my mother. Wait and see. I'll pull Emily into line.'

'George, please don't.'

He gave her one of his scornful looks. 'Do you realize how valuable that land is? Several million at least. What's she going to do with that much money at her age? She's never been a spender.'

'Nor have you.'

'Only because I have nothing to spend. One day I will have. One day you and I will live in style, Marcia. And my aunt is the key. Her inheritance makes my mother's money look like small change.'

She looked at him doubtfully.

'Don't worry. I'll be careful what I do. I won't rush into anything.'

Six

Emily woke with a start as the car stopped. She realized she was holding Chad's hand – again. He was still asleep, so she squeezed his fingers gently to wake him.

When he began to stir, she let go reluctantly and stretched her stiff body. She wasn't even sure he knew they'd been holding hands.

He smiled at her. 'You held my hand even in your sleep.'

So he had known. She was glad and blurted out without thinking, 'I find it comforting.'

He reached out to stroke her cheek with the tip of one finger. 'Ditto. You and I have been through some difficult times together, haven't we?'

'Yes. But we're starting to put our lives to rights now.'

'I hope so. There's a lot still to sort out. And we can get to know one another better as we do it. I'm sure I'll remember some more about myself.'

She wished she could find a way to help him with that; knew how it galled him not to know who he really was. But what he remembered was in the lap of the gods. What the two of them did from now on was in their own hands. 'Where are we?'

Oliver spoke from the front seat. 'I've stopped at the motorway services. I thought we could all do with a comfort break and something to eat. We might be able to buy some food here as well, enough to manage on till you can do some proper shopping.'

'If I know Rachel, she'll be bringing plenty of food. She got into the habit of that when her son and his family were still living in England. She's brilliant. She can put a meal together at the drop of a hat. But you're right, Oliver, we ought to buy a few necessities, in case she's delayed.'

They didn't linger long, grabbing sandwiches and a drink each, then stocking up on tea, coffee, milk, bread, butter, cheese, apples and jam, before setting off again.

Emily was feeling wide awake now and was looking forward to seeing her inheritance. 'How long will it take us to get to Minkybridge from here, Oliver? And what's it like? It's such a strange name.'

'No one knows where the first part of the name comes from, but there is a small bridge over a stream called Minky Brook. The place isn't even a village, it's barely a hamlet – there are a few scattered farms nearby, two rows of small labourers' houses, and a small group of brash newer residences. One of which I live in.'

'You don't sound as if you like the newer houses.'

'I don't. But my wife said old houses were inconvenient and pokey, so we bought a new one. Minkybridge is outside Littleborough on the edge of the moors, just off the road to Todmorden. The older houses are mostly former handloom weavers' cottages. *I* think they're pretty, built of stone with a row of mullioned windows in the third floor to give light to the weavers in the old handloom days before the mills were built.'

'You sound as if you love your history.'

'I love the whole area, and yes, I'm fascinated by our local history. I'm just down the road from your aunt's house and I often stroll along Minky Brook on fine summer evenings. You get some lovely views of Littleborough with Rochdale in the distance from there.'

'Does the house I've been left have a weaver's top floor?'

'No. I'd have brought a photo of it, if things hadn't happened so quickly. No one's quite sure when the pub was first built, though perhaps we ought to call the earlier one an inn. It was for drovers bringing cattle and sheep to market and in the early days, they had a few small fields where customers could put their animals overnight. The land's still there, which is why you have a developer interested in buying it.'

'We do?'

'Didn't you get the letter about that? It's Barton and Halling, a national company.'

'No. George probably has it, and that'll be why he's so interested in taking over my business affairs.' Emily sat fuming for a minute or two, then said, 'Tell me more about the inn.'

He slowed down as traffic began to build up. 'People crossing the moors to Todmorden often stopped there, not just drovers. When hiking became popular in the latter part of the nineteenth century, hikers used it, too, even more so in the 1920s and 30s. The old place continued to operate as a pub offering some basic accommodation right until a couple of decades ago.'

He sighed. 'Not a lot of demand for it, though, and custom tailed off. Motor cars brought new people who were just out for the day, so they didn't need to stay overnight. The locals used to patronize the bar. Some of the older men still complain about it closing. Actually, I agree with them there. I'd love to stroll up the hill for a pint in the evening.'

'Perhaps we should reopen it.'

'You'd not make much of a living and you'd have to work hard. Penelope closed the pub completely after her husband died. She said that sort of life was too hard for a woman on her own. Be warned, though. Hikers still knock on the door asking for refreshments. Penelope used to give them cups of tea, said she enjoyed the company. She was a feisty old dame. I was very fond of her.'

'I liked her the few times I met her,' Emily agreed. 'Did she live there on her own?'

'Yes. People worried about her safety, but she always used to say nothing bad would happen to her at The Drover's Hope. And it didn't. She died peacefully in bed of old age. Ninety-two, she was, and still looking after herself, apart from help with the shopping.'

'Why did she leave the house to me? Do you know?'

'I do, because I drew up the will. She said you were the only relative of your generation who didn't suck up to her to get hold of the property and . . .'

'And what?'

'Well, this puzzled me, but she wouldn't explain. She said you were the right person to have The Drover's Hope. She said you'd bring the old place back to life again, that it'd give you hope and then you'd give hope to others. And I was to tell you that.'

'I wonder what she meant.'

Chad was listening with great interest. 'Sounds a fascinating inheritance. Was the old lady psychic?'

'She had a way of foretelling what would happen sometimes, I must admit. I don't really believe in the supernatural, but sometimes there are things which are hard to explain by logic.'

'I believe there's something beyond this life,' Chad said quietly. 'And I've sensed the presence of ghosts many times, particularly in very old buildings.'

Emily waited, but he didn't go on, only sat frowning, so she asked casually, 'Do you live in an older house, Chad?'

'I have a flat, for convenience, but one day I'm going to live in the country.' He stopped in shock. 'Why couldn't I remember that before?'

'I should think when you stop trying too hard and relax, things will be more likely to come back to you,' Emily said. 'And perhaps your mind will work better now you're away from that horrible geriatric unit. I know it used to make me feel terrible, as if the place was smothering me.'

'I only remember the flat hazily, what my bedroom was like, for instance. I can't remember the address or any useful details. Someone did such a thorough job of beating me up and removing all forms of identification, I have to wonder if they didn't intend me to survive.'

'You were beaten up that badly?' Oliver sounded shocked.

'Yes, I keep getting flashbacks about it.' Chad grimaced. 'Very painful flashbacks. Two men. I can remember some of my bank details as well – at least, I think I can remember which bank it is – but until I remember my name and so on, I won't be able to access my money, will I?'

'It can be arranged once you do remember your name. That's the key.'

Chad shook his head sadly.

Oliver looked at him sympathetically. 'This is an unusual

situation. I really want to help you two, and I will, but at present, I think we should concentrate on getting you settled into The Drover's Hope tonight. Tomorrow I'll pick you up and take you to the bank to take over the accounts, Emily, then we'll go shopping.'

'Thank you. Is all this part of the legal service?' Emily saw his grin in the driving mirror. The expression made him appear almost boyish, in spite of him having very little hair left.

'Heavens, no. It'd cost you a fortune, the way law firms charge for their services by the quarter-hour. No, it'll be my pleasure to help you as a private individual . . . if you want me to, that is.'

'I do want your help. I not only need to get hold of some money, I need to buy a new car.'

'You've got plenty of money coming to you once probate is settled, so there won't be much of a problem with that.'

'I've got enough in my own account to buy a car straight away.'

She turned to Chad, who was looking wistful. 'You've remembered some more things today and I'm sure other information will come back to you.'

'For the first time, I'm beginning to hope. If I can stay with you in the meantime, Emily, I shall be eternally grateful.'

It was strange, Emily mused as they continued driving. Chad had talked about hope just now. Penelope had spoken to her lawyer of Emily finding hope at The Drover's Hope and giving it to others.

Was it happening already? She really liked the idea of doing something as worthwhile as that.

And perhaps, if she were very lucky, George wouldn't pursue her any longer.

She gave a wry smile. It wasn't actually her he was pursuing; it was her money.

Would he stop? Somehow, she doubted it.

Oliver stopped the car by the side of the road that led up across the Pennine range, the backbone of northern England. He pointed ahead. 'You can see The Drover's Hope from here. Look up the slope in that direction!' He pointed. 'That's it, sitting on the rise to the right of the main road.'

Emily leaned forward to study the building – no, several buildings. Mine now, she thought, and something warmed inside her.

The house was far larger than she'd expected, even after Oliver's description, a sprawling, uneven mass of dark slate roofs on a stone building that was two storeys at the front. She couldn't see the rear clearly from here. The building wasn't of any particular style, but she found its irregularities interesting.

Since the traffic heading over the Pennines towards Todmorden was very light, Oliver slowed down to a crawl before they got to Minkybridge. He pointed to a house set back from the road, modern and of a comfortable size. 'That's my home, but I've been thinking of buying a renovator's dream now and working on it.'

'Are you good at do-it-yourself stuff?'

'Hopeless, but I'm sure I could *organize* tradesmen to work on a renovation project. I love watching those home improvement programmes on television. Jeremy – my son – pulls a face when I talk about doing that. But if I ever find an old place that speaks to me, I'll buy it and have a go at renovating. The only good thing about being widowed is that you can please yourself completely about what you do.'

He sounded deeply sad, and there was always a warmth in his voice when he spoke of his wife. Emily liked that.

Oliver speeded up again and shortly afterwards pulled off the road into a typical pub car park, a large, square expanse of crumbling tarmac between the main building and the road. It had potholes here and there, and the edges were crumbling badly. There was no inn sign hanging outside on the wooden post, but the hooks for it were still there in the square frame at the top. There was a smaller sign by the door that read *The Drover's Hope*.

'I like the look of the place,' Chad said. 'It's a real mix-up of architectural styles, but somehow they look attractive together – or they would do if the door and window frames were painted and some of those cracked roof tiles replaced. Shouldn't be a difficult job.'

'You sound as if you know what you're talking about,' Emily said when he fell silent.

'I felt as if I did.' He sounded faintly surprised.

Oliver switched the engine off, then flourished one hand.

'Emily, meet The Drover's Hope. Drover's Hope, this is your new owner, Miss Emily Mattison.'

'Ms,' she corrected automatically.

'Sorry. I usually try to remember. That really matters to you, doesn't it?'

'Yes. My marital status is no one else's business, and when some people say "Miss" to an older woman, they get a slightly sneering look, as if it's wrong not to have been married. It was my choice not to marry, because I've never met anyone I felt I could commit to for the rest of my life.'

She had tried living with a couple of men, and *she* had left them, not the other way round. Both times she'd hoped the relationship would come to something before it was too late for her to have children, but it hadn't. She'd grown tired of the men, decent sorts but not *right*.

Sometimes she mourned the fact that she didn't have any children, but you had to take life as it came. At least she'd had an interesting job, involving travel at times, one that had given her the option of retiring early. To the rest of the world she'd been a secretary, but her job had involved so much more.

And what was she sitting here reminiscing for? Chad and Oliver were waiting for her. She opened the car door and got out to join them, studying the house – *her* house now.

She didn't want to travel any more; she wanted to settle somewhere and put down roots, big deep roots. As she looked at the old house, a voice seemed to say *Here!* in her head, and a warm feeling of coming home had her moving towards it without waiting for the others.

For all its imperfections, she fell in love with the place as quickly as that.

'What do you think?' Oliver asked when he caught up with her.

'I love it. There's something . . . I don't know, appealing about it. I feel it needs to be cherished, so that it can come into its own again, though as what, I don't know. I'd not like to run a pub.'

Silence greeted her remarks so she turned to Chad. 'What do you think?'

'I agree absolutely. I love the look of the house too. It sounds silly, but it feels like a real home.'

He frowned as he turned to stare at the moors that stretched away into the distance, his eyes following the road as it wound higher and higher over the treeless slopes. 'You know, there's something familiar about this sort of scenery. I must have visited Lancashire before.'

'You don't have a Lancashire accent. Yours has a bit of the south-west in it, I think. Not Cornwall or Devon – Somerset or Wiltshire, perhaps.'

'Do you think so?' He stared for a minute longer, then rubbed his temple, as if it ached. 'Damn! Some memory was hovering – I could almost catch it – but it's gone again.'

'Shall we go inside now?' Oliver had been waiting patiently, allowing them time to take things in, but now he moved past them, pulling out a key. It was a huge, old-fashioned metal object like something out of a fairy tale. 'I hope nobody's broken in. It'd be child's play to pick this lock, but Penelope wouldn't let me have more modern locks installed, let alone a security system.'

'If we can do it without damaging the door, I'd not object to putting better locks in and installing a security system as well,' Emily said. 'I'm a big believer in prevention where my own safety is concerned.' Leon had taught her that. She hadn't put an alarm system in her house in Kings Langley because she'd been intending to sell. How strange that she'd instantly wanted to protect this place!

As Oliver continued to fumble with the lock in vain, she held out her hand for the key. It felt comfortable in her hand, as long as her palm and fingers combined, made of rough, blackened iron, very old. It slid easily into the big keyhole and she felt a sense of satisfaction as it turned with a dull clunking sound.

She pushed the door open and stepped inside, then turned to hold out her hand to Chad. 'Come and explore our new home with me.'

He took her hand and they went inside.

Having him here felt right, too, she realized. Very right.

The minute George's car had turned out of the street, Rachel threw the remaining bits and pieces into her own vehicle, switched on the security alarm in her house and set off for Lancashire.

She kept an eye on the vehicles behind her, checking in the

rear view mirror to make sure George wasn't following her. She kept just as careful an eye ahead of her, in case he was taking the same route. But to her relief, she saw no further sign of him.

After a few minutes she settled down to enjoy the drive, not pushing herself too hard. She stopped once for a coffee and snack, and she met no traffic jams, thank goodness, though the traffic was heavy as she circled Manchester on the M64 ring road.

It was late evening when she got to Littleborough. She slowed down to admire some old stone buildings, then followed the satnav's instructions to Emily's pub.

She didn't know Lancashire very well, but she intended to explore it while she was here. She really liked the sight of the moors, great curves of land rolling away into the distance. It didn't overpower you as the French Alps had on her first and only visit there.

She flexed her hands one after the other as the traffic slowed almost to a halt. She'd be glad to stop driving. It had been a fraught couple of days and it had taken all her energy to cope.

When she went into work on the Sunday, Pauline was furious to find that her two most lucrative patients had run away during her weekend break. She called an emergency staff meeting at once.

'How could you let *one* patient escape?' she demanded. 'Let alone two?'

'It happened during the night,' someone muttered, sounding aggrieved. '*We* weren't on duty.'

'And I shall be speaking to the night staff about this, you can count on that. But those two must have been planning this, and I mean to get to the bottom of how they managed to do that without anyone noticing.'

Dead silence. They were avoiding her eyes. She'd hand picked this group of staff, people who'd been in trouble before, who'd do anything rather than upset her or get another black mark on their records. Even Jackson, the most uppity of them all, the one who'd tried to protest about the way she did some things, had been in trouble for insubordination before he joined the unit.

She scowled into the distance. Jackson. Yes, he must have been involved. It'd be typical of him. Too soft by far, that one. Or had he been feathering his own nest at her expense? Had they paid him to help them escape? She'd have to find out where he'd been during the weekend.

When the silence had gone on for long enough, she asked, 'How do you think this reflects on our unit? Badly. Very badly. If any other patient gets out, I'll make sure those responsible lose their jobs instantly, if not their professional accreditation.' She let that sink in, then waved one hand towards the door. 'You may go. Oh, wait a minute. When's Jackson coming back on duty?'

'He started his annual leave at the end of last week,' one of the nurses reminded her. 'So it'll be three weeks.'

How could she have forgotten that? 'Oh, yes.'

They exchanged glances and no one spoke.

'Well? What else do you know that I don't?'

'I don't think Jackson *is* coming back. He's got another job.'

When they'd all left, Pauline sat drumming her fingers on her desk. Jackson Hosier *must* have been involved in the escape. It could only have been him. Why? Why should he care about two old people, who were useless to society?

She checked with HR and found out that Jackson was definitely not coming back to work in this hospital. He must have arranged this without telling her. Which meant the human resources people had been involved.

She noted down the place he was going to. She'd make sure they knew how unreliable he was. How he'd let two old people escape, or even helped them, though she couldn't prove it. However, she was a master of innuendo, if she said so herself.

No one crossed her and got away with it. She'd been vulnerable once, wouldn't let anyone get the better of her again. Never, ever again.

She was enjoying twisting the tail of the system that had denied her promotion. Oh, that gave her such satisfaction!

She had it all planned. Retirement as soon as she was financially secure and to hell with her so-called profession.

Emily stopped to stare round the first room they entered, which must have been the main bar. It was dusty and the shelves behind the bar were bare, but it was a spacious area, and from the windows on either side of the door there were wonderful views right across the moors.

Chad went across to the counter and rubbed a corner of it, studying the wood closely. 'Oak. Years of polishing has gone into developing that depth of grain. You can't get a patina like that overnight, or even in a decade of polishing.'

'I don't think Penelope can have lived in this part. Look at the dust,' Emily said. 'There are quite a lot of footprints in it. Are those all yours, Oliver, or do you think someone else has been in here?'

'It looks as if someone else has been here.'

'An intruder, do you think?'

'Could be.'

'We'll have to be careful, make sure it's locked up properly before night falls.'

'I did check the rear part,' Oliver said. 'All locked up.'

'Good.' She smiled round her new home, still feeling a warmth, as if the house had welcomed her. Strange, that. She wasn't normally fanciful, was noted for her practicality.

She appreciated the way Chad was waiting for her to go first, taking care not to obscure her view. It was a sign of respecting her ownership, well, she thought it was. Was it ridiculous to feel so comfortable with Chad? So safe? Had he always been such a quiet, self-contained person?

The front door opened again and she turned to see Oliver standing in the entrance with a suitcase, smiling cheerfully at them. She hadn't even noticed him going back out again. He pointed. 'The flat's that way. Turn left into that passage and go through the door at the end.'

On one side of the passage was a small open space, only large enough to fit in two tables and chairs. The chairs were stacked now, and one table was piled on top of the other. It looked a mess, all dusty.

She paused before going along the passage to look towards the right and could see another bar behind the front one, a narrower space connected to the front by the serving area. 'Two bars? It must have been quite a busy place once.'

'We'll have to ask the local history centre. The pub had closed by the time Trish and I came to live up here.'

Emily continued along the short corridor, opened the door at the end and stopped just inside. 'Goodness! It's like stepping from the eighteenth century into the twentieth.' Not the twenty-first century, though. The room was like Emily's grandmother's house in style, with carpets, curtains and upholstery in such busy, contrasting patterns, it made her blink.

Oliver came to stand beside her. 'Penelope had this part of the house converted into a flat when she first came here, but once that was done, she never changed a thing. There are several bedrooms upstairs, but I don't think she went up there very often, if at all, in recent years. She found the stairs a bit of a trial because of her arthritis. She did have a new bathroom put in up there, though, so you and Rachel should be OK for showers, Chad.'

The living room was crammed with ornaments and knick-knacks. Every surface was covered with them. There was an electric fire with one of the armchairs set close to it, and a reading lamp positioned in just the right way to focus on a book. The whole room had clearly been set up for one person living alone.

Emily could imagine sitting reading here but would like a seating arrangement that welcomed friends – and definitely fewer ornaments, if any. 'She had lots of books. I like that.'

'This is only a small proportion. There are bookshelves upstairs as well as in the rear bar. You could set up a second-hand bookshop with what she's left you.'

'I shall enjoy reading them.'

'You have quite a few books too, if I remember correctly.'

'Yes. A lifelong passion, especially speculative fiction. I enjoy reading authors' guesses about what the future might be like, though they seem to have got very gloomy lately. I don't think that sort of dystopian image reflects the human soul.'

She moved across to another door to find a good sized bedroom with a wet room leading off it. A kitchen lay at the rear of the sitting room, open plan, with enough space for a small table at one end. The rooms were all spacious and when she pulled back the curtains, she found that the windows in the living area and bedroom looked out on to the road, giving her sweeping views of the moors, while the kitchen looked out on to a large courtyard with empty pots that would look lovely filled with plants.

She could live very happily here, she knew. *Thank you, Cousin Penelope! I'll look after your house. I think you were right. It does feel like a place of hope.*

At the rear of the kitchen was a utility area with a small, square window and a door leading to the courtyard. She tried to open it, but couldn't find the key. 'Didn't Penelope use this door, Oliver?'

He came to join her, frowning. 'Yes, of course she did. I've seen her sitting on that wooden bench in the afternoon sun many a time, reading or simply enjoying the warmth. Before she grew so frail, she used to keep those pots filled with flowers because this area is quite a sun trap.'

He checked around the inside of the door. 'Where's the key gone? Towards the end, I used to come here every few days to check she was all right, and Linda from Minkybridge came in to help with the housework and do Penelope's shopping. It might be a good idea to ask Linda to help you with the housework as well. You can well afford it and I know she needs the money. There's not much employment nearby.'

'That sounds a great idea to me. I'm not at all fond of housework.'

Oliver took out his notebook, mouthing the words aloud as he wrote, 'Contact Linda. Key to flat's back door. There should be a spare at the office. There's a whole bunch of them there. Surely she kept spares here, though?'

He looked at his watch. 'We probably ought to speed up this first tour and make sure we find Chad somewhere to sleep tonight. I'm assuming you'll sleep in the flat, Emily? We only need to put some clean sheets on the bed. Linda stripped it and washed everything after Penelope died. We can go through the rest of the house in detail when we get back from our shopping trip tomorrow.'

He waited, looking at her. 'You all right about this?'

'Oh, yes. I'm sure I'll be very comfortable here.'

'Let's go and check the other bedrooms upstairs for your friends.'

'Isn't there anywhere Chad could sleep downstairs? I'd rather have someone within earshot. It's a big house and I'm still nervous about George coming after me.'

'Surely he won't do that?' Oliver stared at her in shock. 'It'd be a crime.'

'I wouldn't put anything past my dear nephew when he scents money. If he could have kept me locked in that unit or one like it for the rest of my life, he would clearly have done so without hesitation.' She turned to Chad. 'Is it OK if we try to find you somewhere downstairs to sleep, somewhere near me?'

'I'll be happy anywhere. And if you're nervous, I should definitely sleep nearby.'

'Thank you.'

'There's Rachel to think of, too,' Oliver reminded them. 'Anyway, let me show you the upstairs before we decide.'

They went quickly through several bedrooms. They smelled of dust and disuse, with heavy old wardrobes and chests of drawers, standing sentinel round the edges of each room. There was only one bathroom to serve them all. There were clean sheets piled neatly in a linen cupboard on the landing, but the top ones looked dusty too, as if they hadn't been used for ages.

Oliver indicated another set of stairs, much narrower. 'That leads up to the attics.'

Emily stopped at the bottom of them, feeling limp with tiredness. 'I'll wait till tomorrow to explore up there, if you don't mind. Is it just attics not rooms?'

'It's both. There are quite a few rooms, smallish, for the staff probably. The open area is piled with junk that's been dumped there over the years.'

When they went downstairs, she linked her arm in Chad's. 'Where are we going to put you?'

'We can bring a mattress down and I'll sleep in the bar.'

'Are you sure?'

'I'm used to roughing it. I have vague memories of camping out. With children.' He stopped to stare at her. They both knew the implications of that. He must have been married, perhaps still was.

She didn't comment. But if he had a wife, why had she not been searching for him? 'One day you may even have the whole picture, or at least enough of it to see what to do with your life more clearly.'

Chad smiled at her. 'You're very positive. That helps.'

It was another of those moments where she felt so close to him, she wanted to touch him, and lean against his quiet strength.

He had a way of smiling at her that made her feel . . . warm and loved.

Then she remembered Oliver, standing watching them, and felt a little flustered, as if she'd been caught with her clothes off.

Chad turned back towards the nearest bedroom. 'I'll get a mattress.'

'Let Oliver do that. You've pushed yourself far enough for one day.'

'I hate being dependent on others.'

'At one time you were told you'd never walk properly again. Be grateful for the excellent progress you're making.'

Oliver brought down a single mattress. 'I don't think you'll miss having a bed base. This is well sprung and seems unused, brand new even. There's Rachel still to come, though. We should have chosen a room for her and opened the window to air it.'

'We'll let her decide which room she wants. She always knows her own mind. I'd better go and switch that old fridge on now to make sure it works. We don't want our milk to go off, though it isn't the warmest of days, considering it's nearly summer.'

'I'll start bringing the rest of your things in from the car, then,' Oliver said. 'No, leave that to me. I think you and Chad should have a rest. You're both looking pale and weary.'

His words reminded her of a poem and as he went out, she murmured the words:

Ah, what can ail thee, knight at arms,
Alone and palely loitering?

Chad continued it for her:

The sedge has withered from the lake
And no birds sing.

'*La Belle Dame Sans Merci*,' they chorused and laughed.

'Did you have to learn it at school, too?' she asked.

'That and a dozen other poems. It took me years to get over what Mr Robinson did to poetry.' He stopped, and shook his head sadly. 'There. That's a name from the past, but not one that will lead me anywhere, unless I remember the school's name as well.' As she opened her mouth to speak, he held up one hand. 'I know, I know. I should be grateful that I'm remembering anything. But they're such tiny pieces of the jigsaw puzzle of my life that they don't help much. I still don't even know my own name for sure. That is utterly galling.'

Oliver walked in and out, dumping the luggage and bundles in the front bar until the car was cleared. 'This is the last thing. I thought I'd go down to my house now and get you a few spare clothes, Chad.'

'That's very kind. Are you sure you don't mind?'

'It's my pleasure. I have too much stuff anyway. We can buy you some things of your own tomorrow, and don't forget I have an appointment booked for you both with Dr Allerton first thing tomorrow morning. She's coming into the surgery on a Sunday specially, to oblige me. Seven thirty for Emily, eight o'clock for Chad. Can you be up in time to get there? Good. I'll pick you up at ten past seven.'

'Not a problem for me,' Emily said. 'I'm an early bird.'

'I think I am too.' Chad frowned. 'Well, if I wasn't before, I am now.'

'You'll like Jean Allerton,' Oliver said confidently. 'She's one of the best GPs I've ever met. She was wonderful with my wife during that final year.' He sighed and stood still for a minute, his eyes unfocused, then straightened up. 'I'll only be gone an hour or so, or a bit longer if I nip into the office and get hold of the spare keys for the house. Will you be all right?'

'Of course we will.'

When he'd driven off, Emily looked at Chad. 'I know we ought to rest, but I'd like to explore the ground floor more carefully. I don't know about you. Not only am I curious to see my inheritance, but I need to feel secure. I don't want an intruder creeping up on me.'

'I feel exactly the same. Most of all, I never want to be shut away and under someone else's control again.'

She gave in to temptation and linked her arm in his again, standing close.

He didn't say anything. Neither did she. There was no need. They got on so well.

* * *

When they set off again, they walked along the rear bar, to find a door leading to a maze of storerooms and an old-fashioned commercial kitchen. It had an outer door at the side of the house, but once again, there seemed no way of opening it.

'Was this Penelope of yours paranoid about locking herself in?' Chad wondered aloud.

'She must have been if she didn't even leave the keys in the locks. Perhaps she didn't visit the other parts of the house very often.' Emily stood back, brushing a cobweb off her sweater. 'Well, there's no way we can get out to the back or side today and I'm tired. I don't feel like walking right round the house to view the outside.'

'I'm fading rapidly now.'

'I shouldn't even have brought you this far. Let's go back to the flat and rest.'

It was peaceful sitting together, sipping tea slowly, eating a biscuit or two, looking out at the moors and watching vehicles pass on the road that led up and across to Yorkshire. By some trick of acoustics, the sound of their engines was nothing but a faint buzz, with a slightly louder sound coming from the big trucks that chugged more slowly up the hill.

'I'm glad I have somewhere to stay,' he said. 'I don't know what I'd have done without you. Joined the homeless on the streets, I suppose. Anything would have been better than staying in that place.'

'I'm not only glad to have someone around, I'm glad it's you.' She hesitated then shared her thoughts with him. 'I don't know . . . I feel as if we're not done with this business yet. Even though I don't see what George can do to me, I know how tenacious he is. Even as a child, he always wanted other children's toys – and got them too, more often than not. Or broke them.'

'My son was always—' Chad broke off in shock. 'The camping image was right. I have a son . . . No, two sons. They're called—' He frowned, closing his eyes, desperately trying to hold on to the memory.

Oh, she felt for him, she really did.

He groaned. 'It's no good. I can't remember their names. Only their faces.'

'But remembering them at all is another step forward.'

'Yes, but . . .' He looked at her, just looked.

He was an attractive man. Very. Naturally a man like him would be married, she thought. Even George had got married and he wasn't at all attractive.

Only . . . where was Chad's wife?

Once again, Emily had been attracted to a man she couldn't have. She would never break up a marriage . . . Unless he was divorced.

He spoke his thoughts aloud. 'If I have a wife, why hasn't she been searching for me? Why hasn't she listed me as a missing person?'

'I can't imagine.'

'I don't feel as if I have a wife,' he offered.

'But you must have had one at some time.'

'I don't get a good feeling when I think about that.'

She hated the thought of him going back to another woman. Hated it! From now on, she must control her emotions and keep in mind that when all the fuss had settled down, she'd very likely be left here alone. Well, she'd been alone for a while now, in that sense, knew how to live a perfectly satisfactory single life.

But this time, she'd been hoping . . .

Sometimes she wondered what was wrong with her. Why hadn't she ever been able to find a life partner?

Chad gave a little shake of the head, as if dismissing some unhappy thoughts, and turned back to his mug of tea, clutching it tightly and staring down into it. 'We shall just have to wait and see,' he said at last. 'And hope for the best.'

She concentrated on her own mug. She'd wait, yes. And hope. But not hope for too much. Didn't dare.

Then she realized she'd used that word again. Hope. Was there hope for them? Please let there be.

Seven

Rachel had an easy drive up to Lancashire. No traffic jams, one quick stop for refreshments, and on she went, singing along to the radio when a song came on that she liked, wincing when the broadcast was interrupted for hurtfully loud traffic announcements.

It felt good to be going away somewhere, whatever the reason. She'd been a bit down in the dumps since her son and his family left for Australia, even though he'd tried to persuade her to follow them later. That had posed, and still did pose, a dreadful dilemma. She didn't want to leave England and live so far away from all she knew, but oh, she didn't want to be parted from Tim and his wife Abbie, let alone little Sophie. She missed her granddaughter so much!

People got excited about emigrating, but what about the families that were broken up by it, the ones who were left behind?

She didn't know why she was dwelling on this. Hadn't she promised herself to accept Tim's choice? She would, after all, be able to visit them in Australia. One day. If she saved hard. Or got a part-time job. She'd been retrenched and tossed into early retirement unexpectedly. The money she'd received, and the reduced superannuation because she'd worked for fewer years than she expected, wouldn't cover expensive trips to the other side of the world.

Her ex would easily be able to afford it, but he probably wouldn't bother. He had a new family now.

She pushed those useless regrets to the back of her mind and concentrated on her driving.

It was late evening when she reached Littleborough. She slowed down to admire some old stone buildings, then followed the satnav's instructions to Emily's pub. She didn't know Lancashire very well, but she intended to explore it while she was here. She really liked the sight of the moors, great curves of land rolling away into the distance. It didn't overpower you as the French Alps had on her first and only visit there.

She flexed her hands one after the other as the traffic slowed almost to a halt. She'd be glad to stop driving. It had been a fraught couple of days and it had taken all her energy to cope.

As she stopped in front of Emily's new home, she let out an involuntary exclamation of surprise. Oliver had told them it had once been a pub, but it still looked like one, and a seedy, run-down place at that. And it was on its own out here, not in the cosy village she'd pictured.

Getting out of the car she stopped for a moment to breathe deeply, enjoying the crisp moorland air after being shut in the car for hours. Then she suddenly felt impatient to see her friend, and turned to grab her handbag and one of her bags of food.

The front door opened and Emily came hurrying out to join her.

'You don't look too bad, considering you've had a hard day's travelling and need to settle in,' Rachel decided aloud. 'You look much happier, that's for sure.'

'I am. Anyone would be. I'd expected you sooner. There wasn't a problem, was there?'

'Only George arriving at your place an hour or so after you'd set off.'

'Oh, my goodness! What a narrow escape!'

'I had to wait till he'd left before I dared go out to my car. You should have seen the black looks he threw towards my house.'

Emily shuddered. 'He wasn't supposed to return till tomorrow. Was he furious to find the house locked up?'

'Furious is a mild word. He turned dark red and looked like a volcano about to erupt. And you know what? From the way he looked back at your house, I don't think he wanted to leave it. Marcia looked disappointed as well.'

'Well, tough. It's *my* house and I still can't believe he moved in like that against my wishes. I hope he'll stay out of my life from now on. I don't think even he would have the cheek to turn up here.'

'I wouldn't put anything past him. Look how he slashed my tyres.'

'It could have been vandals.'

'I'm quite certain it was him. After all, he'd just been threatening me.'

'Let's forget about the obnoxious George. Come inside. I'm so glad to see you.'

Rachel grinned as she gestured to the house. 'Are you sure you've enough room to put me up? Or had I better look for a B&B?'

Emily linked her arm in her friend's. 'I still can't believe a place this large is really mine.'

Rachel turned to click the remote that locked her car. It might be the only vehicle in a bare, windswept parking area, but better safe than sorry was a good motto for a woman on her own. 'I'll come back out for the other boxes and bags in a few minutes. I want to see the house before we do anything else.'

They stopped in the front area and Rachel said simply, 'Wow! Your very own bar.'

'No booze behind it, though. Well, I don't think there is.'

'That can be remedied.' Rachel felt inside the bag she was carrying and placed a bottle of white wine on the dusty bar. 'There. Our favourite viognier. If you feel up to it tomorrow, we'll have a little party, starting with a nice glass of white wine.' She shivered. 'We won't even need a fridge to chill it. Not a very warm day, is it, considering we're almost into summer now?'

There was the sound of a car pulling up outside and Rachel felt Emily stiffen. 'Don't be nervous. We won't let anyone cart you away again.' She went to peep out of the front door and flung it wide open. 'Anyway, it's only Oliver.'

He came in carrying some bags plus a bouquet of flowers, which he presented to Emily with a mock bow. 'Welcome to your home, *madame*.'

For a moment she felt as if the room was filled with light and warmth, then the illusion faded. But still, the flowers made her feel good. 'Thank you.' She smiled down at the bouquet.

'Now that's what I call a nice gesture,' Rachel said.

Emily watched him smile at Rachel and her friend smile back, and drew her own conclusions. 'I'll have to look for a vase. Come and have a cup of coffee, you two. I've only got instant and I know you like fancy coffee, Rach, but it'll be hot and comforting, at least.'

Chad had already put the kettle and electric heater on, so the sitting room of the flat felt cosy and welcoming. They sat for a few minutes, drinking the coffee, not saying much, then Rachel bounced to her feet and demanded to be shown round.

Oliver studied Emily and Chad. 'Let me do the honours. You two should take it easy for a while.'

When they'd gone, Chad sighed and let his head fall back. 'He's right. I'm exhausted.'

Emily watched him fall asleep, then allowed herself to follow his example. You could push yourself so far, but in the end you simply had to give in to your body's demand for rest.

'They look so tired and pale,' Rachel said quietly. 'Is that for lack of sun, do you think, or for another reason?'

'Lack of sun, I hope. They've both been shut away for a few weeks.'

'Are they going to be all right now, do you think?'

'I've got them booked in to see a doctor first thing tomorrow morning. She's a good one, too. I'll have to pick them up at ten past seven.'

'Ouch!'

'You can either come with us or stay here.'

'I think I'll stay here and do some cleaning and tidying. I don't like hanging round, waiting for people, and if Emily's got you, she'll be all right. Where am I sleeping?'

'You can pick your own room.' He showed her the first-floor bedrooms. 'Chad will be sleeping downstairs because Emily's a bit nervous.'

'Hmm.' Rachel inspected the rooms, then chose one whose door had a lock on it. 'I feel a bit jumpy too, after all that's been going on.' She rattled the door. 'That's nice and solid, though.'

'Perhaps I should come and sleep here, too?' He was fiddling with the curtain as he added, 'I don't want to be left out now that I've been involved in the Great Escape.'

'Perhaps you should stay.' She looked at him speculatively. She hadn't met a guy she fancied for a while. Oliver didn't hit you in the eyes as what she called a 'possible', because he wasn't sexy looking, but his kindness and enthusiastic approach to life grew on you quickly. He had a particularly warm smile. She was a sucker for smiles, and his was getting to her.

Oliver had clearly loved his wife.

She liked that about him, too.

Oh, she was being very fanciful. He probably had a lady friend already. There was a shortage of men in her age group.

* * *

In the morning, Emily woke early, lying in bed listening to birds calling, wondering where she was. Sunlight poured round the edges of the faded curtains and her eyes settled dreamily on its brightness.

Then she remembered everything in a sudden rush of images. That had been the pattern ever since she came out of the coma. She woke each morning to a brief disorientation, then too much information cascaded into her brain.

She decided to have a quick shower and make herself a cup of tea before they left. Maybe some toast, too. She was hungry, something that hadn't often happened in hospital.

She chose a blue denim skirt, rather than jeans. It was one of her favourites, her lucky skirt, she always thought. With it she wore a white T-shirt and a darker blue cardigan. She looked at herself in the mirror. She normally kept herself in pretty good shape for a woman of her age, because she was fortunate and had never had a problem with weight. Now she'd have to work on getting her fitness back.

Once she was dressed, she went into the kitchen to find Chad yawning as he waited for the kettle to boil.

'You can shower in the bathroom in the flat, if you like.'

'Thanks. I'll do that in a minute.' He poured the boiling water into their mugs and began to jiggle the teabags, staring blindly into space and swirling the bags around for far too long till she took them from his hands.

He watched her finish making the tea, then said in a rush, 'I'm not looking forward to seeing another doctor. Are you?'

She shuddered. 'Not at all. But if Oliver vouches for this one, she must be all right, don't you think?'

'I expect so. He's a great guy, Oliver. I really like him.'

'I do too. Do you want something to eat before we leave or aren't you hungry yet?'

'I wouldn't mind a piece of toast.'

Emily got out the bread. 'We must go shopping after we've seen the doctor. It feels strange to have nearly empty cupboards. Thank heavens for the stuff Rach brought.'

'Maybe next week I can get some money from social security until I remember who I am, then I can pay you something at least.'

'Don't do that. Not yet, anyway. You'll have to jump through all kinds of hoops and until you're certain where you stand . . . Well, better safe than sorry. Your memory *is* returning, even if only in fragments. I'm sure it won't be long before you can access your own money. In the meantime, I have plenty, truly I do. I'll lend you some.'

'I hate borrowing from you.'

'I don't hate lending it to you.' Her eyes met his and again there was that warmth between them.

'Well, we'll keep a careful account of everything and I *will* pay you back as soon as I can, Emily, I promise.'

'I know. Now, how about you grab that shower?'

Before they left, Emily went upstairs to wake Rachel, but had to wait for her friend to unlock the bedroom door.

Rachel got back into bed and took the cup of coffee Emily had brought her. 'Thanks for this.' She took a big slurp. 'I'm not good in the early mornings. Sorry. I'll get myself going in a minute.'

'It's all right. You don't have to go anywhere.' She heard a car and went to look out of the window. 'Oliver's here. Go back to sleep if you want. Long drives can tire you out. We'll lock up as we go.'

Emily ran lightly down the stairs, feeling much better physically this morning. As she went out to join Oliver and Chad, she paused for a moment to look up at the moors.

'It's beautiful here,' Chad said quietly as she got into the car.

Oliver smiled over his shoulder. 'I wouldn't live anywhere else. People seem to think Lancashire is only made up of grimy industrial towns but this Pennine territory that it shares with Yorkshire has its own beauty. Once you two are fitter, I'll take you walking across the moors, if you like.'

'Love to.'

He turned round and drove off.

His two passengers were quiet, enjoying the scenery.

Dr Jean Allerton was grey-haired and brisk. Oliver went in with them to explain the situation they'd had to escape from.

She looked increasingly angry as the tale unfolded, but didn't comment except to say, 'You must lay a complaint. We can't let that sort of abuse continue.'

'Let's wait a while before we take action,' Oliver pleaded. 'My clients need time to get over their experience. We don't want people haranguing them to prove their case yet. Chad is starting to remember some details now, but if he gets stressed, that might stop.'

'We'll see. Perhaps you gentlemen will wait outside while I examine Ms Mattison?' She turned to Emily. 'You understand that I can only give you a quick check-up at this stage.'

'That's all right. I'm recovering well, physically and mentally, so I don't think I need any treatment other than rest and lack of stress.' She gave a wry smile. 'More than anything, I need you to confirm that I don't have Alzheimer's.'

'Not easy to give a hundred per cent assurance, but you certainly don't seem to have that slightly bewildered look.'

'I was in a coma after a fall down some stairs, though I don't remember that. But I'm not confused about anything that's happened since, or about my life before the fall. I just . . . don't want anyone to lock me up again. That's what worries me most, being helpless and in someone else's power.'

'Would they do that to you again, do you think? Surely it was all a terrible mistake?'

'I don't think it was a mistake. I'm quite sure it was deliberately done.' She explained some of the tricks played on her to make her look forgetful. 'My nephew George would lock me away again like a shot.'

'What you do about your nephew is not my concern, but it sounds as though you have grounds for a formal complaint about the way you were treated by the health system.'

'I doubt I could prove it'd been done on purpose, and if I did complain, my nephew's part in it would come out. That'd upset my sister, who is very frail. The main thing is, thanks to Oliver, I'm out and living my own life again.'

'Others may still be locked away. You owe it to them to make some sort of complaint.'

She sagged in her chair. 'I hadn't thought of that. I'll have to give it some thought.'

She let the doctor take her blood pressure and check her physically, answered questions and when it was all over, had a question of her own, the most important question of all. 'Do you think I seem . . . all right mentally? I mean, *I* feel right, but . . .'

The doctor patted her arm. 'You seem perfectly compos mentis to me, Emily, and I'm sure you'll soon regain your former fitness, but try to do that gradually. If you have any health worries at all, any sudden changes in what you can or can't do, come and see me, or go to the A&E at a hospital.'

'What if George . . . comes after me?'

'Get in touch with me straight away. We'll sign you up at the practice, so that I'm officially your doctor from now on. And if there's any further trouble, we'll bring in a geriatric expert I know, who specializes in dementia.'

When the doctor had finished with her, Emily went to sit with Oliver while Chad went in for his check-up. She got so lost in her own thoughts that Oliver's voice made her jump.

'Sorry. Didn't mean to startle you. Jean didn't find anything wrong with you, did she? You look worried.'

'About George. Or Sister Pauline. Or both of them. They might come after me *and* Chad.'

'I've been thinking about that. I've been joking about moving into The Drover's Hope, but maybe I should do that for a while, just in case? That way, I'd be on hand to deal with any problems as your lawyer.'

'Would you mind doing that?'

He gave her one of his boyish grins. 'I'd be delighted. I don't want to miss a thing. Have you told anyone where you are?'

'No. None of my other friends and definitely not my sister.' Not even Leon, who would want to be kept informed. Or maybe he already knew about her accident and had accepted that she'd been brain damaged?

She shared the reason for her worries. 'The trouble is, George intercepted the letters from your son and you gave the hospital security men your business card, so he knows exactly where I am.'

'Oh hell, yes! I'd forgotten that.'

'But do come and stay, if you can stand the primitive conditions. It'd be good to feel more secure. If it's not too much interruption to your life, that is?'

His expression grew sad. 'I don't have much of a life at the moment. It took a while to get used to being without my wife and I still miss Trish greatly. I shouldn't have retired when she fell ill, just taken leave of absence. But you can't go back, only press onwards.' He gave a slight shrug. 'I'll move in today. I can help you sort out the place as well, if you like.'

After a moment, he added, 'Rachel isn't – um, in a relationship, is she?'

'No. It's about time she was, though.'

He didn't comment but his beaming smile said it all.

They were all summoned back into the doctor's room when Dr Allerton had finished examining Chad.

'I'd like to sum things up for you,' she began. 'I'm using the word "seems" because this is the first time I've seen you, but I'm fairly certain of my initial diagnosis.'

When everyone nodded, she continued, 'Emily seems to be recovering well from the coma. If she had physical injuries, they couldn't have been major, because there's no sign of them now. Chad seems to be suffering from retrograde amnesia due to a head trauma. The fact that he's starting to remember things is a good sign.'

'What can we do to help him?' Oliver asked.

'The mind can be difficult to treat. Often time is the only healer. I think Chad needs peace and quiet above all, but I gather there may be further problems brewing for him and Emily.' She looked questioningly at Oliver.

'We're not sure, but there could be, hence this visit to you.'

'Well, I'll be happy to support you in any way I can. I don't feel it's necessary to prescribe drugs, unless either of you has difficulty sleeping – and even then, only the mildest of sleeping tablets.'

Emily shook her head. 'I never take the things. They leave you dopey in the morning and I hate that.'

'Me too,' Chad said.

Dr Allerton stood up. 'Well, then. If you'll just go to reception, I'll find you a form to fill in for signing up at this practice, then give it to the records officer tomorrow.'

When they'd done this, she showed them briskly out. 'I'll let you get on with your day. I have ten people coming for Sunday lunch.'

Oliver lingered to say, 'Thanks, Jean.'

'Keep me in the loop. It's an intriguing situation. You don't think there's any chance that they're exaggerating? About the nephew and the sister in that unit, I mean?'

'No.'

'I get furious every time someone misbehaves in our poor overloaded health system. And the elderly seem to cop a lot more abuse than any other group.'

He grinned suddenly. 'Don't let Emily hear you calling her elderly. She hates it.'

'The word does have bad connotations, doesn't it? As if everyone over a certain age needs looking after, when most don't.'

She walked across to the door with him. 'Look, Oliver. If Emily and Chad don't lay a complaint soon, I shall have to do it myself and ask for the matter to be looked into. If they're right about what happened, it must be stopped, and the sooner the better.'

'Give them a few days to find their feet, at least.'

'Till Thursday. I mean it, Oliver. I care about looking after my patients . . . and I won't condone others maltreating theirs.'

'You always were a firebrand, even at school. Give my best to Charles. Is his new job going all right?'

'He loves it.'

Marcia looked at George in puzzlement. 'But you said you didn't want to stay at your mother's again.'

'Well, I've changed my mind. Mum's the trump card in all this, because Emily won't do anything to upset her. You'll see.'

'But—'

'Leave it to me.' He opened the car door for her. 'Let's get away from this seedy hotel.' He cast a glance of loathing at the place where they'd stayed overnight. 'At least when I worked in the Middle East, we could live in proper comfort and be served by people who really know how to look after you.'

'I'm going to miss that.' She sighed.

When they got to his mother's house, they found Liz about to go out to the shops with a friend who had a car.

'I'll take you to the shops later, Mum,' he said. 'Thanks for looking after her, Mrs Rawton. I'm afraid something's come up and I need to speak to Mum straight away.' He put his arm round his mother's shoulders and guided her firmly back into the house.

'Did you see Emily?' she asked as they sat down together.

'No. She'd already gone up to Lancashire.'

'Why would she do that when she's only just come out of hospital?'

'She's inherited a house and land near Littleborough from Cousin Penelope.'

'Emily's inherited it?' Liz frowned. 'But *I* was the one who got on best with Penelope. Why, I had her to stay here several times because you said I should cultivate her. I'd not have done that if I hadn't truly liked her.'

'Yes, well, it never hurts to seize the moment, which Emily must have done. But you'd have thought Penelope would have remembered you in her will as well.'

'It would have been such a help,' she said wistfully. 'I do wish my share dividends would improve. It's not much fun having to be careful of every penny.'

Marcia scowled at him.

'They are starting to improve, Mum. I could increase your monthly allowance a little. But we have to go carefully.'

'That'd be such a help, George. Prices will keep rising.'

'That's not what I've come about, though. I think we should go and visit Emily. She's rushed off to the north and she's not really well. You must be worried about her. And she'll need help dealing with her inheritance, I'm sure.'

Liz smiled at him. 'You're such a caring person, dear. Emily is very capable, but she's a bit too independent, if you ask me. You've offered to help her before.'

'I certainly doubt she's used to handling large sums of money.'

'It'd be nice to have the chance. Um . . . You said once that Penelope's land might be worth something one day.'

'That day has come. Which is why I need to see my aunt and make sure she doesn't let anyone cheat her.'

'Oh, I don't think she's in danger of that.'

'Unfortunately she's got in with some rather questionable types. I thought if we went up to Lancashire together, you could help me persuade her to accept my help. How do you fancy a trip to Littleborough?'

His mother's face lit up. 'I'd love that. I haven't been away for ages.'

Rachel was enjoying her lie-in when she heard a sound downstairs. Footsteps. There had been no sound of a car, so it couldn't be Emily and the others returning. Her heart began to pound. Was there an intruder?

She got out of bed and slipped her jeans on over her pyjamas, then a fleecy top, before looking round for something to defend herself with. To her annoyance, she could only find a large and very ugly jug standing on the hearth. Shrugging, she picked it up. It'd slow someone down, at least.

At the door, she hesitated. Should she really go out and confront the intruder or ought she to stay here, behind a locked door? She jigged about impatiently from one foot to the other, then picked up her mobile and put it on speed dial for 999. If she had to call the police, she'd be ready to do it quickly, but somehow, she just couldn't stay in the bedroom while the intruder was doing heaven knew what downstairs.

Taking a deep breath she opened the door and listened intently.

The sounds were only faint, but they were definitely coming from Emily's flat.

I'm either a fool or a heroine, she thought, and started creeping down the stairs, ready to dash back to her bedroom if necessary. A couple of the treads creaked under her and each time she froze, but whoever it was didn't seem to have noticed.

When she came to the entrance to the flat, she could tell that the intruder was in the kitchen, which was a strange place to look for valuables . . . unless . . . unless the person was hungry.

She tiptoed across the living room and peeped into the kitchen. An unkempt youth was stuffing his face with bread and jam, gulping it down as if he hadn't eaten for a long time.

She spoke without considering what she was doing. 'What are you doing here?'

It would have been hard to say who was the more scared, herself at what she'd risked by speaking or him at the sight of her. For a moment they both froze, then he whimpered and cowered back, as if he expected her to thump him.

It was then she realized he was intellectually challenged, or whatever you were supposed to call it these days. And he was showing no sign whatsoever of attacking her. On the contrary, he looked as if he was expecting her to thump him.

Her fear lessened considerably. 'Why don't you sit down properly at the table and go on eating? It'd be a shame to waste the food. Would you like something to drink with it?'

He looked at her as if she'd spoken gibberish, then studied her face, as if he could read what she was like from it. His expression slowly cleared and his body relaxed a little, as if she'd passed some sort of test. He took the chair furthest away from her, sitting down on the edge, as if ready to flee.

She walked across to the kettle, hoping she was doing the right thing. 'Do you want tea or coffee?'

'Tea, please.'

The 'please' reassured her further. She put the kettle on then turned back towards him. He half stood up as if about to run, so she said quickly, 'I have some apples in the fruit bowl. Would you like one?'

Another of those searching, wary glances, then he nodded. 'Yes, please, miss.'

Well, at least he had good manners. She took an apple from the bowl and set it on the table a short distance away from him. 'I'm going to make myself some cheese on toast first. Would you like some too?'

His face brightened. 'Yes, please, miss.'

As she worked, she chatted, choosing her words carefully. 'My name is Rachel. What's yours?'

'Toby.'

'Where do you live?'

He was on his feet in an instant.

'Please don't go. I'm not going to hurt you.'

Slowly he sat down, but only on the edge of the chair. She was quite sure that if she frightened him, he'd flee. She opted to continue chatting. 'This house belongs to my friend Emily. She'll be back soon.'

'I'm not going back. I'm not!'

'No, of course not. Don't run away. You'll like Emily.'

'This is Miss Penelope's house.'

Penelope? He must have come here to visit the previous owner. 'Miss Penelope gave her house to Emily.'

'Don't tell the supervisor!' he said suddenly. 'She locks me in cupboard. Miss Penelope hides me. Don't tell!'

'We'll hide you too,' she promised rashly, upset at how afraid he looked. 'We won't let anyone hurt you.'

Who had the previous owner been hiding this youngster from? Was someone ill-treating him? He didn't seem dangerous or badly behaved.

'There.' She put a plate of cheese on toast near him and set the other one down at her own place. As he grabbed it, she said hastily, 'Eat it nicely, Toby.' She didn't think she could face any more of that face cramming and gulping.

He watched her and began to eat slowly, taking a bite when she did. The poor lad must have been ravenously hungry.

When they'd finished eating, she wondered what to do with him. He looked exhausted.

'Do you want to lie down and have a sleep? There are some beds upstairs. Or you could lie on the couch here.'

'I lie here. Nice, nice.' He lay down, letting out a deep sigh as he closed his eyes. He was asleep almost immediately.

He looked much younger now, gaunt-cheeked with dark circles under his eyes and an unshaven jaw. She guessed he'd not been eating properly for some time. She wrinkled her nose in distaste because he smelled sour and everything about him was grubby.

Oh, well. No use worrying about that now. She had to keep him here till Emily came back. Unless she was much mistaken, this was another runaway in need of help, only it was Emily's house, so Rachel didn't feel she could offer him a place to stay.

How strange! Wasn't that what Penelope had said in her will: that Emily would give hope to others?

Rachel chose a novel from the bookcase and began to read. She'd intended to start cleaning the house, but it seemed better to stay with Toby. She had to keep him calm when the others returned.

Who was he hiding from? Would Oliver know?

Eight

Oliver took them for a hearty snack at a café he patronized regularly, then on to do some shopping.

After buying several bags of food at a big supermarket, and some basic jeans, tops and underclothes for Chad, they set off back to The Drover's Hope.

Emily noticed a large car sales yard ahead. 'Could we stop here, please, Oliver? I need to buy a car.'

'Today?' He looked surprised, but slowed down.

'The sooner the better as far as I'm concerned. I don't like being dependent on others, even friends. Unless this isn't a reputable place for second-hand cars?'

'Well, I've bought my last three cars here, though they were new ones, so obviously I find this company good to deal with. Don't you want a new car? You can easily afford it.'

'Not really. A nearly new one is best, I reckon. It won't lose as much in depreciation.' No matter how much money she had, she didn't intend to spend recklessly. It simply wasn't in her nature.

She got out and studied the place. It had 'Quality New and Used Cars' in big red letters along the front above the showroom. The outside looked well tended, as if business was good, with rows of well-polished cars gleaming in the weak sunlight. There was a row of what looked like new luxury vehicles inside the showroom, cars like Oliver's.

A young man came out of the office and changed direction to join them.

'Something wrong with the car, Oliver?'

'No. It's running beautifully. Good to see you again, Mark. These are two friends of mine, Emily and Chad. Emily needs a car.'

'Pleased to meet you.'

Mark waited for her to speak, which was a good sign. She hated pushy sales people. 'My old car was involved in an accident and is a write-off, so I have no trade-in. I'm looking for something no more than two years old, automatic, air conditioning, not too low slung and not too small. Apart from that, I'm open to suggestions.'

'You seem to know your own mind, at least. Some people turn up with no idea what sort of car they want, apart from the colour and the sound system. So . . . let me see.' He surveyed the rows of vehicles. 'There are probably three which would suit you, and of course I'll offer a good price to any friend of Oliver's. Come and have a look at them.'

An hour later, after two test drives and some consultation with Chad, who seemed to know about cars, Emily bought a neat hatchback with an excellent safety rating. Mark offered to bring the car to the pub the following day, since she didn't have transport.

As she settled back in her seat, she smiled in satisfaction. 'That's good. I've hated not being mobile. I really value my independence.'

'Why does that not surprise me?' Chad teased.

Oliver started up the engine. 'You must both be tired now.'

'I'm not too bad today,' Chad said. 'Nothing a short rest won't put right, anyway.'

'I'm the same,' Emily agreed. 'Most of all, I'm hungry. I want a big plate of fresh salad and crunchy vegetables, with some good quality cheese, both of which were in short supply in that hospital.'

When they got back to the pub, she exclaimed, 'Goodness! It feels like coming home!'

'It feels like that to me, too.'

Chad sounded even more surprised by this than she was.

The front door of the pub was locked and there was no sign of life, even though the window of the sitting room looked out on to the front. Unfortunately, because of the sloping land, it was too high to look inside, but Emily would have at least expected Rachel to peer out and check who had turned up. She must have heard the car, surely?

When they got to the door, Oliver took the big, old-fashioned key out of his briefcase and inserted it in the lock. 'I'd expected Rachel to open the door for us.'

'She's probably exploring the house.'

But when they went inside, they heard voices coming from the flat. A man was arguing with Rachel, sounding very stressed.

'Let me check the situation first.' Chad pushed past Emily and hurried forward, stopping in the doorway for a moment to see what was going on.

Rachel was trying to calm an agitated young guy, who looked as if he'd been living rough.

'I know him. Let me through,' Oliver said in a low voice, then shouted, 'Toby! It's all right. No one is going to hurt you.' He moved past them into the sitting room.

The young man gulped but stopped struggling to get away from Rachel.

'Where have you been, Toby? Your house supervisor will be looking for you.'

He immediately tried to push past them and Rachel grabbed his jacket.

'Not going back. Not going back! Miss Penelope hide me.'

'I think someone must have been ill-treating him,' Rachel said. 'He was very hungry and he's got bruises on his lower arms.' She turned back to Toby. 'It's all right, really it is. This is my friend Emily. It's her house now.'

He calmed down a little, staring at Emily.

'She'll let you stay here.'

Oliver opened his mouth as if to protest, but shut it in response to a quick warning glance from Rachel.

Emily moved forward, smiling. 'It's nice to meet you, Toby. Shall we all sit down? I'm really thirsty. I've got some fizzy water in my shopping. Do you like fizzy water?'

He blinked and looked at her warily, then nodded.

'Oh, good.' She bent to fumble in the bag she'd put down and handed him a bottle. 'Could you open this one for me, please? The tops are always very tight.'

For a moment all hung in the balance, then he reached out and took the bottle, opening it carefully, tongue poking out at the side of his mouth as he concentrated. The water fizzed up and a little spilled.

He cringed. 'Sorry, sorry, sorry!'

Clearly he was expecting someone to hit him. Emily hated to

see his fear. 'That's all right, Toby. I spill too sometimes. If you get a cloth, you can wipe it up. It's only water.'

'Miss Penelope not get mad, not shout at me, not hit me.' Tears began rolling down his cheeks. 'I want her back.'

'She can't come back, but I'm here. I can help you.' Something made her add, 'Just like she did.'

He looked at her, neither trusting nor mistrusting, evaluating . . . waiting.

Beside her Oliver muttered, 'It's not as easy as that.'

Emily gave him a very determined look. 'Chad and I know what it's like to be helpless and afraid, Oliver. I'm not letting a friend of my cousin be ill-treated by anyone. Whatever it takes.'

He let out his breath in a half-groan. 'I can see you're going to be as bad about it as Penelope was.'

'What do you mean?'

'Collecting waifs and strays. Helping them.'

Emily opened her mouth to protest that she didn't do that sort of thing, but the words died unspoken, because she knew she was definitely going to help Toby . . . and she was already helping Chad. How strange! Had the coma changed her?

There was a sudden feeling of warmth around her, as if someone was hugging her. The light in the kitchen seemed to grow brighter for a moment or two, then faded.

Her imagination working overtime again. It must be. Lights couldn't grow brighter and dimmer on such a grey day.

Rachel intervened. 'I'll put some lunch together. Will you help me, Toby?'

He nodded vigorously. 'Help you.'

'Oliver, you can come and talk to us while we work, if you like. I think those two need a rest.'

The lawyer nodded, looking resigned now.

Emily and Chad both went into the living room.

'Infuriating, isn't it, to be so weak?' he murmured.

'Every day in every way . . .' She smiled, cocked her head to one side and looked at him, waiting.

'. . . I'm getting better and better,' he finished. 'And so we are. How many more people are you going to rescue, Emily Mattison?'

She smiled at him. 'As many as I can. Will you help me?'

'Of course I will.' A shadow passed over his face. 'If I can.'

'I know.'

He gave her a sudden hug and she clung to him for a moment, then remembered he might still be married and stepped back.

'I know what you're thinking,' he muttered. 'But I don't *feel* married. I just . . . don't.'

After a wonderful meal of really fresh food, they decided to explore the house and its outbuildings properly.

Emily followed a hunch. 'Toby, will you show us round?'

He looked at her, his face scrunched up in thought, then nodded and led the way out.

In the rear bar, he tugged at her sleeve. 'You need keys.'

'Where are they, Toby?'

'Hidden. So no one can come in.'

'It's time to give them to Emily, don't you think?' Rachel said gently. 'This is her house now, so they're her keys.'

Emily watched him think that through slowly, then nod.

'I show *you* keys, Emily . . . just you.'

'Very well.' She looked at Oliver, knowing he'd stop her if he thought she was at any risk from their young intruder.

He threw her a resigned look and shrugged.

Toby led her through the rear bar, past the entrance to the pub kitchens, then along the corridor. It was lined with several walk-in store cupboards whose shelves were bare. He ignored those and went into a small room near the end.

She followed and let him close the door behind them.

On the shelves that covered the left side of the storeroom were piles of plates and stacks of wire trays filled with glasses. All were thick with dust. The wall to the right was covered in wood panelling, which looked old and in need of a polish. There were two wrought iron candle holders on the wall – eighteenth century, she'd guess. How wonderful that they'd not been removed!

When Toby went across to one of them and twisted it so that it was slightly skewed, she reached out to stop him damaging it, but then realized that the candle holder had moved easily, so it must have been intended to move. He went to twist the other one, tugging it downwards, and a section of the panelling behind it opened with a small click, revealing a shallow cupboard about a metre square and thirty centimetres deep.

He put one finger to his lips. 'Secret place. Miss Penelope said I tell next lady. You're next lady.'

When she nodded, he looked at her very solemnly. 'She left a message. She hid it. I know where.'

'Can you show me?'

He nodded and felt inside the cupboard, pulling out a dusty envelope.

She opened it carefully and read the beautiful copperplate handwriting.

> *This house is yours now, Emily. Look after the old inn. It's been in our family a long time.*
>
> *It's always been a place of hope. Look after the people who come here for help. Give them hope.*
>
> *Be happy here, as I have been.*

Toby looked at her anxiously. 'I remembered. I did it.'

'Well done.'

He nodded, beaming at her now, then turned back to the cavity, pulling out what looked like a ledger and a battered tin box which rattled. 'Miss Penelope's book. For you. And the keys. All in the box. Two keys for each door.'

He thrust both items into her hands, then pushed the secret door shut and twisted the second candlestick, which seemed to hold it in place.

Again that sense of warmth and approval surrounded her like an embrace and Emily stood for a moment, welcoming the feeling. Was The Drover's Hope haunted? She had never believed in ghosts . . . until now. Perhaps it was Penelope's spirit still lingering? Whatever it was, it certainly didn't feel as if it meant her any harm.

She jumped in shock when someone called from the corridor, 'Emily? Are you all right in there?' The door rattled but seemed to be sticking, so she opened it.

'I'm fine. Why are you worried? Toby and I have only been getting the keys to the back doors.'

'We called out several times and you didn't answer,' Oliver said.

'Oh. I didn't hear you. How strange!'

'And the door seemed to be stuck. Chad said we should wait a little longer, but I was starting to get worried.'

'Toby and I were getting these out, the keys and Penelope's diary. We need somewhere to tip the keys out. There are quite a few.'

'How about we do that on the bar top?' Chad suggested. 'And I noticed a box of envelopes on one of the shelves in the flat. Shall I fetch them and something to write with so we don't mix up the keys again?'

He took longer than they'd expected and Emily was just going to go and look for him when he came back, looking dazed.

'Are you all right?'

'Yes. Only . . . I've suddenly remembered my first name. It's not Chad. That's just a nickname. It's Edward . . . Edward John . . .' Another long pause, during which he rubbed his temple as if it ached, then shook his head. 'That's all I remembered, though.'

'It's another piece of the puzzle, an important one.' Emily smiled reassuringly at him. 'Though I prefer Chad to Edward.'

'So do I. It's what my friends call me. I wonder if it's a shortening of my surname? Chadwick? Chadderton? They don't sound right, though.'

'Give it time.'

He looked down at the packet of envelopes in his hand. He'd been clutching them so tightly he'd crushed them. 'Here we are. Envelopes and a pencil.' He smoothed them out. 'They're not too bad. Let's get started on the keys. Toby, will you tell us which keys are which? Then I'll write it down on the envelopes. We can leave one copy of each key in the box and put the others on a key ring once we have some labels.'

The lad shuffled his feet and looked at Emily. When she nodded encouragingly, he sorted out two keys which were alike. 'Big green door to back yard.'

Chad wrote on two envelopes and put the keys in them.

When all six pairs of keys had been identified and labelled, Toby started on the padlock keys. To Emily these looked very similar to one another, but he had no trouble telling them apart. This was his home, she realized, and he should stay here. It was what Penelope would have wanted. She was quite sure of that.

They returned a set of keys to the secret compartment and Emily asked the others to stay with her to explore her new domain.

It was giving her hope, too, being here.

Before they could make a start, however, there was a hammering on the front door.

She saw the panic on Toby's face. No, not panic, utter terror! She went across to put her arms round him and give him a hug.

'Not go back! Not go back!'

'No, you can stay here.'

'I'd better answer it,' Oliver said.

Emily was about to let him do that, then decided it was cowardly and thrust the box and book at him instead. 'No, I'll do it. It's my house and I don't intend to hide behind others.'

She hurried through to the front door, hearing someone start hammering on it again. When she flung it open, she didn't even have time to speak.

'It took you long enough to answer the door.'

The woman who stood there was large and angry. Emily was so startled by this rudeness from a complete stranger she couldn't speak for a moment.

'Is he here?'

'Who?' But of course she guessed.

'That idiot, of course. Toby Jones. I'm Mrs Corrish, his house supervisor. Don't believe anything he's told you. He's more trouble than the other seven put together, that one is.' She waited, arms folded. 'Well, is he here?'

Emily didn't oblige her with an immediate answer, because she wasn't sure how to deal with this. She could see Oliver shaking his head at her.

The woman didn't wait for an answer. 'I knew the old lady had died, so when Toby ran away again, I waited for him to come back of his own accord, because this time there was no one here to feed him. He likes his food, that one does. Eats like a pig. Only he didn't come home and when I drove here to find him a couple of days ago, the place was all locked up. Then a friend told me someone had moved in, so I came back.'

'We've only just got here,' Emily said.

'I heard you got here yesterday.' Mrs Corrish looked round

scornfully. 'Not much of an inheritance, a ruin like this. Still, the developers will knock the place down and the sooner the better.'

'Developers?'

'Don't play daft. You must have heard from them.'

'I'm surprised you know about it.'

'Word gets around. Everyone round here knows. Barton and Halling have had their surveyors traipsing all over the property.'

Without my permission, Emily thought. How dare they?

Mrs Corrish was off again. 'I came to put a stop to Toby sneaking off here, once and for all. I'm not having you or anyone else hiding him from me, listening to his lies, blackening my name. I treat him well. I look after them all properly. He's just a troublemaker.'

On the other side of her, Chad stirred as if about to speak, his expression showing suppressed anger. Emily put one hand on his arm, shaking her head slightly. If Mrs Corrish was angry enough to pour out her feelings, let her. They might learn something. 'I don't know anything about that.'

'I think you do. There's nowhere else Toby could be. He used to visit the old lady whenever he could get away, and she filled him full of stupid ideas. He has to learn to behave himself, *he* does, to fit in as much as someone like him can. He's lucky to have a place in a modern group home, you know. So I'll ask you to fetch him out. And after this, please do not encourage him to come here.' She stood there, arms folded, impatience in every twitch of her body.

'Is this Toby a prisoner at the group home, then?' Emily asked. 'Isn't he allowed out on his own?'

'He's in my charge, so it's for me to say what he does and where he goes. Look, I'm a busy person, so stop pretending. I know you've got him hidden away. If you don't fetch him now, I'll report him and you to social services.'

Emily was furious at such rudeness and she could see why Toby was afraid of this bully. But she wasn't afraid. 'I only arrived here yesterday afternoon. I haven't even managed to explore the whole house yet. I'm sorry, but I don't know where your Toby is.' Which was true. Sort of. She started to close the door.

Mrs Corrish's hand shot out and she shoved the door open again with such force, Emily was jerked backwards. 'I'll come inside and check that for myself, thank you very much. Who knows what you may be doing with him?'

Chad moved forward, barring her way. 'You'll do no such thing.'

'You either let *me* come in and look for him, or I'll be back with the police and his social worker. Either way, I'm not leaving him here.'

Oliver moved forward to where she could see him. 'Do you remember me, Mrs Corrish?'

She didn't answer beyond glaring at him.

'Yes, I see you do. I was Miss Penelope's lawyer and now I'm acting in the same capacity for Ms Mattison. You shouldn't try to push your way in or *we* might be the ones to call the police and report you for trespassing and causing a nuisance.'

She gave him a dirty look but took a step backwards. 'I might have known *you* would be involved. You Taptons have certainly dipped your fingers into the Mattison pot.' She shrugged and waved one hand in a dismissive gesture. 'All right, then. Please yourselves. I *will* be back and I've got the law on my side.'

Emily waited in the doorway, watching the woman walk away.

Mrs Corrish opened the car door and took out some cigarettes, lighting one and tossing the match away. She took a deep drag and turned to get into her car. A gust of wind suddenly blew up from nowhere, whipping the cigarette out of her hand and sending it flying into the vehicle. With a shriek she dived into the car after it, cursing and yelling as she hunted for the lit cigarette. It took her a while to find it and pinch it out.

'Serve her right,' Emily muttered. Only after Mrs Corrish had driven off did she sag against the nearest support, which happened to be Chad. 'Phew! What a harridan! Where's Toby? Does anyone know?'

'He ran off towards the back of the house the minute he heard that female,' Rachel said. 'I didn't try to stop him.'

'I don't know where the hiding places are,' Oliver said. 'Penelope kept her secrets. I've had to deal with the Corrish woman before. She wasn't making idle threats. She'll be back with the police. She knows every trick in the rule book when she wants something.'

'Why does she bother if she dislikes Toby so much?'

'She's paid to look after him. She gets all sorts of perks and extra payments because the members of the group are intellectually challenged. The trouble is, Toby's operating at a higher level than the others and needs a more stimulating life. Penelope tried to have him assigned to her instead, but the authorities said she was too old to look after him, and I'm afraid they were right. But *he* used to look after her in some ways. They both acted as if she was his grandmother, and a beloved grandmother at that.'

'Hmm.' Then Emily remembered something. 'What exactly do these developers want to do with my property?'

'I don't know. It was my son who was dealing with your inheritance, and Jeremy only brought me in when he needed someone to rescue you. I have the file at home, because I was going to look through it. Shall I go and fetch it? Barton and Halling are a national company, as you must know. If they're interested in buying this land, they'll be willing to pay an excellent price, I'm sure.'

'*If* I want to sell.'

'Yes. Your choice. I believe Miss Penelope refused to sell to them last year.' He checked his watch. 'Shall I fetch the file? I can bring some of my other things too and move in.'

Emily nodded. 'Yes, please.'

He still lingered. 'One or two people approached Penelope over the years about selling them parts of her land. But they weren't developers, just individuals. I was acting for her then and the only place anyone could have got permission to build was where the outbuildings are, so that it wasn't a new dwelling exactly, just a replacement. She didn't want strangers living so close and always said no.'

'The rules for building in green belt areas are a lot more flexible these days,' Chad said. 'Burton and Halling build good quality homes, at least, if you do want to sell part of your land and stay here.'

Emily glanced quickly his way. He'd sounded so sure of himself. But she didn't comment on that. 'It's far too soon for me to know what I want to do. I haven't even seen all the outbuildings yet. I'd love to see that file, Oliver.'

'Food will be ready when you get back,' Rachel told him. 'But don't expect a fancy meal.'

'I usually warm up a frozen dinner.'

She grimaced. 'That's not my idea of an even half-decent meal. I can do better than that.'

'Great.' He beamed at them all and hurried across to his car.

'That's a lonely man,' Rachel said abruptly.

'I worry that we're taking advantage of his kindness.'

'Don't. He's enjoying being involved with us.'

'I think you're right.' And her friend was a lonely woman, Emily knew. But she didn't comment. If something happened between Oliver and Rachel, she'd be happy, but she didn't approve of deliberate matchmaking. She'd been the target of it a few times herself, from well-meaning friends, and hadn't enjoyed being pushed into dating some guy who didn't attract her in the slightest. Or worse still, set up with a man at a dinner party, with everyone else watching how she got on with him.

She'd met Chad without anyone's help and she was hoping something would come of it. If he was free. If she was lucky.

She hoped Rachel would find someone too.

After they'd gone back indoors, she locked the front door carefully. 'Let's get a cup of coffee then continue exploring the house. We'll probably run into Toby on the way.'

Emily relaxed as soon as she entered the flat. It was cluttered and old-fashioned. The whole building was dusty, in need of repairs and not at all like a normal house, but for some weird reason, she felt at home here. Her other house had never made her feel like this. Indeed, she'd been going to sell it and look for somewhere more interesting to renovate once she'd retired.

Strange, that The Drover's Hope had fallen into her lap like this. She wasn't usually so lucky.

George went to sit in his car to make the phone call, not wanting anyone to overhear his conversation. He struck lucky first time. She didn't always answer her mobile when she was at work.

'Ah, Sister Pauline. George Pilby here. No, don't hang up. Can you talk or should I ring you later? You are still interested in certain outcomes, I take it? Good. I'll ring you in two hours, then.'

He put the phone down with a smile of satisfaction. He'd

hooked her again. Well, she didn't take much hooking. She was a bitter woman, whose main focus was making money.

When he went back into the house, Marcia looked at him, an unspoken question in her expression.

'The person I was ringing will be available in a couple of hours' time,' he said quietly.

'I don't know how you do it, George.'

'Do what?'

'Find people willing to bend the rules.'

He grinned. 'Bend them? Pauline was smashing every rule she could, even before I turned up.'

'You're still taking a big risk.'

'It'll be well worth it this time. There's far more at stake here than there was with my mother. And Emily's not as easy to manipulate. Which makes her more interesting to deal with.'

Liz rejoined them just then and the conversation became general. And boring.

George sat it out, grateful for Marcia, who seemed able to maintain inane conversations for hours on end.

Nine

Oliver came back just as they were about to set off exploring the rest of the outbuildings. They'd already looked at the pub's kitchens and other service areas, though they'd left the cellar till later. He was clutching a briefcase, from which he pulled out a folder and gave it to Emily.

'Before we start, perhaps you'd look through these copies of recent letters sent on behalf of your cousin Penelope? I've put a marker at where she died and we sent a letter to inform you, as the heir. Barton and Halling made an offer for The Drover's Hope almost immediately after her death.'

She read them through quickly then looked at him in bewilderment. 'I didn't receive any of these earlier letters.'

'They were sent to your home.'

She pointed to the date. 'I wasn't at home then. I was staying with my sister.'

Rachel leaned across to look at them. 'I forwarded all your letters to Liz's for the first fortnight you were away. There were some business letters with *Tapton and Associates* on the back.'

'No need to ask who got hold of them, then,' Emily said grimly.

'Intentionally intercepting an individual's mail is illegal, unless the power to do so has been gained through an interception warrant,' Oliver said. 'And the home secretary has to authorize that.'

'George was probably dealing with his mother's mail and my letters were forwarded with it.'

'Nonetheless, opening someone else's post is still illegal, even if it has been delivered to your address.'

'And if I accuse him of that, make my complaint official, it'll upset Liz. He relies on that. He insists he's only trying to look after her since her husband died.'

'Does she need looking after?'

'I'm afraid so. She's always been a bit of a weak reed.' Emily tapped the papers. 'I need to think about these.'

'And the offer to purchase your inheritance?'

'My immediate inclination is to say no. I know I haven't been here long, but it feels like home – or as if it could become my home. I was looking to sell my other house and move somewhere anyway.' She glanced out of the window. 'I love the views, the feeling of peace, and I've always fancied doing a renovation.'

'I think we'd better contact Barton and Halling, then, to let them know that their earlier letters went astray. Shall I do that for you in my official capacity?'

'Yes, please, Oliver. But while it's still light, let's go and do some more exploring. We keep getting interrupted and I'm dying to see the rest of the house. Oh, and we must find Toby and reassure him that he's safe here.'

In the rear bar, Oliver explained about the three exits from the rear of the pub into the courtyard. 'There's an exit from the utility room of the flat, which you've already seen, this one behind the bar, and another one from the other side of the old barn, which is at the end of that corridor. There's a sort of circuit through the outbuildings, which are the oldest parts of the dwelling.'

He hesitated, then added, 'I know there are some secret hidey-holes and perhaps even a secret passage, or how else would Toby have managed to stay hidden?'

A flurry of rain against the rather dirty window panes at the rear of the bar made Emily say, 'Let's try the undercover circuit first or we'll get soaked.'

Oliver took them past the storerooms and stopped to point to the ground, where there were some large footprints. 'Toby's, I should think.'

'Then we'd better rub them out.' Emily moved to scuff her feet across them. 'I'm not giving that woman any clues if she comes back with the police.'

'You really shouldn't shelter him,' Oliver said. 'And definitely not if the police are involved.'

'I feel I should. I don't know why, but it seems important. Do you really think she'll be back with the police?'

He shrugged. 'I wouldn't be surprised. If so, I'll probably know the officers and can help you deal with it all. After all, Mrs Corrish can't prove that Toby is here.'

'No, but she seems pretty sure. What about Toby's social worker?'

'He's called Kevin and he's OK. Does his best for the lad but the trouble is, he has too much work on his plate, what with the recession and the cuts in services. And to make matters worse, there are no other facilities in the district to shelter younger people like Toby, who can live fairly independently but still need overseeing. So it's a choice between Mrs Corrish or lodgings, or even an old folks' home, I'm afraid.'

'Surely they wouldn't put a young man like him in an old folks' home?'

'It isn't a perfect world and money is stretched thinly. They do what they have to.' Oliver unlocked the door at the end of the corridor but didn't open it. 'Now, this is a rather special part of the house, so I'll let you go first.' He smiled expectantly.

She moved forward into what had looked from outside like a

tumbledown barn. From inside it wasn't like any barn she'd ever seen. It must have measured twenty metres by ten, and had a high ceiling in the centre. But the walls were only one storey high. Four huge timber posts, arranged in two pairs, stood in the central area and from their tops, big wooden beams were attached to hold up the roof. Daylight showed here and there through the tiles at the far end, and clearly the roof leaked there, but she was awe-struck by the beauty of the place. 'Are my eyes deceiving me or is this part very old?'

'They're not deceiving you.'

'Is it a listed building?'

'No.'

'But surely it ought to be?'

'Penelope didn't let anyone in here unless she trusted them absolutely. She said if it were listed, the heritage people would take it over.'

'It needs a lot of TLC. Perhaps they ought to take it over. Look at the droppings. The birds obviously get in and out at the far end.'

'Yes, but for some reason they stay down there and don't come to this end, nor do they stray into the rest of the outbuildings.'

'Can't we do something about that end part to make it waterproof and bird proof?'

His smile was wry. 'It'd take a lot of money to set things to rights. You've inherited a pleasant amount of money from Penelope, but I doubt it's enough to repair this place, let alone restore it as the heritage people would insist.'

'Yes. I can understand that. But surely I could make it waterproof without telling them?'

'Using what sort of tradesman? You don't want someone to do it wrongly and harm the rest of the structure. As Miss Penelope always said, it's a very special place.'

'Oh dear.'

Chad moved forward, slowly turning round on the spot to study the barn. 'I could probably do some minor temporary repairs for you. I know enough not to damage the historic structures.'

Emily held her breath. Had he remembered something else? She glanced sideways at Oliver, who raised one brow in a silent question. She could only spread her arms slightly to indicate her ignorance.

Chad didn't notice their exchange, he was so intent on examining the area. He walked across to the nearest of the four wooden pillars and ran his fingers over the rough surface. 'Beautiful. It's oak, of course. Seventeenth century, possibly earlier.'

He came back to join them. 'I think Toby's hiding in the far corner on the right. There's a low wooden fence, with some stuff stored behind it. I caught a glimpse of his shirt behind them. We'll have to find a better place for him to hide than that.'

'I didn't hear you.' Oliver moved a short distance away.

'I'm definitely going to hide him,' Emily said. 'And if I decide to stay here, I'm going to ask the social worker whether Toby can come and live with me.'

Chad looked at her in surprise. 'He's a nice lad, but that's a big responsibility.'

'Yes, but I think it's what Penelope meant by giving hope to others, as if this house is a trust. I'd enjoy some young company. I've lived alone for too long. And I'm sure he could make himself useful. He seems very strong and I'm not strong, physically. I'm too small. He could help us clean the place up and maybe even do the basic maintenance once it's repaired and—' She broke off to gaze at him in dismay. She'd said 'us' and that was a bit premature. 'If you're able to stay . . .'

'I very much want to stay . . . for several reasons.'

His eyes caught hers and for a few moments they smiled at one another, important messages passed and understood.

Chad looked back at their surroundings. 'I must have had something to do with renovations and old buildings. I can't remember what, but I *knew* how I'd start on your roof, knew exactly what to do first to stabilize that back corner.' He tapped one fist against his temple a couple of times. 'If I can remember that, why can't I remember my own surname?'

Emily couldn't help giving him a quick hug, he looked so forlorn.

He pulled her against his chest and didn't let go for a moment, then drew back and gave her a look that curled her toes and sent heat rushing round her body. He laughed softly, as if he knew exactly how she was feeling.

Oliver pretended to be examining one of the posts.

After a moment or two, Chad said in quite a different tone, 'Come on! Let's go and tell Toby it's safe to come out.'

She slipped her hand into his as they walked across the floor, and their feet beat out a duet of soft echoes on the worn wooden planks. He didn't take his hand away until they got right to the other side.

'You can come out now, Toby,' she called. 'Mrs Corrish has gone. But in case she comes back, we need to find you a better place than this to hide.'

He peered out from behind some piles of wood and oddments of old furniture, casting a careful glance round the barn before sliding out fully. 'Hide in secret room? Am I allowed without Miss Penelope?'

Her breath caught in her throat for a moment. Was there really a secret room? She'd always dreamed of finding one as a child, had loved to read about them in adventure stories and envied the imaginary children who had such adventures. 'Yes, you're allowed to hide there, Toby. Can you show me where it is in case I need to hide in it too? We should show it to Chad as well, because he's going to help you.'

'I'll wait for you in the flat,' Oliver said at once. 'It's better if I don't know where the hiding place is at this stage, though later I'd love to see it.'

Toby gave Chad a wide, trusting smile. 'This way.' He took them into what seemed to be merely a derelict outhouse, the sort people didn't think twice about knocking down. But when she looked at the walls and saw how old the bricks were, narrower than modern bricks and crumbling with age, she realized it was very old.

The rear room was in a somewhat better state of repair. It must have been a dwelling at one time, she thought, because it had a fireplace.

Toby stopped to fumble with a wooden bench that was standing by one wall.

When Emily looked closer, she saw it was attached to the wall. There seemed nothing remarkable about it till Toby's fiddling caused it to swing outwards at one side, taking some of the wooden wall with it. He beckoned to them then crouched down and vanished inside the opening.

Emily felt excitement rise in her as she bent to slip into a low-ceilinged space. Even she couldn't stand upright here and the two tall men looked very uncomfortable in their gorilla-like crouches.

'Stand here.' Toby moved to one side, then reached up and put his hand into a crack above the entrance. The door by which they'd entered swung slowly shut, leaving them in darkness.

Emily moved closer to Chad, clutching his arm. She hated being shut in dark spaces, hadn't taken that into account in her hunger for adventure.

There was a soft click, like a gently closing door, then a faint grating sound. Opposite them another doorway began to open, letting in enough light to see, thank goodness.

The new room was narrow and not very big, but at least they were able to stand fully upright again. Daylight and fresh air filtered in through some narrow gaps in the wall near the ceiling and as her eyes grew accustomed to the dimness, she saw a long bench down one side. On it were some neatly folded blankets, plus packets of what looked like biscuits and a metal cup.

She turned her head to find the source of a dripping sound and in one corner saw a small basin into which water was welling up then overflowing gently, to slide away down a drain hole.

Toby followed her gaze. 'It's a spring. Water comes out all the time.'

Chad knelt to examine it. 'Amazing that it's so clear.'

Toby sat on the bench. 'It's safe here. Miss Penelope said so.'

'I'm sure it is.' Emily was still feeling jittery and short of breath. She didn't think she could bear to be shut in here on her own, even to hide from an enemy. 'How do we get out again?'

'Go back to the wall.' He showed them how to pull down on another of the rough old planks at the top to activate the mechanism that closed up the secret room. Again they had to crouch in darkness till the inner door shut and the outer one opened again.

When Chad put his arm round her shoulders, she realized she was shaking. 'I'm . . . a bit claustrophobic about small dark places. I didn't expect it to be so . . . cramped.'

'I didn't like it, either. But you kept control of yourself brilliantly.'

'It was an effort. I don't like to react in foolish ways when my brain tells me I'm perfectly safe. I'm glad to be out of there.' She turned to Toby. 'If you need the secret room, you can use it any time.'

He nodded solemnly.

'I think that's enough exploring for today,' she said. 'Let's go back to the flat and have something to eat. I've been feeling hungry nearly all the time since we escaped.'

Toby's face lit up at the thought of food. So did Chad's. That felt so blessedly normal.

Rachel and Oliver were sitting in the living room, looking comfortable together. Emily wished they hadn't had to interrupt them.

Her friend jumped up. 'Secrets revealed?'

'Not all of them, but we were tired and hungry so we came back. We still have to explore the end part in more detail.'

'How far did you get?'

'To a room with a fireplace.'

'The old cottage,' Oliver said at once. 'Beyond it are the former stables. Both places are in very poor condition, but they could be renovated and rented out to fell walkers as accommodation, if you felt like making some money from the place.' He lowered his voice. 'What about Toby?'

'He's staying here. Oliver, will you ask the social worker if *we* can take care of him instead of that horrible woman?' She knew this was more impulsive than her usual decisions about life, but somehow it felt right. Toby belonged here just as much as she did.

'Kevin would be happy to let you do that, but there are protocols to be gone through which would reveal where you two have come from. That might work against you having any chance of being given the responsibility for Toby. Are you ready for where you've been to be revealed?'

'Damn!' Chad said softly. 'I'm definitely not ready yet. Maybe we can wait a few days until I get my memory back? Or at least my identity? That may change things.'

'All right.' Emily made her mind up. 'But we'll let Toby—'

Oliver raised one hand. 'Don't tell me what you're doing about Toby.'

'Well, you can tell *me* what you're doing,' Rachel said at once, 'because I'm on his side any time where that horrible female is concerned.'

'I didn't say I wasn't on Toby's side.' Oliver gave Emily a wry smile. 'But as your lawyer, I'm in a ticklish position. If I know no precise details, I can probably keep quiet about what I've seen and heard.'

Emily nodded and he turned back to Rachel, as if seeking her approval as well.

'You're forgiven, then.'

Rachel smiled at him warmly as she spoke, then caught Emily watching her and blushed. 'OK. Let's eat. It's just cold stuff and salads.' She bustled off to serve the meal.

Two hours after his earlier call, George went out to his car and rang Pauline's mobile again. 'We need to talk. And I need your signature on something, so if we're in agreement about helping one another, we need to meet as well.'

Her voice was sharp. 'Tell me what you want first. Your aunt escaped your clutches so I don't see how I can be of any further use.'

'But my aunt didn't escape before she'd signed a document, which you witnessed.'

He heard a sharp intake of breath and smiled. *Gotcha!*

'You think that will work?'

'Sure of it. And my head's on the line as well as anyone else's. Trust me on this.'

'How much is it worth?'

'Five hundred.' He heard a sharp intake of breath.

'All right.'

'Where do you live, Pauline?'

She told him and he grimaced. About an hour and a half's drive away. He noted down the address. It meant he'd have to stay with his mother for another day. Oh well, couldn't be helped.

'Marcia and I will be there in a couple of hours' time. She can witness your signature.'

He went back into the house. 'Sorry to do this, Mother, but Marcia and I have to go and look at a house. The agent is letting us view it before it's advertised.'

'If it's round here, I should come with you. My friend Janet drives me around sometimes. We like to take tea in pretty villages, so I know which are the really good areas.'

'It's over in a little village called . . . um, Upper Bampstead. I don't think you'll have heard of it. Much better if you have a good rest. We'll eat out, so don't make anything for us. We'll be back in time to share a nightcap. I'll just go and change. Don't want to look crumpled.'

Liz sagged back in her chair, disappointed. She'd been looking forward to an evening with her son and his wife. And she would have loved a drive out. She was stuck here so much of the time. Even with library books and visits from friends, time could drag.

Voices floated down the stairs and she frowned. This cottage was such a small place, it was a good thing she lived here alone. It would be very irritating to hear other people's conversations all the time.

She switched on the television news. There. That was better. Sometimes George and his wife had rather sharp exchanges, and he could be brutal in the way he talked to Marcia. No doubting who was master in that household. Her husband had been just the same.

Liz hated to overhear people quarrelling.

They found Pauline's house quite easily, but George drove past and parked round the corner. He winked at his wife. 'Can't be too careful.'

Pauline stood in the doorway for a moment, scowling at them. 'I shouldn't have anything more to do with you, Mr Pilby.'

'Oh, but you should, Sister. You'll be well paid for one small favour. The final one of our dealings.'

Still she hesitated. 'I have a bad feeling about this. Your aunt must be very cunning to have got away from a locked ward. Things may continue to go wrong when you deal with her.'

He laughed. 'I doubt it. She's a fool who got lucky, that's all.'

When Pauline still didn't move, he asked, 'Well? Are you going to help me or not? If you don't need the money . . .'

'Oh, come in.' She held open the door and showed them into the dining room. 'Now, explain exactly what you want me to do.'

'Just witness my aunt's signature on a document.'

'What sort of document? Are you asking me to commit a crime?'

He leaned forward. 'Isn't what you've done already a crime?' After a short silence, he held out the paper. 'Here. No need to read it. You simply sign at the bottom. Put the twenty-fifth as the date. I was at the hospital that day, so it all fits in.'

She turned to the front page of the folded document and he snatched it from her, putting it back with only the last page showing.

'I like to check what I'm getting into,' she protested.

'And I like people to mind their own business. You can always say you weren't allowed to read the document if anything goes wrong.'

Marcia said quietly, 'It won't take a minute, Pauline, and George does know what he's doing. There's five hundred pounds waiting to be paid to you. Well worth it, eh?'

Pauline hesitated, biting her lip, then scrawled her signature and wrote the date he'd requested.

'Thank you.' George stood up. 'I doubt we'll need to trouble you again.' He held out an envelope.

'I'd prefer to count the money before you leave.'

The minute Pauline nodded and put away the wad of notes, he left without a word of farewell. As they walked back towards the car he smiled at his wife. 'That went well.'

'I suppose so. I—'

There was a man standing by their car, about to put a piece of paper under the windscreen wiper.

'Hoy! What are you doing?' George shouted, hurrying forward.

'Warning you not to park here again. This is a residents only parking area and you've not got a sticker on your car. Besides, I'd know you if you lived here. I know everyone in this street.'

George bit back his annoyance. 'Sorry. We were in a bit of a hurry and I didn't see the signs. We'll leave straight away.'

'You do that. And don't come back again or I'll report you to the authorities and you'll be fined,' the man yelled after them.

'Stupid fool.' George drove round the corner and speeded up. 'There. That was easy, wasn't it?'

'Too easy. I have to agree with Pauline. I don't feel good about this, either, George. Look, there's still time to change your mind and—'

'No way. It's exactly the windfall we need to top up our retirement fund.' He grabbed her arm and gave it a little shake. 'I've not let you down before, have I?'

She bit her lip. 'No, but – George, watch out!'

He narrowly avoided a cyclist, who made a crude sign. 'Stupid fool.' He added more quietly, 'How many times do I have to tell you to leave money matters to me, Marcia? My aunt will find it difficult to get the better of me. And long term, well, she has no children and I'm her only nephew.'

'Yes, but—'

'And now that I know she isn't brain damaged – or not much – she'll be as well cared for as my mother is. I'm not a cruel man. I'm making sure you're well looked after in your old age, too. That's what you care about most, isn't it?' He waited and when she didn't answer, said quietly, 'I know what I'm doing, my dear.'

'I just . . . worry sometimes.'

'Worry about keeping my mother happy. You've done brilliantly so far. She must be the biggest bore on the planet.'

'I think she's rather sweet.'

'I think we need to find a proper house for ourselves, but not too close to her. That's our next job once I've sent off the contract to Barton and Halling. You can start studying the market and deciding where you want to live. It won't be long now before I can retire, thanks to Barton and Halling.'

'Emily will deny signing the contract to sell.'

He smirked. 'She can deny it all she likes. I'm rather good at forging signatures, and I've made sure the dates on the various documents tie in with my visits. Pauline will back me up on that.'

As she still looked doubtful, he added, 'Give me a few months and I'll pull my aunt into line permanently. Perhaps she should live with my mother? They can bore each other to death then.' He laughed heartily at his own joke as he turned into his mother's street.

Ten

Late on Monday morning, Oliver brought more of his things from home to add to his clothes at The Drover's Hope. He looked as excited as a schoolboy as he carried his computer and several boxes up to the bedroom he'd chosen, yelling, 'Down in a minute!'

'You did say you wanted internet access?' he asked Emily when he joined the others in the flat.

'I was going to look into it today.'

'No need. I've arranged in your name for some technicians to come this afternoon to update the telephone system, which is archaic, as well to make sure you're connected to the internet. I didn't think you'd object.'

'Object? I'm delighted.' She couldn't resist giving him a hug. 'How on earth did you manage that? I wasn't even sure we could get on the Net out here.'

He tapped his nose, grinning. 'If you don't ask, I won't have to tell you any lies. Let's just say that thanks to being a member of a certain organization, I've got friends in useful places.'

'Wonderful. I'd better set my computer up ready to go, then. It's about time I checked my emails. George won't have read them all, thank goodness, because they were protected. Goodness knows what people have been thinking about me not replying.' She shivered at the thought of her nephew.

Chad looked at her in concern, moving closer as if offering unspoken support. 'Does he still frighten you?'

'Yes. I hadn't realized he could be so . . . ruthless. He grabbed hold of me once while I was in hospital and shook me hard, warning me to do as he said or else. Now that I have you and a built-in lawyer, I feel much better about facing him, but I still worry about how ruthless he can be.' She looked across at Oliver.

'Even George isn't above the law, but he's got away with so much already.'

'Some people do manage to twist the law in their favour, I'm afraid. No system is perfect. But we won't let George get you in his power again, will we, Chad? One or the other of us will stay near you until we've got everything settled.' Oliver frowned. 'It's an unusual case, though.'

She sighed. 'I wish it weren't. I wish things were absolutely straightforward.'

'If they were, you'd not need me. Oh, and I'd better warn you: I don't think you'll hold Dr Allerton back for long. She's itching to follow up on the way you were treated, because she takes a pride in the NHS.'

'You're an unusual lawyer, Oliver. I'm lucky to have you at my side.'

'I'm only a part-time lawyer now, but I do believe in justice. And actually, I'm enjoying myself, in a strange sort of way.' His eyes turned towards Rachel as he said that, then he looked back at Emily. 'I think we should visit my office this afternoon. We need to go through some of the final formalities for handing over the estate.'

'I have to wait for my new car before I go anywhere. If it's delivered in time, I can drive you there and practise finding my way round Littleborough. I need to get back into the swing of real life again, not expect people to look after me. And we have to stock up the house with food and cleaning materials. I know we've bought a load of food and things, but they seem to have vanished without trace.'

Chad moved towards the kitchen. 'I'm ready for a coffee. Anyone joining me? Good.' He put the kettle on.

Oliver lowered his voice. 'I need to ask one thing as your lawyer: are you still happy to have Chad living here?'

Emily looked at him in surprise. 'Oh, yes. I'm enjoying getting to know him. We're . . . attracted to one another.' She hesitated, then confided, 'The only thing is, Chad's remembered that he has two sons so we don't know if he's still married or not.'

'Ah.'

'If he could only remember his surname, surely we could check out who he is?'

'Yes. I'll use a search engine once we've got the internet up and running, see if I can find anything useful. If he's right about his first names and we put in Chad as well, that should help, surely?'

There was the sound of a vehicle drawing up outside, sending the gravel crackling and scattering. She looked out of the window and forgot her problems as she watched Mark get out of the car and move towards the house. 'It's here! My car's here.'

She set off running, collecting Rachel on the way and stopping next to the car, her hand out to touch it. She felt a little foolish at showing such childish excitement and when she looked round, the three men were watching her in amusement.

Oh, what the hell! Let them smile. The car represented freedom of movement, something she hadn't had for a long time. She stroked its glossy silver paintwork, bent to examine the grey and maroon upholstery of the driver's seat and gave in to the temptation to sit in it, adjusting the seat to suit a shorter person.

'Everything all right?' Mark came round to smile down at her.

'It feels great. I need to drive it, to check that it runs OK.'

'Oh, it will, I promise you. I'm hoping you'll drive me back to work as a test run.'

'I'd love to.' She rushed up to the house to grab a cardigan and her handbag. 'I'm driving Mark back.'

Oliver grabbed her arm. 'I should go with you.'

'It's only into town and back.'

'Till we're sure you're safe, you really shouldn't go anywhere alone.'

Her joy faded abruptly. 'I suppose you're right. Come on, then.'

She cheered up again as she drove carefully into Littleborough, following Mark's clear directions to bring them to the car yard.

'I must seem silly to you, getting so excited about my car,' she said to Oliver as he moved into the front passenger's seat.

'Not at all. You've been through a terrible experience. Getting back to normal must feel wonderful.'

'You're very understanding.'

'I try to be. We could go and sign those papers now at the office. I'll introduce you to my son while we're there and brief him on what's happened so far.'

'Great.'

As they parked, he cleared his throat, avoiding looking at her. 'Um . . . your friend, Rachel. She isn't . . . you know, in a relationship?'

Emily smiled, not surprised by this question. 'No. But I think she might be ripe for one if she could meet the right person.'

There was no answer, but when she glanced sideways she saw him looking happy.

After she'd signed some papers, she drove them back, more confident of the route to take, humming along with one of her favourite songs on the radio.

They spent the last part of the morning cleaning up the bar area outside the flat, keeping the front door wide open to air the place.

Work stopped abruptly as Emily saw a large four-wheel drive come up the hill, slow down and turn into the car park. It had the *Barton & Halling* logo on the doors. It stopped in front of The Drover's Hope and two men in dark suits got out. Both were carrying briefcases.

'What now?' Emily wondered aloud. Couldn't she have even half a day without crises?

The others came to join her from where they were working, so the visitors were faced by a group of three.

'Miss Mattison?' the taller man said crisply.

'*Ms* Mattison,' she corrected at once.

His lips tightened for a moment or two, as if he was annoyed by this, then he repeated 'Ms' in a bored voice and held out his hand. 'Colin Gressam and my personal assistant, Louis Tompkins. We're from Barton and Halling, as you may have guessed.'

She wondered if they'd come to make an offer for the house, but played dumb. 'Why should I have guessed that?'

'Well, you were told things would happen quickly. My colleague and I have come to do a preliminary walk round the pub and take some photos, so that we can get started on planning the demolition and—'

'I beg your pardon?'

'The pub has to go to make way for the entrance to the new estate. Anyway, look at it.' He waved one scornful hand towards the building. 'It's in a dreadful condition.'

'I haven't the faintest clue what you're talking about.'

The two men exchanged knowing glances.

'You've agreed to sell this property to our company, so—'

Emily could only gape at them for a moment or two, then she pulled herself together. 'I can assure you I've made no agreement to sell. And since I'm the owner, I—'

'Your nephew said you were becoming a little forgetful, which is why he's helping you with the sale. Perhaps we phone him and check that, dear? I have his number on my mobile.'

She was furious at his tone. 'Don't you *dear* me! I'm not a child. This has nothing to do with George and I've no intention of phoning him.'

Their expressions said they still thought she was losing her wits.

'George is lying. I am *not* suffering from dementia. And I've signed nothing.'

Oliver moved forward, his voice crisp. 'I'm Ms Mattison's lawyer. Perhaps we should go inside and discuss why you believe this? Is that all right with you, Emily?'

'Yes. And as for George—'

'We won't try to ascribe blame at the moment,' Oliver said firmly. 'We'll start by finding out the facts.'

What she wanted to do was tell the two men to get the hell out of her house. She might have known George was still working to undermine her and get hold of her inheritance.

Oliver turned back to the visitors. 'If you'd come inside?'

'Certainly. We need to see what the old place is like, anyway.'

'Well, you won't be going beyond this front room today!' Emily snapped. She stopped just inside.

Gressam looked round the front bar and grimaced. 'No wonder it closed down.'

Oliver pulled two tables together and made sure Emily and Rachel had chairs.

When everyone was seated, he took charge. 'Could you please tell me why you feel Ms Mattison has accepted your company's offer to buy?'

'I have a copy of the memorandum of agreement and—'

'Go through the whole process that's been followed, if you don't mind.'

'Surely she remembers what she did?'

Emily leaned forward, glaring at him, speaking slowly and clearly. 'It's rather difficult – to remember something – you have not done.' She looked up. 'Ah, Chad. Do come and join us. We're having a very interesting discussion about things these men imagine I've done.'

Chad, who had been surveying the barn with an aim to doing some emergency repairs on the roof, immediately sat down.

Oliver waited until he was seated, then went on, 'Tell me the exact process you went through to reach this so-called agreement.'

'The memorandum of agreement, duly signed and witnessed. Several weeks ago we sent a letter out to Ms Mattison and—'

'Which I never received,' Emily snapped.

Oliver patted her arm. 'Let them go through it all, then we'll say our piece.'

He was suddenly rather impressive, no longer the genial friend, but a calm professional with a crisp and authoritative way of speaking.

She couldn't believe this was happening. Was George so far ahead of her at every step that she had no hope of winning against him? Would he gain control of her and her money as he had with his mother? Not if she could help it.

'Your nephew replied to head office in response to our offer to buy, explaining that you'd been involved in an accident and were unable to respond yourself. He made a counter-offer on your behalf, and entered into negotiations to push up the price. By the time we were in agreement, you'd come out of your coma, so we sent you a memorandum of agreement, which you signed. We received it this morning and as we're eager to proceed, we came here immediately to check a few things out.'

Oliver held up one hand. 'Just one small point. If you wish to come here in future, please make an appointment.'

Gressam gave a long-suffering sigh. 'Very well. Anyway, even though contracts haven't been exchanged, the sale can now be considered binding.'

He fumbled through some papers in his briefcase. 'This is a copy of the memorandum. We sent you the contract itself about a week ago and your nephew has just finished discussing the final details.'

'I didn't receive the contract, either.'

Another sigh. 'It was sent to your home address and signed for by your nephew.'

'I didn't authorize George to do that. Nor did he show the contract to me.' She frowned. 'Don't I remember that it's illegal to open someone else's mail?'

'It is indeed,' Oliver said.

'Since you'd authorized your nephew to negotiate on your behalf, this is all unnecessary and you won't make us increase the price any further.'

Emily said loudly and slowly. 'I did not authorize him to act for me. I have my own lawyer.' She indicated Oliver. 'And I do not wish to sell.'

Oliver took the memorandum from Gressam and spread it on the table between himself and Emily. Chad got up and stood behind them to read it. His hand was a comforting pressure on Emily's shoulder. At the end of the table, Rachel folded her arms, scowling at the two men.

'Is this your signature, Emily?' Oliver asked.

'It looks like my signature, but I definitely didn't sign this memorandum.'

'You've been in hospital, I gather, a geriatric assessment unit.' Gressam studied her, frowning.

'Only because the rehab unit had no free beds. *I am not – suffering – from dementia.*'

Her voice seemed to echo into the silence.

Oliver cleared his throat to get their attention. 'I must remind you to deal directly with my client from now on. I shall send you another memorandum, stating that George Pilby has no authority whatsoever to negotiate on his aunt's behalf.'

'That's rather shutting the stable door after the horse has escaped, don't you think?'

'No. Because we deny that anything has been signed. We shall need details of precisely which days the offer, memorandum and contract were sent out and returned. Actually, I'm not sure we shouldn't put this in the hands of the police.'

There was another silence heavy with hostility, which he allowed to continue for a few moments before speaking again. 'In the meantime, I shall be applying for an injunction preventing any further steps being taken about this sale by your company – or by Ms Mattison's nephew.'

Chad leaned forward. 'Has the contract been returned to you?'

'Not yet.'

'As it hasn't arrived here for signing, and as Ms Mattison has been with one or the other of us every hour since the night she left the rehab unit last Friday, you have three witnesses who can swear that she hasn't seen the contract during that time, let alone signed it.'

'It was sent well before she left the unit, should have arrived at her home on the previous Monday.' Gressam stared at Chad. 'May I ask who you are?'

'A good friend of my client,' Oliver said quickly, then looked at Emily. 'All right if I ask them to deal with this through me from now on?'

At her nod, he pulled out a business card and gave it to them. 'Use my mobile phone number. I shall be staying here until this matter is sorted, as will everyone present. Ms Mattison is, rightly in my opinion, nervous of being left alone in such a large and isolated building.'

'Let me phone head office,' Gressam said.

Oliver stood up. 'You can do whatever you wish once you're outside the house. We've listened to you, and I hope you've listened to us. Please leave now and don't return without an appointment.'

As they got to the door, the assistant pulled out a phone and aimed it at Emily to take a photo.

Chad moved quickly forward and knocked the phone aside.

Oliver's voice rang out sharply. 'Do not take any photos of my client, or I'll take out an injunction within the hour to prevent you from using them or harassing Ms Mattison further.'

The assistant scowled at him, but its flash had already gone off.

Chad twitched it out of his hand.

'Hey! What are you doing?' He tried to grab the phone back but Rachel moved to block his way.

Chad pressed some buttons, seeming to know exactly what he was doing. 'There. Photo deleted. Nothing else touched.' He handed the camera back.

'You had no right to do that!'

Oliver leaned forward. 'And you had no right to take any photos after I'd asked you formally not to. Now, the discussion is finished and your presence is no longer welcome here. You should let me see the original documents you claim have been sent and signed, then let me have photocopies.'

He followed the men out, standing in the car park to see them off.

Gressam looked back over his shoulder, scowling at Emily, as he got into the passenger seat.

Emily linked her arm in Chad's, something she loved to do, and smiled at Rachel. 'You two were quick off the mark there. Thank you. You're obviously familiar with modern cameras, Chad.'

'Yes. I need to photograph stuff for my work. Antiques are . . . are . . .' He broke off. 'Damn! It's gone again.'

'Another piece of the puzzle has slotted in, though. Antiques.'

Oliver came back inside, picked up the memorandum of agreement and frowned at it. 'It looks very much like your signature, Emily.'

'I know. But I definitely didn't sign it.'

'We shall need to call in handwriting experts if this gets to court. But our first line of defence will be to gather evidence about George dealing with your mail without your authorization. We shall also need to know exactly where you were each time he claims to have seen you or had something signed. I wonder what he's intending to do with the contract now.'

'Sign it in my name, I suppose. But surely he can't get away with that, or get hold of the money if he does manage to push a sale through?'

'I'm hoping the date it's signed is after you left the geriatric unit.'

'So am I.' After a pause, she added, 'But I doubt he'd be that stupid.' She paced up and down the room, stopping to spread her hands wide and exclaim, 'I still can't believe any of this is happening.'

'I can. I've seen some terrible cases while I've been a lawyer, cases where I believed the defendant, but was unable to prove the person's innocence. Cases where old people were robbed blind by their relatives and I couldn't prevent it. The law isn't always able to deal out justice, unfortunately.'

'Well, whatever George is trying to do now,' Rachel said, 'it only reinforces our decision that you must be with someone every minute of the day, Emily. And it wouldn't hurt to be with someone during the night as well.' She looked meaningfully at Chad, but both he and Emily shook their heads.

'You can't tell me you don't want to sleep together!' Rachel said indignantly. 'Anyone can see that you've got something going. And you're both consenting adults, so I don't know what's holding you back.'

Emily could feel herself flushing.

'I may be married to someone else,' Chad said. 'I don't believe in being unfaithful.'

'And I don't believe in sleeping with another woman's husband,' Emily added.

Rachel rolled her eyes. 'Then I'll have to sleep on your sofa, Emily.'

'I'm doing that already,' Chad said at once. 'No one will get past me. I'm a light sleeper. And you should stay with someone all day, Emily.'

'Surely there's no need for such extreme measures?' Emily asked.

'I'm afraid there is.' Oliver's voice was still firm, but it had regained its quiet, friendly tone. When he was with them, he seemed like a different person from the man who'd spoken so confidently to the men from Barton & Halling.

'Oh, very well.'

Oliver received a phone call from a Janice Ryling in the legal department at Barton & Halling.

He listened intently, then said, 'We'll come in to see you immediately, then. I wish to see the original documents before I accept the photocopies.'

More discussion, then, 'Very well. We're on our way.'

But before they left, he rang his doctor friend and arranged for Emily and Chad to see a geriatric specialist. 'Just in case,' he said as he put his phone away.

The thought of what that implied made Emily shiver. She couldn't help it. She was terrified of being shut away again, and this time she was sure she'd be doped into submission.

Barton & Halling occupied one floor of a new, three-storey

office building. As the three of them stood in the lift, Oliver warned them not to volunteer any information whatsoever, but to look to him for guidance on every point.

Emily nodded, but she still felt a bit shaky.

'It'll take a while to get past the memories of that place,' Chad said softly. 'But we'll get through it.'

Would they get through it together, though? That was becoming increasingly important to her. She'd never met anyone she felt so comfortable with.

Unsmiling, Oliver accepted seats at one side of a shining wooden board table, opposite a man and a woman. The woman was clearly in charge of this encounter.

'We do not appreciate all these delays,' she said as a preliminary.

Oliver held up one hand. 'To whom are we speaking?'

'Is that relevant?'

'Oh, yes.'

'I'm Janice Ryling and this is Mr Korton, my PA.' Her voice took on a sarcastic edge. 'I'd like to state as a preliminary that your client's claim not to have signed the memorandum won't make us raise our price at all.'

'As my client doesn't wish to sell, that's irrelevant.'

'She *has* agreed to sell.'

'No. She definitely hasn't.'

Once again there was a sense of hostility, as each side waited to see who would continue.

In response to a glance from Ms Ryling, Mr Korton broke the silence. 'These are the papers you wished to see.' He pushed them across the table. 'And these are photocopies of them all.'

'I prefer to make my own photocopies once I've read the originals.' Oliver gave a wolfish smile. 'Otherwise I'd have to read all the photocopies as well in order to compare the two. That might take up even more of your precious time.'

From the look on the man's face and the way he pulled back the photocopies, Oliver felt instantly suspicious. Or was he reading too much into the action? Well, you couldn't be too careful.

He read through the two-page memorandum, passing each page to Emily, then started on the rest of the correspondence.

Emily read on steadily, passing the papers to Chad. When she'd finished, she turned to Oliver and waited.

'Have you ever seen any of these papers before, Ms Mattison?' he asked formally.

'No, never.'

Oliver turned to the two lawyers. 'Do you have a copy of the contract? Mr Gressam said you'd drawn one up and sent it to my client, though I'd like it on record that she didn't receive that, either.'

Ms Ryling sighed and pushed some stapled papers forward. 'This is a copy of the contract, which was delivered to her home and signed for by her nephew.'

'Who had no right even to open it. I'll study it at my leisure.' He turned to Emily and pushed the last paper towards her. 'Did you sign this memorandum?'

'No, I didn't. How could I? I never saw it, let alone signed it.'

'Miss Mattison herself said it looked like her signature,' the PA said at once.

'Ms,' Emily corrected.

He looked at her in exasperation. 'Does that matter now?'

'It does to me. I never allow people to call me Miss.' She smiled, suddenly realizing her name was written on the memorandum as 'Miss Emily Mattison' each time it appeared. She tapped that word with her forefinger and looked at Oliver, who nodded his understanding of her silent message.

He stood up. 'Perhaps you'd show me to a photocopier, now.'

After he'd finished making copies, he collected Emily and Chad, and led the way outside, shaking his head to indicate they should wait to discuss anything.

When they were in the car, she said, 'I thought you'd point out that the contract was for Miss Mattison, something I'd never accept.'

'Not yet. We'll keep it in reserve.'

'It's one of my quirks, refusing to be addressed as Miss, and I can get several people from my former employer to vouch for that. I might let it pass occasionally, but I'd never, ever allow anyone to call me *Miss* in a formal document.'

'I doubt that would be enough to change matters in law,' Oliver said. 'But it might be useful as corroborative evidence. In the meantime I'll take the necessary steps to get an injunction to prevent your nephew from approaching you or your dwelling, but that'll take time, I'm afraid. It has to be served on him so that he can respond.'

'The sooner it can be applied, the better.' Emily was surprised at how afraid she was of what her nephew might do next.

Oliver rubbed his hands together briskly. 'Right then. We'll go and see Dr Allerton now. She kindly agreed to stay on a little longer after her session ended at the practice, because her friend Ms Patel, who's a geriatric specialist, has made time to join her.'

At the doctor's surgery, they were taken into a small meeting room. Emily wanted Chad to be present, as well as their mutual lawyer, to back up if necessary some of her statements about what had happened in the geriatric ward.

Once they were all seated, the two women studied her so carefully before she even spoke that she felt as if they could see right through her. As they started to question her, she decided it wasn't a hostile gaze, but an assessing one. She felt certain these two wouldn't be fooled by anything she said or did. Luckily, she had only to tell the truth.

When they stopped asking questions, they turned to Chad to ask him to corroborate certain claims she'd made about what had happened in the geriatric unit.

'Everything Emily's said is true. I was treated in a very similar manner, including being sedated unnecessarily. It was seeing one another spitting out the tablets they gave us that first drew us together.'

Afterwards Emily expected them to confer, but Dr Allerton looked at her colleague and nodded as if to say go ahead.

'In my opinion, as a first assessment only of course, you're not suffering from dementia, Ms Mattison,' Ms Patel stated quietly.

'Thank you.' Emily knew she wasn't, and yet she felt enormously relieved to have this reassurance from an expert in the field.

The two doctors turned to Chad, studying him in exactly the same careful way and asking Emily to verify a couple of things he said.

He answered their questions about himself calmly when he knew the answer, admitting his ignorance when he didn't. He had no trouble with general questions and displayed good knowledge of a range of subjects.

'Since you're still remembering the odd detail about yourself, Chad,' Ms Patel said, 'there is a likelihood that you'll retrieve further information. One can never be quite sure how much, but there's nothing I or anyone else can do to speed it up, unfortunately. And there's no guarantee how much you'll remember. You seem to me to be in full possession of your mental faculties, however.'

She smiled gently at the relief on his face. 'That's my expert opinion and I'm prepared to swear to it in court.'

He let out a long sigh. 'I find that very reassuring. Thank you. I'm lucky to have found such good friends at this difficult time.' He looked at Emily and Oliver as he said that.

Chad had spoken with dignity, Emily decided. She'd guess he'd been a figure of authority, though in what area was not yet clear: he'd shown considerable knowledge of old buildings, photography and antiques. Or were those simply interests? How had he earned a living? And why had no one come forward to report him missing or respond to the requests for information?

The two women went on to question both of them about the details of their confinement at the unit.

'That's it, for now,' Dr Allerton said eventually.

Ms Patel nodded agreement. 'You were right, Jean. There's something very wrong there and we can't let it continue.' She looked at Chad and Emily. 'Would you two be willing to testify in court about your treatment?'

'Definitely. In fact, it'd give me great satisfaction,' Emily said at once. 'Though I don't remember what happened when I was in a coma, of course.'

Chad nodded. 'I'm much the same. I remember the later details of my incarceration very clearly, but not the earlier ones, like how I got there. I was semi-conscious for a while, apparently, and under heavy sedation. Once I'd stopped swallowing the tablets, things became much clearer.'

Emily suddenly remembered something. 'I think I may have two of the tablets they kept dishing out stuck in the pocket of an old dressing gown they gave me. It wasn't my own, but no one would believe that, because George insisted it was. I was wearing it over my clothes when I fled.'

'Excellent. If you could let us have them . . .'

'It'd be no proof in law,' Oliver said at once. 'She could have got them anywhere.'

'It'd give us some idea of what they were using and therefore where they might be getting their supplies from,' Ms Patel said bitterly. 'I want this place and all others like it closed down. We're here to *care* for older patients, not abuse them or dope them to the eyeballs.'

'If I can do anything to help, I will, believe me.'

'Thank you.'

Emily shivered. If she hadn't met Chad . . . If she hadn't had her friend Rachel to help . . . she might still be there.

Eleven

George walked round the rental house, then returned to the living room, dividing his scowls equally between the room and his wife. 'The rooms aren't big enough. I don't know why you're even considering this rabbit hutch.'

Marcia gestured to the agent to leave them alone. 'George, there isn't much available in the area to rent at the moment that's any better, not without paying an absolute fortune into someone else's pocket. This house will be all right for a few months, while you're working in England. It's a reasonable size, very conveniently situated for transport and in a good area. Plus they're prepared to give us a three-month lease, with monthly renewals.'

'No wonder! It's downright shabby. Look at that lounge suite! My aunt's house was far better than this.'

She didn't comment on that. He still seemed aggrieved that he'd had to leave Emily's house, but Marcia had been relieved. She'd never felt right about taking the place over when his aunt might well recover from her accident – as she clearly had, whatever George still claimed.

She sighed. She wished she knew what he was up to. He was planning something, she could tell, but what? She wrenched her thoughts away from that to the present problem.

'The furniture here is adequate.' She went to sit on the offending lounge suite. 'Actually, it's quite comfortable. Come and try it.'

He joined her on the sofa, wriggling about, still scowling. 'I think we deserve more than merely *adequate*.'

'Of course we do . . . long term. But this is by far the best house we've seen, and you know how good I am at making a home out of a rental. We should take it, just for a few months. It'll give you time to see what your next permanent project will be. You said you'd probably continue working with that company a while longer. After all, you *are* an expert on industrial pumps and they do pay you rather well.'

'So they should.'

'Once we retire, we can decide where we want to live permanently and take our time finding a house that's just right. We'll both enjoy that.' She hoped.

'Hmm.' He got up, shoved his hands deep in his pockets and went to stare out of the window.

She waited. It never did to hurry George.

'I suppose you're right. This place is in a decent area, at least. And you usually work miracles with the interiors, I will admit.'

Silence followed, which she didn't interrupt, then he shrugged. 'Oh, very well. I'll go and tell that fellow we'll take it.'

'Ask him how quickly we can move in. It might be worth staying with your mother for another day or two if we can move here quickly, rather than wasting time, effort and money changing to a hotel.'

He grimaced. 'I suppose so. I wish my mother didn't fuss so much, though.'

'It's because she cares about you. Just be a little patient with her.'

When he'd gone to talk to the agent, Marcia let her head drop against the back of the sofa, closing her eyes briefly. It was always like this when they were looking for a house. George wanted the best, the very best. He acted as if he were a multi-millionaire. He was going to be a devil to deal with when it came to buying a place of their own. She hoped he had a lot of money saved, wished he'd involve her more in the financial side of their life, so that she knew what to aim for.

She could usually manage him when it came to their day-to-day living, but she wasn't fool enough to interfere with his major long-term plans. Not if she wanted a comfortable early retirement, as he'd been planning for several years now. It had become quite an obsession with him, especially when they were living in the Middle East.

She couldn't disagree with his focus. When she remembered how her parents had had to scrimp and save in their old age to manage on the state pension, and how limited their life had been, she knew she'd do anything rather than go down the same path. Not only had her parents lived in a mean little council house nearly all their lives, but they'd died in a road accident because they were driving an old rattletrap of a car that had few safety features.

She shuddered. She didn't ever intend to live as they had. Which was why it was worth putting up with George's autocratic attitude towards her – all women, come to that – not to mention his moods. She enjoyed her comfortable lifestyle very much indeed.

After leaving the doctor's, they stopped to buy some more food, then Emily drove them home, enjoying the comfort of her new car. She kept wondering what Oliver's legal tactics would be, but didn't want to discuss that while she was driving.

Once they got back, she didn't have to wait long to find out what he was planning.

'We need to talk,' he said abruptly as they finished a scratch meal.

'I'll clear away and leave you three in peace,' Rachel offered. 'Toby, you'll help me, won't you?'

'I do the washing up. Miss Penelope showed me.' He began to clear the table. There wasn't much food left to put away. Between his appetite and Chad's, the dishes of salad and plates of cooked meats had been cleared quickly, plus all the French loaf.

'Let's go into the front bar, so we've space to study the papers we've got.' Oliver took their consent for granted and led the way out of the flat. 'First we should check the dates on the letters they sent and the dates you're supposed to have signed the memorandum, then we can tie them in to events.' He spread the pieces of paper out.

Emily picked up the earliest letter. 'This must have been forwarded to my sister while I was in hospital.'

Rachel nodded. 'Yes, that's my handwriting on the envelope. I forwarded all your mail, Emily, as we agreed.'

'George must have arranged to have Liz's mail forwarded to him. I'm amazed she let him do that.'

'Do you think she knew?' Chad asked.

'Perhaps not. But if he said it was necessary for business, she'd agree. It's suspicious how short of money she always seemed, because I'd understood that Nigel had left her well provided for.'

'In any case, there was no excuse for your nephew opening letters addressed to you, even if they were forwarded to him. It's against the law and you never agreed in any way whatsoever that he should act on your behalf once you recovered consciousness, did you?' Oliver looked at her, pen in hand, ready to note down her answer.

'I was in no state to agree to anything at first. But after I'd recovered, I did try to stop him handling anything. The trouble was, he refused to bring in my mail and that sister refused to put me in touch with anyone who could help. I felt so helpless.'

'I overheard Emily asking for her mail, and her purse, and several times asking them to stop George interfering,' Chad said. 'I used to sit in the day room for hours and I had little else to do but watch what was going on, since I was supposed to be sedated.'

'Your testimony could be very useful.' Oliver made another note then turned back to Emily. 'And your nephew never mentioned the letters from Barton and Halling, let alone discussed the offer with you?'

'No. Definitely not. He'll say he did, of course.'

Chad leaned forward. 'I'd guess he'll get Pauline to bear witness to that. But I may be able to help there as well. I overheard most of his conversations with Emily, and some of his conversations with Pauline, too. They were rather lax about that.

Over-confident.' He smiled. 'I couldn't help overhearing what they said, because your nephew has a very loud voice.'

'Overhearing some of their conversations won't provide enough evidence of collusion,' Oliver said. 'It'll be their word against yours, two against one. And they'll claim you weren't in your right mind.'

'I also saw him hand Pauline an envelope on three occasions. They didn't realize how half-open glass doors can sometimes act as mirrors.'

'Hmm. Would you have any idea exactly when George came to visit, Emily?'

She frowned. 'It's hard to remember dates, because we weren't allowed newspapers, but after his first visit, George only came to see me on Tuesdays and either Thursday or Friday, so that should narrow it down.'

'We must make a chart of the weeks you were there, with George's visits noted, and anything else you can remember.'

'There wasn't much happening to mark the passage of time.' Emily couldn't help feeling bitter as she remembered the long, dreary hours, her despair at being in that unit.

Chad suddenly snapped his fingers. 'Jackson might remember things better than we do, and he's no friend of Pauline's.'

Emily shook her head. 'He helped me a little, guessing I was going to try to escape, but he was adamant that he didn't want to be a whistle blower, said his career would never recover from that.'

'Sadly, he could be right,' Chad said. 'But it might be worth tracing him and trying to persuade him to reconsider.'

Oliver made another note. 'I'll be frank with you. It's not going to be easy to prove your case unless the handwriting expert provides some evidence in our favour.'

Emily stared at him, disappointment surging through her. 'That settles it. I'm going to phone my former boss and ask for his help.'

They looked at her in surprise.

She could feel herself flushing. 'I used to work in – um, let's call it one of the government's security units. I was only doing research and clerical work – well, most of the time – but Leon is still in charge and he's a very clever man. I'm sure he'll help me if I ask him.'

'Security?' Chad said. 'You were working in MI5 or something?'

'Or something. It was a small unit that wasn't in the public eye. It was interesting work, though of course I can't tell you about it.'

'Why do you think this Leon guy will help?'

She couldn't control her blushes. 'Because he and I were . . . well, we were involved at one stage. It didn't work out. He's wedded to his job, has already had two failed marriages. I wanted more than that from a partner. But we didn't split up in an acrimonious way and we've remained good friends. I'm sure he'll help if he can.'

She let out a huff of laughter. 'We had an argument once and I swore I'd never ask him for help. But I'll do whatever I have to, to save this house and stop George controlling me. Leon will crow about that.'

She saw Chad's face and stifled a sigh. She hadn't wanted to reveal details of her past affairs; no new lover liked that. She turned towards Oliver again. 'Please don't say a word about this. I wasn't supposed even to mention my former job to anyone.'

'We won't. But if you think Leon can help in any way, you should definitely contact him.'

'I'll do that straight away.' She left the room and went into her bedroom, using the telephone to ring a special number she'd never forget. It rang three times and a mechanical voice said, 'Number received. You will be phoned back shortly on a more secure line.'

She put the phone down and waited. Two minutes later it rang. She wasn't surprised at how quickly they'd got back to her. He unit was nothing if not efficient.

She was surprised that it was Leon himself calling. 'Emily?'

'Yes.'

'Are you all right?'

'Yes. What had you heard?'

'That you were in a coma. They said you had brain damage. Your nephew wasn't very optimistic about your recovery. We checked with the sister in charge of the unit and she said much the same thing, in medical jargon. We were all a bit upset. You're sure you're all right now?'

'Positive. George didn't want me to recover so that he could take over my finances. Don't believe a word he says. And the sister in charge of the unit was working with him to keep me sedated.'

She heard a low, soft whistle of surprise. Leon didn't question what she'd said, though. He knew she'd not lie to him.

As she was trying to work out how to ask for his help, he chuckled. 'You never did like asking for help, Emily Mattison.'

'No. But now I really need it.' She summarized the situation. 'I know this isn't job related, and I'm not with the unit any longer, but I'm desperate. Can you help in any way?'

'Definitely. I'll take charge of helping you myself . . . for old times' sake.'

'There's just one thing . . . I'm involved with the guy who escaped with me.'

'I'll tread carefully.'

She heard rustling sounds, then what sounded like keys clicking on a computer keyboard. He'd be checking his schedules.

'Give me two or three days to sew up the current project. Unless things become desperate, in which case you should call the emergency number straight away.'

'I don't think anything that desperate is likely to happen. We do, after all, have a lawyer working with us, and Chad and I are away from their control now. Once we've sorted out my problems and got George off our backs, maybe you can find some way to help Chad recover his lost identity. Then I'd know . . . if he's free.'

'You sound very taken with him.'

'I am. He saved my sanity in that place and . . . we're comfortable together.'

'Then I wish you both well and I'll help in every way I can. Take care. And Emily . . .'

'Yes?'

'I'm glad you rang, glad you're not incapacitated. Really glad.'

She put the phone down and sat for a moment or two, remembering Leon. How much had he changed in the couple of years since she'd retired? Not much, from the sound of it. How much had she changed? A lot. She'd hoped at one stage that they'd stay together . . . but she'd gradually realized Leon would never give any woman the sort of love she wanted, and she would never settle for less. Which was why she was unmarried. Too idealistic, her mother used to say. Too picky.

Would Chad be able to give her that love? She wouldn't know till they found out about his wife – ex-wife, she hoped – and until her business affairs had been settled.

How complicated life could get!

She went to join the others in the bar. 'Help will be with us in two or three days. I doubt anything serious will happen before then.'

'From this Leon fellow?'

'And the unit. He doesn't work alone. He has . . . resources at his disposal that we couldn't match.'

The following morning at nine o'clock there was the sound of a car drawing up outside The Drover's Hope.

Rachel immediately went to look out of the window. 'Damn! It's that Corrish woman again. She's sitting in her car. Why isn't she getting out? I bet she's waiting for someone. Hey, Toby!'

He came out of the kitchen.

'You'd better go and hide. Mrs Corrish has just turned up again.'

He gulped and tears filled his eyes.

Emily hated to see how he changed at the mere thought of his house supervisor. 'Go and hide in the secret room, Toby. She won't find you there. Here. Take a packet of biscuits with you.'

He grabbed the biscuits and dashed off towards the rear of the house.

Oliver came down the stairs just as Toby rushed through the bar. 'Where's he going in such a hurry?'

'Avoiding madam.' Rachel pointed out of the window.

'Ah. I'll go back upstairs and join you after they come in. Good thing I don't know where Toby is right now.'

She went back to watching their unwelcome visitor, standing behind the dusty old curtains and keeping up a running commentary. 'Ah. Here's another car. Two men getting out of it. One has "council official" stamped all over him. The other is a plump guy and he looks unhappy about something.'

When the doorbell rang, Emily went to answer it. She didn't open it wide, just stood in the narrow gap and said curtly, 'Yes?'

'I'm from the local council. We have reason to believe that you're concealing a runaway lad who is in care. We need to speak to him at once.'

She didn't hurry to answer, wondering what best to say. As she opened her mouth, she heard someone coming towards her and turned as Chad joined her.

'Do you have ID?' he asked the visitors, his voice cooler than she'd heard it before.

Both men began to fumble in their pockets.

Chad waited beside Emily, his face expressionless, his arm round her waist.

'You're just wasting time!' Mrs Corrish snapped. 'You know perfectly well who I am and you must have realized I'd bring back people with the right to search for Toby.'

Emily studied the men's IDs and nodded. 'Do come in.'

They entered the hall, but Chad stepped in front of Mrs Corrish, barring the way. 'You haven't shown us any ID yet, nor do we know what right you have to enter this house.'

Her face went bright red. 'That must be obvious. I'm Toby's carer.'

'So you say. I thought you were the group supervisor.'

'It's the same thing.'

'It doesn't sound the same to me. And we still want to see some form of identification.'

'I don't *need* to produce ID since you know who I am.'

'We've not seen any official proof of the position you claim to hold.'

Oliver came down the stairs and walked across to join the group. His words showed he'd been listening. 'You do need to produce some ID, Mrs Corrish. My client doesn't take kindly to people pushing their way into her house, as you tried to do last time.'

She fumbled in her handbag, muttering to herself, then went through the bag again. 'My ID card is at home. Kevin Hansford will vouch for me.' She indicated the worried looking man standing in the hallway.

'That's not good enough, I'm afraid.' Oliver smiled at her and closed the door in her face, ignoring the yells, the sound of the doorbell and then the knocker. He turned to the two men. 'Mr Hansford. Mr Pointer. Nice to meet you again.'

He offered his hand and they could do nothing but shake.

'I think it'd be better if Mrs Corrish joined us,' Pointer said. 'She is, after all, Toby's carer.'

'Supervisor, not carer,' Oliver corrected. 'He seems to me to be functioning at a high level for someone with Down syndrome and I'm sure he looks after himself physically.'

'You know him?'

'I've met him here a few times. Miss Penelope used to have him round to tea.' He looked at Kevin. 'Toby was always very hungry, and sometimes upset by the way Mrs Corrish had been treating him. As his social worker, I'd have expected you to do something to change his situation.'

'I wasn't aware till recently. But I'm working on it now, which is why I'm here. Um . . . you've seen him since she died?'

Emily spoke. 'Rachel and I have. He was hungry and very upset when we saw him. We gave him food. But he ran away when Mrs Corrish came to the house. He seems terrified of her.'

'You don't know where he is now?'

'Why should I?'

'Mrs Corrish is sure he's hiding here. We really do need to see him and get his side of the story.'

'After which you'll send him back to that woman while you look for new accommodation? He'll only run away again, and I don't blame him.'

Kevin sighed. 'You know what it's like.'

'You two can look round the house, but not her,' Oliver said.

'*She* isn't coming inside without a police warrant after her rudeness to me last time,' Emily put in. 'And I sincerely pity anyone in her care.'

'She claims that you're suffering from dementia and have also escaped care,' Pointer said, staring at her as if it was true.

Emily looked at him in astonishment. 'How would she know anything about me? I've only met her twice and until recently, I lived in the south.'

'She says your nephew is looking for you because he's worried about your safety.' His eyes flickered to Chad then Oliver.

'I can't think how that woman ever got in contact with my nephew. I've certainly not told her anything about my family.'

Both visitors looked surprised.

'You should ask her how she came by this information,' Oliver said. 'This is starting to look like harassment by the nephew. For your information, my client was in hospital after an accident that left her in a coma, but she is not suffering from dementia and never has been. She's now fully recovered from the accident and—'

'But—'

'Let me finish. Fully recovered and in view of her nephew's . . . concerns about her health, has voluntarily been checked by a geriatric specialist, who also found no signs of dementia.'

Kevin looked even more unhappy. 'I'm sorry to be troubling you, then, Miss Mattison, and I do apologize for the misunderstanding.'

'*Ms* Mattison.'

He smiled wryly. 'Sorry. *Ms.* My partner prefers that form of address, too. I usually remember.'

'What on earth does that matter?' the official said. 'We need to see Toby. Surely we don't have to get a warrant to search the house for him?'

Oliver waved one hand in a gesture of encouragement. 'No need for a warrant. Go ahead and look round.'

He looked even more suspicious. 'Don't you want to accompany us?'

'Why should we? I trust Kevin and I'm sure he'll keep an eye on you, Mr Pointer. I gather Miss Penelope showed you round once or twice, Kevin.'

'Yes. It could be a lovely old place if it was looked after. That barn is wonderful.' He looked at Emily. 'If you're sure it's OK? Right then. This way, Mr Pointer.'

'Shouldn't someone go with them?' Rachel worried once they'd left.

'No. Let them fumble their way round. It's a confusing house.' Oliver grinned. 'I don't care if they get lost.'

'Someone should keep an eye on Mrs Corrish,' Chad said.

'I'll do it,' Oliver said. 'But I'd love a cup of coffee.' He moved to stand by the window. 'She's on the phone. I wonder who she's speaking to.'

'Probably stirring up more trouble,' Rachel sighed. 'It'd be nice simply to settle down for a while and deal with this house. Emily and I both love those renovation programmes on TV. And antique shows.'

'I have a few pieces of antique furniture. They belonged to my grandmother,' Oliver said. 'They're in storage because my wife preferred modern stuff, but I couldn't bear to part with them. I've been going to get them valued.'

'I could do that for you and—' Chad stopped, looking surprised. 'I keep saying things that make me suspect I have some connection with the antique business. It's as if I'm looking through a curtained window and the curtains are growing more transparent all the time. But I don't feel I have a wife. Not now, at least. I don't get the faintest sense of any emotional attachment to a woman in my previous life.'

'Let's hope you're right about that.' Emily smiled at him. 'I wonder how our visitors are getting on.'

'I should think they're very hesitant to poke around too much without the Corrish woman to urge them on,' Oliver said smugly. 'Kevin's a great bloke, really. Just a bit hamstrung by lack of facilities for someone like Toby. And his partner's been unwell for months. She's due to have a baby soon and there are complications.'

'Poor thing. I was sick all the time when I was pregnant, which is why I only had one.' Rachel shuddered at the memory, then shrugged her shoulders. 'As if you want to know that. Going back to Toby, perhaps if he could get a job he might be better off? Why hasn't he done that, or at least worked in a sheltered workshop? He knows his tasks here well enough, so could obviously learn a simple job.'

'Lack of work round here, or sheltered workshops. I wonder . . .' Oliver looked thoughtful.

'Wonder what?'

'If he knows anything about gardening. Or would like to learn. I could do with some help to keep my place in order till I sell it.'

'And I could do with some help to get this place in order.' Emily's voice softened. 'I'd be happy to employ him. Giving people hope, Penelope said. I'd like to do that, Oliver. I'd like it very much. Maybe if you help us, I could start with Toby.'

'You can't do anything till we've sorted out the legal situation for yourself.'

She sighed. 'No. I keep forgetting that.' She glanced at the clock. 'I wonder what those two are doing.'

Kevin led the way round the house, hesitating at the back when he found the outer doors locked. 'We'll have to go and get the keys.'

'Someone should have come with us,' Pointer said sourly.

'We're disturbing their day. They're not going to be happy to see us. Why should Toby come here anyway, now the old lady is dead? He doesn't know these new people.'

'But that lawyer said he'd seen him here.'

'Yes, and that Toby ran away.'

'Mrs Corrish is a hard worker. She keeps the group house immaculate.'

'She's more concerned with that than with letting the occupants move in and out of society.' Kevin sighed. 'It's not easy, but Toby—'

'She says he's a trouble maker.'

'Toby? No, he isn't. He's a nice young fellow who wants something more stimulating to occupy himself with.'

Pointer scowled. 'Well, this isn't getting that door open.'

'I'll go back and ask for a key.'

Left on his own, Pointer began to walk up and down the barn-like room. When a breeze ruffled his hair, he swung round, expecting to see Kevin returning and the door open. But the door was still closed.

Another breeze lifted the debris in the corner and swirled round him, throwing dust in his face.

'What the hell—?' He edged backwards, annoyed with himself for feeling nervous, but unable to help it. This place made him feel uneasy.

When a faint glow began to shine in a corner where there were no light fittings, he turned and fled back to the main house, nearly bumping into Kevin and Chad a short distance down the connecting corridor.

'Something wrong?' Chad asked.

'No. Just . . . Well, it felt a bit spooky in there. Why would there suddenly be a breeze? And a light.'

'I can't imagine where the light came from, but I know what you mean,' Chad said. 'The old barn has definitely got a spooky atmosphere. A lot of these old places are like that. Anyway, I'll open the doors for you and you can look round outside.'

'You could show us round.'

'If you want. But I don't know the place very well myself, yet.'

Pointer moved outside, waiting for Chad to join him. 'You're a friend of Ms Mattison, are you?' Chad didn't seem to have heard, was wedging the outer door open with a big stone.

Kevin said in a low voice, 'I can show you round the outhouses, Mr Pointer. I've been here before. No need to trouble anyone.'

'You stay there by the door, Kevin. Just in case Toby tries to slip back into the house. I'm ready, Mr . . . what is your surname?'

'Oh, just call me Chad.'

Pointer frowned at this. He didn't intend to let any tricks like those just played spook him. They must have been tricks. Things like that couldn't happen without human assistance.

The social worker shrugged and leaned against the outer wall, raising his face to the weak sunlight.

Pointer followed Chad around the back yard, opening every cupboard door in the old buildings, looking round suspiciously every now and then.

But there was no sign of Toby.

'Satisfied?' Chad asked. 'There are no other buildings.'

'I suppose so. But Mrs Corrish won't be. She's convinced Toby came here, says there's nowhere else he could go.'

'I wouldn't know about that. I've only just arrived.'

'Close friend of Ms Mattison, are you?'

'None of your business.'

Pointer blinked his eyes in surprise, saying nothing else as they went back inside.

Chad locked the outer door. 'Let me show you out, gentlemen. I think you've disturbed Ms Mattison enough for one day.'

Mrs Corrish bounced out of the car and hurried across to them as they came down the steps. 'Well?'

'No sign of him,' Kevin said.

'Did *she* show you round?'

'No. We went round on our own, then Chad joined us for the rear part.'

'They're making fools of you. Don't listen to a word she says. I have it on very good authority that she's losing her marbles, which is why they're so protective of her. As for this Chad person, he claims to have lost his memory and says he has nowhere else to go. He's using that as an excuse to cosy up to her. He wants to get his hands on all this.' She waved her hand at the old pub.

Kevin frowned. 'How do you know this?'

'A friend of mine told me. Miss Mattison's relatives are worried about her. My friend is helping her nephew and sister by keeping an eye on things. He's a private investigator, that's how seriously they're taking this. It seems Miss Mattison was all set to sell this place at a profit till these people intervened. She'd have had enough money to be looked after comfortably for the rest of her life. Why would she change her mind about that so suddenly?' She answered her own question. 'It's these people she's met. They've persuaded the poor old thing to act against her own interests. You should do something about that. You're a social worker.'

'It's none of my business. Ms Mattison isn't my client. But she doesn't seem like a "poor old thing" to me.'

'You're a typical bureaucrat. Close your eyes and stick to the regulations. Don't lift a finger to stop people robbing an old woman blind.'

Kevin moved a few steps away from her, throwing her a look of disgust.

Pointer glanced from one to the other, shaking his head. 'Well, there's not much more we *can* do here if there's no sign of Toby. As Kevin has pointed out, *he* is our client, not Ms Mattison.' He turned to the social worker. 'I have other work piling up. Let me give you a lift back to the offices.'

As they drove out of the car park, Kevin twisted his head to look behind. Mrs Corrish was on the phone again. Who was she ringing and about what?

Who was telling the truth here?

He sat lost in thought, thanked Pointer for the lift when they got back, and decided to make a couple of phone calls himself.

Not till later, though. After he got home. After he'd thought this through.

You could sometimes achieve a lot more by acting informally than formally.

Twelve

George and Marcia arrived back at his mother's house and went upstairs to freshen up before joining her for tea.

His mobile phone rang as he was about to go back down. 'I'll take this call first.'

'I'll wait for you.'

He was already speaking, his back turned to her and didn't seem to have heard what she'd said. Marcia hesitated then stayed where she was. It was hard to find out exactly what he was doing, so she eavesdropped whenever she could.

'This Mrs Corrish actually rang *you*?' George sounded surprised. 'She's been inside the place?'

He fell silent, listening intently, nodding occasionally. 'Good, good. Looks like she could be useful, then.'

Whoever it was certainly had a lot to say, Marcia thought, keeping very still and trying not to attract her husband's attention.

'Mmm. Well, thank you for calling so quickly. We must make sure my aunt doesn't mess things up this time, poor old thing. She doesn't realize how the coma has affected her judgement and brain. She had no idea how to deal with business matters even before this, so I'm trying very hard to protect her now that she's so vulnerable.'

He listened again. 'Are you sure they're all staying with her? The lawyer as well? Why on earth would he do that? I don't like the sound of it. They're taking advantage of her. If you can find out anything about them . . . Well, I'll pay whatever it takes within reason, but I'll want daily updates.'

He ended the call and turned to see Marcia still standing in the doorway. 'I thought you'd gone downstairs.'

'I couldn't help overhearing and I *am* involved in this, so I need to know something about what's happening.' She took a deep breath and burst out, 'You're going too far, George. Your aunt isn't losing her memory and judgement, you know that.'

He grabbed her by the shoulder and squeezed hard. 'Did we not agree that *I* would deal with the business side of things?'

'You're hurting me, George.'

'I will hurt you if you interfere. My aunt has no need of all that money and would just waste it. It's *family* money. Penelope was my relative too.'

'I don't think so.'

'Well, my mother's first husband's relative, which amounts to the same thing, since the old hag had no children to leave it to. The money should have gone to my mother, or at least have been shared with her, and then naturally it would come to me.'

'But George—' She whimpered as his fingers dug in.

'*Stop interfering!*' He held on for a moment longer, tightening his grip.

Marcia was betrayed into a yelp of pain. 'George, stop hurting me. *Please*. I won't interfere again.'

Only then did he let go, gesturing with one hand towards the door.

Rubbing her shoulder and trying to fix a smile on her face, she left the bedroom.

Downstairs, Liz had heard her son's voice as he answered the phone. She'd intended to switch on the radio, because she hated eavesdropping. But what she heard stopped her in her tracks, one hand stretched out towards the set.

She froze as his words sank in, and her hand went up to press against her mouth, holding in a cry of protest. She wouldn't have believed it if she hadn't heard their conversation herself. Not George. Not her son.

But then Marcia's yelp and plea to her husband to stop hurting her proved that this was only too serious, that George definitely wasn't . . . behaving nicely. And when Marcia cried out again and promised to keep quiet, Liz knew she couldn't close her eyes to the situation.

Her son was a bully!

And he was trying to take money from Emily. *Steal it.*

She'd wondered if George was being too careful with her money, but now, for the first time, she had proof that her son was withholding money from her for no reason. She'd been surprised when her income had dropped drastically after her husband died. What was George doing with her money?

And if he was stealing it, what could she do?

She wanted to weep, to cry out to him not to do this to her sister, but she couldn't. She'd been slightly nervous of upsetting George ever since he became a teenager. He was so . . . powerful. Aggressive sometimes.

She clapped one hand to her chest as her heart began to flutter.

They were coming down the stairs now. How was she to deal with them without betraying that she'd overheard what they were saying? She was sure her face would show how upset she was.

Her heart beat faster, the room whirled around her and she let out a cry as blackness overwhelmed her.

Kevin got himself a glass of red wine, took a deep breath and phoned Oliver Tapton. He trusted the lawyer. Increasingly, he didn't trust Mrs Corrish. But his main concern was as the social worker for his client, Toby. That above all. He felt guilty that he hadn't realized things had got so bad for the poor lad. He'd been too tied up in his own troubles.

'I hope it's not an inconvenient time to call you, Mr Tapton.'

'Not at all. Always happy to talk to you, Kevin. And I thought we'd agreed you were to call me Oliver.'

'I got used to calling you Mr Tapton when I was a lad. I can't seem to think of my parents' friends by their first names.'

'Well, call me whatever you're comfortable with. How can I help you?'

'It's about Toby, of course. I really do need to talk to him, Mr Tapton. I'm worried about this running away. It's happened too often. I knew he wasn't exactly happy, but I hadn't realized he felt quite so bad. When I spoke to him at his group home, he didn't say anything, even though we were alone.'

'He may have been afraid to. Someone may have been eavesdropping.'

Kevin couldn't think what to say to that. Oliver's voice was quiet, but it brought him back to attention.

'Toby's very frightened of Mrs Corrish, far more than is reasonable.'

'Oh, dear. We were so proud of the amenities when the group home opened,' Kevin said wistfully.

'It's people who make the world happier. I think they're far more important than amenities.'

Kevin let out another gusty sigh. 'Amenities help, though. Mrs Corrish came very highly recommended and she does look after them physically. The place is always immaculate and they're well turned out. The food's good, too.'

Oliver chose his words carefully. 'But perhaps not enough of it. And maybe Toby needs more stimulation. But you're right, of course. You do need to speak to him. Look . . . if he gets in touch, I could perhaps arrange a meeting with you on neutral territory, somewhere he'll feel safe and able to talk. My house, perhaps? What do you think?'

'As long as I can talk to him on my own.'

'Of course. You can talk to him outside in the garden, if you like. No fears of eavesdroppers there, eh? He should feel safe to talk freely. Come to think of it, I'm looking for help in the garden. If Toby had a little job, that might help him settle down. I can teach him what to do.'

'It'd be perfect for him to work with you. And if he *is* afraid of her, I may have to find him some temporary lodgings, move him out of the group home quickly.'

'Emily might offer him a bedroom here at The Drover's Hope. There are several rooms not being used. He seems to feel at home here, often called in to see Penelope. And Emily says she'll need help too, a general handyman and cleaner sort of job.'

There was a silence then Kevin said, 'I gather Ms Mattison has her own problems. And it's not certain she's . . . well, fully recovered from the coma, mentally that is.'

'How do you know so much about Emily? She'd never been to Littleborough until I brought her here and she's certainly not a client of the local social services system.'

'A friend of her nephew spoke to Mrs Corrish and she passed on the information to me, for Toby's sake.'

Oliver couldn't control a snort of annoyance. 'Oh, yes? Purely altruistic to pass on hearsay evidence.'

'It was what she said that made me go to The Drover's Hope. It seems the nephew's really worried about your client. He sounds to be a very caring person.'

'I don't think so.' Oliver bit off further angry words, forcing himself to speak calmly. 'Look, Emily doesn't get on with the nephew, and he's trying to interfere in her life and finances without justification. I already told you, she'd visited a geriatric specialist recently to have a check-up and got the all clear.'

'Does her nephew know that?'

'No. George hasn't seen her since she left hospital. And we've applied for an injunction to stop him approaching her, because he makes her nervous. She just wants to live here in peace.'

'But her nephew says she was all set to sell it and move nearer to her sister. He says she signed the papers.'

'As her lawyer, I can guarantee she has no such plans and never did have. She's signed nothing.'

'That's all very strange. But if you say so.'

'Yes, I do. And you know I'd not lie to you. I'd appreciate it if you'd not discuss Ms Mattison with anyone else until we get this matter straightened out. Now, back to Toby, who is your business. I'll be in touch if I can find him.'

'Yes. Thank you, Mr Tapton. You've – um, given me a lot to think about.'

Oliver ended the call and turned to the others.

'You seem to trust Kevin,' Emily said.

'I've known him since he was a child. His parents are close friends of mine. Kevin's a good guy, caught in an imperfect system, which is nonetheless doing its best for people like Toby.'

'I've been caught in an imperfect system, too. It can be terrifying when things go wrong.'

'You were at the mercy of someone who could possibly have been committing crimes, which is a bit different. That unit must be investigated and the abuse stopped before anyone else is hurt. They're not all like that. Now, I really must nip across and check on my house. I'll only be an hour or so.'

* * *

Soon after Oliver had left, the phone rang. Rachel was close to it, so looked questioningly at Emily.

'Go ahead. But I don't want to speak to anyone.'

'Hello. Drover's Hope. Ah. Isn't it rather late for a business call?'

Someone went on talking at the other end.

'Well, I'll just see if she's free.' Rachel covered the phone with one hand. 'It's that guy from Barton and Halling, Gressam.'

'Oh, no! Don't I get a minute's respite?'

Rachel handed her the phone.

'Hello?' Emily listened intently, then said, 'I didn't sign anything, and I'm not discussing it with you now. This sort of thing is for my lawyer to deal with, as you've been informed.' She ended the call abruptly, looking at the phone and letting out an angry huff of air.

'What is it?' Chad asked. 'Anything I can help with?'

'The contract arrived by courier this afternoon. It has my signature on it. And it's just like the other signature. Gressam said I must have forgotten I'd already signed it.'

She looked at her friends in dismay. 'This is like a nightmare. I know perfectly well I didn't sign anything at all.'

'Oliver will sort it out.'

'Gressam seemed pretty certain the sale is in the bag. Told me we have to be out of here within the month. Demolition starts the day after we leave.'

'He's that sure the sale will go through?' Chad frowned. 'They're certainly pushing hard, and treating you as if you don't count.'

'I'd like to strangle my nephew!'

Chad smiled. 'I'll help you.'

Rachel looked from one to the other, hid a smile and stood up. 'I'm going to find another book. I've finished this one.'

Emily nodded, but she wasn't really paying attention and her frown didn't diminish. After a few seconds she looked at Chad. 'What if they manage to persuade the authorities that I did sign the contract?'

He held out his arms and she walked into them. 'Then at the very worst, you'll have the money.'

'I don't want the money. I want to live here and make the old place come to life again. I'd thoroughly enjoy doing that. Leon said I was too young to retire and he was right.' She looked up at Chad. 'I've been hoping you might find that sort of project interesting, too.'

'I would. Especially working with you.' He bent his head to kiss her.

When they drew apart, they went to sit on the sofa, his arm round her.

'Something else is upsetting you,' he said quietly. 'Want to share it?'

'It's George, of course. It'd do him no good for me to get the money for this place. And he's no altruist, believe me.' Another pause, then, 'So what else is he planning?'

'I don't know.'

The front door opened just then and Oliver called out a greeting.

'Let's discuss it with Oliver.'

When Liz recovered consciousness, she found herself lying on the sofa with Marcia kneeling beside her and George standing staring at her from near the window. He was silhouetted against the light, so she couldn't see the expression on his face very clearly, didn't want to.

'Do you often faint?' Marcia asked gently.

Liz was thankful being unconscious had masked her distress about her son's behaviour. 'Not often, no.'

'How often?' George demanded.

'Oh, just once or twice.'

'Then you shouldn't be living on your own.'

He gave a slow smile and as his face was mostly in shadow, his teeth showed most clearly and gave him a sinister look.

'I think you and Emily should find a house to share, Mother,' he went on. 'It's what sisters do, isn't it? Live together in their old age, look after one another.'

She gathered her courage together. 'Emily has a new house and a life of her own. I wouldn't dream of imposing on her. And . . . and we don't like the same things.'

'Oh, she's going to sell the new house soon. It's almost derelict.'

'How do you know that?'

'I have friends in the industry. She's already signed the contract. She's getting very forgetful, so I'm still keeping an eye on her. She *is* my aunt, after all. Family need to stick together.'

'Yes, they should. And she's a close relative. You should remember that and treat her fairly.' Liz closed her eyes, afraid she'd said too much. 'I think I'll go to bed early, if you don't mind. I feel exhausted.'

'Shall I come up and help you?' Marcia offered.

'No, thank you. I'm quite capable of managing on my own.'

'What did she mean by that remark?' Marcia worried when Liz had gone upstairs.

'What remark?'

'She said "You should remember that and treat her fairly" when she was talking about your aunt.'

'Why should she mean anything special? She's not a devious woman. In fact, she's rather simple-minded.'

'Shh! Keep your voice down. This is a small house.'

He shrugged but lowered his voice. 'It's a good idea, isn't it? Keeping them both together?'

'Not if they don't want it.'

'If *I* want it, that's what they'll do.'

Marcia didn't say anything else, just rubbed her shoulder, which still hurt.

Upstairs, Liz buried her face in her pillow to hide her sob. Simple-minded, was she? No, she hadn't been mistaken in her son. He was ruthless, cared nothing for people . . . not even her. The sobs nearly overflowed but she held them back, somehow.

But what was she going to do about it? How could she go against him? How could she regain control of her money and life?

Was it even worth the hassle?

Oliver entered the old inn, whistling happily, a big bunch of flowers in his hand. He stopped in the doorway of the flat to extend the flowers to his hostess. 'These looked so beautiful, I picked enough for a couple of vases.'

Then Emily's miserable expression sank in. 'What's wrong?'

She shook her head in a helpless gesture. 'Gressam rang again. B&H have received a copy of a contract they say I signed. I *knew*

George wouldn't let it go. They say the signatures match and we have to be out within the month.'

Oliver stood perfectly still, as if all his energy was focused on processing the information. 'I'll ring them.' He had the number on speed dial, put his phone on speaker and they all stood listening to it ring . . . and ring.

In the end, it rang out. He didn't try to redial. 'We can't do anything tonight. They must have closed immediately after they phoned you. Deliberately leaving you in suspense, I should think.'

'Yes, that's what I thought. They left it till the very last minute to call me. They're in league with George, they must be. Breaking the law.'

'Not necessarily. They're just looking out for their own interests. I'll ring them first thing in the morning.' He went across to give Emily a hug. 'We'll find a way through this, I promise you.'

Chad was frowning. 'We're both wondering how this is going to benefit her nephew.'

'George won't let me get the money,' she said. 'I know he'll have something else planned.'

'He may get a few surprises,' Oliver said grimly. 'I haven't quite lost my touch.'

Emily went to bed early, exhausted beyond reason. The others moved into the bar.

Later, when everyone separated to go to bed, Chad brought his mattress in, intending to sleep on the floor of her living room.

She listened to him moving around, trying to be quiet, then went to the door of her bedroom and stood there. Did she dare take the initiative?

As soon as he noticed her, he stopped his preparations and waited.

'It's a double bed,' she said quietly. 'I don't want to be on my own tonight.'

'Are you sure?'

'Oh, yes. Very sure.'

'You still know very little about me.'

'I know enough to love you, Chad.'

'I love you too.'

Then his arms were round her and she was pulling him towards the bed. Who knew where comfort ended and loving began? Who cared about anything but being together?

It felt so right. And he was as gentle and caring in bed as he was in everything he did.

In the morning she woke before he did and lay looking at him, memorizing each line of his face, wanting to touch him. A lean, intelligent face, silver hair, pale blue eyes. Not good looking exactly, but a very attractive man, nonetheless.

Did he find her attractive? She'd never been good looking, never thought looks the most important thing, but she wished now that she was prettier for him.

Chad opened his eyes, coming fully awake instantly. He smiled at her and ran one fingertip down her cheek. 'I love you, Emily. That won't change, I promise.'

Whatever happened today, or in the future, she would cling to that thought, remember the look in his eyes as he said the magic words. He had definitely meant it.

As she did when she replied, 'I love you too, Chad.'

Oh, the joy of being with him, of love igniting passion, of being as close as is possible for two people.

Thirteen

Breakfast was a quiet time, with very little conversation. Most of the group were lost in thought.

Emily still felt anxious about what was going to happen, and not at all sure that she would escape George's machinations.

She'd made one decision, though. 'I'm going to give all of you the emergency number for Leon, just in case anything happens to me. You need to memorize it, and promise never, under any circumstances, to write it down.' She repeated the number and saw them moving their lips as they muttered it or did whatever was necessary to commit it to memory.

To her amusement, she saw Toby mouthing the number as well. She doubted he'd remember it, but if he wanted to try, there was no harm done. 'Don't tell anyone else the number,' she repeated, looking particularly at him.

He nodded several times. 'Won't tell anyone. I know how to use a phone.'

She turned back to the others and explained how the automatic system would note their number and ring them back. 'They only speak on very secure lines. I don't understand the technology but they seem pretty certain the line they call you back on is safe.'

With a sigh, she pushed her plate away. 'I'm not very hungry this morning.'

'You need to keep up your strength,' Rachel said automatically.

'Something bad is going to happen,' Toby said suddenly. 'Very bad. I can tell.'

'That's guaranteed to cheer everyone up,' Rachel muttered.

He ignored her and finished his meal, eating more slowly than usual and frowning. For the first time, he didn't ask for seconds.

The table was cleared by Toby, who seemed to have taken that task upon himself, doing it in the same patterned way every time and getting upset if anyone tried to change his methods. After he'd finished, Oliver explained to him that his social worker wanted to talk to him. 'We can go to my house and talk to Kevin there.'

'I'm not going back!' Toby said at once. 'Not going back!'

'No. But if Kevin finds somewhere else for you to live, you won't need to go back to her. And there's another thing: I need help in my garden and I thought of you. I'd pay you for doing it.'

'A job?'

'A small job, just one day a week.'

'I wanted a job. Mrs Corrish said I couldn't. She said no one would give me a job.'

'She was wrong.' Oliver looked at the others. 'I can't leave the Toby situation as it is, so I'll arrange for a meeting as soon as Kevin can come to my house.' He went out into the bar and they could hear him speaking into his phone in a low voice.

'Well, let's hope that one of our problems can be sorted,' Emily said, trying to sound more cheerful.

Just then, the doorbell rang.

'I'll get it,' Chad yelled.

* * *

He opened the door, gasping at the sight of the woman standing there, arms akimbo, looking at him as if he'd just committed a major crime. He couldn't for a moment or two speak or even think straight, as images and memories cascaded through his brain.

'Edward John Chadderley, what the hell are you doing here?' she snapped. 'Why did you run away from the hospital? Have you any *idea* of the trouble you've caused me?'

He took a step backwards, his hands going up to his head, which was throbbing and hurting. Unable to hold back a groan, he staggered sideways just as Emily came into the hall. She ran forward in time to steady him, calling, 'Oliver! Oliver, come quickly!'

'Get your hands off my husband!' yelled the woman in a very piercing voice, following them into the building.

Emily ignored her and guided Chad to a nearby table. He sank down on a chair, continuing to hold his head. Small sounds of pain still escaped his control.

'Who are you?' Oliver asked the woman.

'His wife.' She pointed to Chad.

'Oh. You'd better sit down, then.'

'I certainly had. It's obvious that my husband shouldn't have left hospital and I intend to make sure he goes back and gets the treatment he needs.'

She marched forward and yanked Emily's hand away from Chad's shoulder. 'Leave my husband alone.' She tried to put her arm round Chad's shoulders, but he pushed her away.

Letting out a long, quivering sigh, he looked from one side to the other. Emily had folded her hands in her lap and was waiting, as quiet and composed as ever. Oh, how admirable her calmness, especially in the face of his wife's anger and shrillness.

Her name came back to him. 'Marina.' With it came images of quarrels and shouting.

She frowned. 'They said you wouldn't remember anything else.'

'They were wrong.'

'You should go back and let them help you.' She wasn't shouting now, but her voice had a sharp edge to it and the looks she gave Emily would have soured milk.

'I'm not going back. They weren't helping me.' Why was she

urging him to go back to the hospital? Was it possible . . . had she too been paying Pauline to keep him locked away?

'What *do* you remember?' she demanded.

'Not much, but I'm remembering more every day. Only I don't remember our life together, just quarrels and shouting. Why can't I remember being *with* you?' He saw an expression of relief cross her face, or thought he did.

'How the hell should I know why you remember one thing and not another? I'm not a doctor.'

'If you knew about me, knew I'd lost my memory, why didn't you come to visit me in hospital? Why didn't you identify me, bring me clothes, books, all the sorts of things a person needs to make life comfortable?'

'I did come to visit you. When you were first moved to that place.' She shuddered. 'You were sedated, in no state to remember anything, and that sister said you likely never would. She suggested I wait for a while, see if you could recover.'

'She told me no one had come forward.'

Marina shrugged. 'I asked her to say that. You and I hadn't been getting on too well. I thought the sight of me might upset you. I took over the business and left you to the medical experts. Pauline would have let me know if you'd remembered who you were, if it was time to visit you.'

But Marina was avoiding his eyes. 'I don't believe you,' he said in a voice flat with certainty.

'I don't think you're in a fit state to make judgements. Someone had to run the business, after all. You should be grateful to me for that.'

'What business?'

'You haven't remembered much, have you, if you don't remember your precious business?' She jerked her head in Emily's direction. 'But you've recovered enough to go back to your old ways and find yourself another woman. You always do.'

He turned to Emily. 'I haven't remembered much, but I do remember this about my so-called wife. *Don't believe a word she says.*'

Marina threw back her head and laughed harshly. 'Trying to take the moral high ground, are you? Well, it won't work. Who'll believe an idiot who didn't even remember his own name until I told him?'

She looked past him to Emily. 'I hope you haven't been stupid enough to give him money, or it'll vanish. He's very good at getting money from people. He looks as if butter wouldn't melt in his mouth, but he's a clever con artist.'

'What business?' Chad repeated.

She let out a scornful sniff. 'I'll tell you more when you remember – or when you go back to let the experts help you.' She stood up. 'Here. After you've got your wits together, phone me and we'll go into things.'

He glanced at the card. 'This isn't a business card.'

'No. It's just my mobile phone number. I'm not having you coming back and messing things up just as I'm sorting them out.' She looked at Emily. 'He's a lousy businessman, too. Don't trust him an inch.'

Emily studied them both and then linked her arm in Chad's. 'I trust him absolutely.'

'More fool you.' Marina stood up and made her way towards the door.

'Aren't you going to go after her, insist she tells you more about the business?' Emily asked.

'No. I don't want anything to do with her. I intend to deal with her formally.' He pulled her suddenly close. 'Thank you.'

'What for?'

'Believing in me.'

Oliver had followed Marina out and now came back inside. He fished out a pencil and notebook and wrote something down in it. 'Just taking note of her car number plate. It might be of some help. Who knows?'

Chad stood up. 'I need to think. On my own.' He looked at Emily. 'You won't . . . do anything rash?'

She returned his gaze. 'For what it's worth, I wouldn't buy a used car from her.'

He gave her a wry smile, then walked out, going through the back bar towards the barn.

Rachel fanned her face as if she was too hot. 'Phew! A thrill a minute here. Mind you, I'd not buy a used car from her, either. There was something about her face that I didn't like.'

She followed Emily's gaze. 'I can see why Chad needs to be on his own.'

'So can I. But I want to help him.'

Rachel smiled gently. 'You have helped him and you're still helping him, but he needs to stand on his own feet if he's to keep his self-respect, don't you think? Especially after what she said.'

Chad wandered into the old barn. Small birds were flittering in and out of the narrow gaps in the roof at the far end, chirping softly to one another, dancing in the air almost. His mind was in turmoil and his head was aching furiously, but the sight of the birds and their happy little sounds began to soothe him.

Memories continued to trickle back. Of a younger Marina, her face contorted with anger. So many quarrels. Cheating, too. With other men. Taking money from the business. Marina doing what she'd accused him of.

Was she really still his wife? How could he have stayed married to a woman like that?

Surely they must be divorced? But she hadn't said that, and however hard he tried, the facts wouldn't fall into place.

Something else slipped into his mind. Memories of their sons. Two sons. Grown up now. Living their own lives. Curtis . . . tall, talking fast and gesticulating, his eyes alight. Lennox, shortened to Lex, to his mother's disgust. A quieter young man, more like his father in nature.

Chad decided to go on line and find out about himself, then see if he could contact his sons. Surely they'd be on one of the social web sites? Everyone else their age seemed to be there, hanging out their lives for the world to see.

What had their mother told them about him? Did they even know he was missing or had she given them some excuse to explain his absence?

His mind was jumping about, not functioning properly. Come to think of it, Chad himself would have a presence on line, surely?

And the business she'd talked about. What sort of business was it? She hadn't said, and he'd been in too much distress to answer. He was still not in a condition to pursue the point, because his head was throbbing painfully. What he needed was a rest and some quiet time.

He couldn't decide what to do next until he had more information and could think clearly.

When he went back to the flat, he found that the others were also tired and not feeling like doing much. Rachel wanted to watch a programme on TV. Oliver wanted to nip across to see one of his friends who lived nearby.

When he'd left, Emily looked across at Chad. 'You all right?'

'Yes. Only I'm not feeling very sociable. I need to move about . . . think . . . be quiet.'

'There's plenty of room here for you to do that. I hope it helps.'

What helped immediately was the easy way she'd accepted his needs and let him follow them.

So Chad spent the evening wandering round the house, moving mainly from the bar to the old barn, letting the memories trickle back as he walked. It seemed to help to walk – or was he imagining that?

When it came time to go to bed, he returned to the flat, to find that Emily had gone to bed half an hour ago, and since the light in the bedroom was out, he assumed she was asleep.

Rachel was still sitting there.

'I didn't want to leave her on her own. I'm going up to read in bed now that you're here to keep an eye on her, Chad.'

'Oliver not back?'

'No, not yet.'

So Chad lay down on the mattress again and left Emily in peace. He felt drained and weary, needed to rest.

If he could fall asleep.

If he could stop worrying about his wife . . . who might not be his wife now . . . who didn't feel like his wife . . .

Morning was a long time coming. The blackness eventually became charcoal, then grey. The greyness grew slowly lighter, and the room slowly filled with bright light that promised a sunny day.

And the central memories he desperately needed were still eluding him. What was his business? Why was Marina trying to muscle in on it? Where were his sons?

Fourteen

Chad ate a quick breakfast with the others, then said he wanted to check something in the old barn. He looked at Emily. 'Do you have a minute or two?'

'Yes, of course.' She walked with him and when he took her hand, she felt a warmth that was far more than the touch of his skin; a closeness of the heart.

The old barn seemed filled with sunshine this morning, beams of light slanting down, small birds flying about at the far end, dust motes dancing in the air.

'I haven't got enough memories back yet to know where I stand,' he said abruptly. 'But I know one thing instinctively. I'm not still with her.'

'Good.'

'So I want to make it clear to you that I want to be with you. Long term. Whatever we have to go through to get there.'

A sigh of relief escaped her. 'I want that too.'

'You've never married?'

'No.'

'Are you against it or will you consider marrying me?'

The light seemed to glow around them as he spoke.

She had no hesitation with this man. 'I'd love to marry you, Chad.' She put her arms round his neck, kissing him, melting into his embrace as he kissed her back, framing his face with her hands.

As he pulled away, he touched her cheek gently, then brushed her hair back behind her ear. 'Good. We'll get through this mess somehow and then we'll decide what to do with our lives.'

'Sounds a good plan to me.' She glanced at her watch. 'I think I'll leave you in peace for a while, though, if you don't mind. I need to go on line. I'm behind with everything in cyberland.'

'May I borrow your computer later and go hunting for myself on line?'

'Of course. You don't want me to try?'

'No. I'd rather do it myself.'

Oliver watched Chad and Emily leave the flat, exchanged knowing smiles with Rachel then went back to his toast and honey.

'I think they're good for one another,' she said. 'I envy them.'

'So do I.' He started fiddling with the crumbs on his plate. 'I'm not good at making important decisions quickly.'

'I'm not either. At least you were happily married. I wasn't. So take your time. I'll need to do the same.'

'Thank you for being so understanding.'

They hadn't said anything important, yet Oliver felt they'd said everything.

When they'd finished eating, Toby again got up and cleared the table without being asked, then Oliver explained to him that he'd arranged a meeting with Kevin at eleven o'clock.

'I don't want to.'

'You have to.'

Toby moved towards the door.

'You mustn't run away. Not this time.'

'I want Chad. I want him to come too.'

Oliver looked at Rachel. 'Stay with Emily and don't open the door to anyone till we get back.'

'No, Daddy!'

'I have no desire whatsoever to be a father figure to you.' He was delighted to see her cheeks go pink.

She changed the subject hastily. 'I wonder what Emily and Chad are talking about. I know what I'm hoping for. Those two belong together. Anyone can see that.'

'It can happen very quickly. Meeting someone, liking them in a special way.'

Chad stayed in the barn, letting the peace he always felt there soothe him. When he heard the sound of footsteps, he wondered if Emily had returned, but it was Toby, hesitating by the door, looking worried. 'Do come in. Is something wrong?'

Toby stopped a few feet away from him, surprising him by saying, 'You're feeling sad. I can tell.'

'Yes. I am a little. I've forgotten who I am. I'm starting to remember. But it's hard.' Images were still clicking into place in his mind, such a random selection. It was hard to get to grips with the present when the past kept jerking at his attention in a haphazard way.

'I'm sorry you're sad.'

'Thank you. Can't be helped.'

Toby rocked from side to side, then said in a rush, 'Oliver says Kevin is coming. I have to speak to him. I don't want to. Don't want.'

'Kevin's your social worker. He needs to make sure you're all right.'

'I'm all right here.'

'He can find you somewhere to live away from Mrs Corrish.'

'I want to live *here*. Miss Penelope said I could. She promised. Then she died.'

'You'll have to ask Emily about living here. But you still need to speak to Kevin first.'

A big sigh was his only answer, so he waited for a few moments, not pressing for a decision. Then Toby surprised him, 'You come with me. To speak to Kevin. I feel safe with you.'

Chad hesitated. He knew they'd agreed not to leave Emily on her own. But Oliver's house was only a few hundred yards down the hill, and Rachel would still be here with Emily. Toby was looking at him so hopefully, Chad couldn't say no. The meeting with the social worker surely wouldn't take more than an hour or so. He could spare an hour to help someone else who wasn't finding life easy.

'We'll go and ask the others if it's all right for me to come. I don't want to leave Emily on her own for too long.'

Toby nodded and as he was turning round, he grabbed Chad's arm. 'Look!' he whispered, pointing.

A row of small birds was perched on one of the beams and seemed to be watching them. 'They fly away if someone bad comes in. Don't fly from me. Don't fly from you.'

'What sort of birds are they?'

'Meadow pipits. Miss Penelope loved them. They're always here. I like them.'

'Do they have nests in the barn?'

'No. Nests outside. We watch them through binoculars. Don't go near them. Don't frighten them.' Toby smiled at Chad and repeated, 'They like you. I like you.'

It was ridiculous how much better that made Chad feel, even though there was probably no connection between him and the birds' visits to the barn.

Or perhaps it was Toby's trust that made him feel better?

Emily decided to enjoy a couple of hours of quiet reading. She'd discovered lots of interesting books in Penelope's collection and was reading a mystery set in the 1920s. She was near the end and wanted to find out who'd committed the murder. She thought she'd guessed but wasn't sure.

'I'll leave you to your book. I want to go up and sort out my clothes. I think we need to hold a grand washday tomorrow.' Rachel grinned. 'I might just have a little nap while I'm at it. I didn't sleep all that well last night. Will you be all right?'

'Of course I will.'

'Don't open the door to anyone, mind! And yell if you need me.'

Emily read for a few minutes, then snuggled down in the big armchair, feeling drowsy and not even trying to keep her eyes open.

She was jerked from a deep sleep by the sound of someone hammering on the front door. Her mind was still blurred. Since the accident, she'd had trouble waking up quickly.

The person didn't wait long to knock again and for some reason this annoyed her intensely. It had been so peaceful here until now.

Grumbling under her breath, she went to the door and, not thinking, opened it without checking who was there.

'Ah!' George set his hand on the door and pushed it wide open, sending her stumbling backwards. 'I thought so. You *are* living here.' He turned to beckon to someone.

She looked beyond him to see Marcia helping Liz out of the car. The yell to Rachel for help died in her throat, because even George wouldn't hurt her in front of his mother, surely? But if Emily caused a scene, it would definitely hurt Liz.

He grinned at her, a nasty, triumphant expression. 'Careful

what you say and do, Auntie dear. We don't want to upset someone with a dodgy heart, do we? Mum fainted yesterday.'

'You should be careful, too!' she tossed back at him.

'Oh, I will be. Much more careful than last time I dealt with you.'

From across the car park, her sister waved to her, then began hurrying towards the pub. Now, that was strange. Liz wasn't wearing her usual smile. What was going on here? Something was definitely wrong.

Emily moved past George and ran lightly down the steps to throw her arms round her sister.

Liz kissed her cheek and hugged her convulsively.

'Better come inside, everyone.' But when Emily looked, George was already inside. As they went in, she saw him standing with legs apart, turning slowly round to study the outer bar.

'What a dump! Good thing you're going to sell it.'

'Whatever gave you that idea, George? I have no intention of selling this place.'

'Then why did you sign the contract with Barton & Halling?'

'I didn't.'

'Oh, but you did. Just shows how bad your memory has become.'

Liz's hand tightened on her arm. She shot Emily a quick, shocked glance, then looked down, trying to hide her agitation, but unable to stop tears welling in her eyes. Fortunately, her son had resumed his survey of the bar and didn't notice as she quickly wiped the tears away.

There was an exclamation from the stairs at the rear of the bar and Emily looked round to see Rachel standing nearly at the bottom, staring at them in shock. Before her friend could move, let alone turn back to the safety of her bedroom, George ran across and grabbed her by the arm.

'Do come and join us, Mrs Nosey Parker. You don't want to miss the final scene.'

'Let go of me!'

He only did that after giving her a shake and saying, 'I thought I told you to leave my aunt alone. Your interfering has only confused her.'

Liz made a sound part way between a gasp and a sob.

She's guessed he's doing something wrong, Emily thought. *Does he realize that?* She didn't think so from his smug expression as he resumed his survey of the bar.

Had Liz guessed he was creaming money off her retirement fund as well? Well, even if she had, she probably wouldn't have the courage to stand up to her son.

George's wife went to look out of the window.

She's opting out, Emily decided. Doesn't want to rock the boat. Or was Marcia wholeheartedly behind her husband in what he was doing? Who knew? Marcia had always been cool and distant, good at hiding her feelings.

'Where in this hovel of a place do you live, Auntie dear? Mother needs somewhere more comfortable to sit down.'

'My flat is over here.' Linking her arm in Liz's again, Emily led the way. She slowed down as she saw George flourish a mocking bow in Rachel's direction and point, waiting till her friend had gone into the flat before following them.

He stared round again, his face showing further disdain. 'Why on earth are you putting up a fight about selling this place? No one in their right mind would want to live in such a dump.'

'I like it here. I shall enjoy renovating and remodelling it. And if I ever do sell it, I don't intend the money to go to you, George.' She saw another upset expression on her sister's face, but once again George didn't notice that. He seemed to be growing careless with what he let his mother see. Emily wondered if she could push him into revealing more.

He gave her one of his wolfish grins. 'The money won't be going to me. It'll be going into a trust which I'll be managing for you. As I manage my mother's trust.'

Liz's eyes filled with more tears but she didn't say anything, just sat there, shoulders drooping.

It was obvious to Emily that Rachel had missed none of this. She sat down close to Liz and patted her back.

Emily remained standing near the fireplace. She glanced at her watch, worrying about what might happen if Chad and Oliver returned. They'd notice the car parked outside but would they come rushing in and get into a fight with George, either verbally or literally?

She didn't know what to do, how to react.

George was so confident, and seemed to have won every trick so far.

Why had he come to the north? What was he planning this time?

After the three men left The Drover's Hope, they drove straight down the hill to Oliver's house. Kevin's car was already parked there and he got out, waiting for them.

Toby didn't come with the others, but stayed in the back seat, hunched up and looking miserable.

Chad opened the back door for Toby, saying quietly, 'Kevin won't hurt you. There's no need to be afraid.'

With a doubtful look, Toby got out. But he stayed as far away as he could from his social worker when they entered the house.

Oliver gestured to one side. 'You and Toby can use the morning room, if you want to be private, Kevin.'

Toby stopped dead.

Kevin spoke gently. 'I need to speak to you on your own, Toby. I'm not going to hurt you or force you to go back to the home.'

'I want Chad with me.'

Chad could see Kevin start to shake his head. 'How about I stay in the hall, just outside the room? You can call me if you're frightened.'

Toby looked from one to the other, heaved a sigh and waited for Kevin to go into the room first.

'Where do you want to sit?' the social worker asked.

As he closed the door behind them, Chad heard the lad say, 'I'll sit here. By the door.'

He felt sorry for Toby, but you could only buck the system so far, and Toby did need caring for in some way.

Oliver poked his head out of a door at the rear of the hall. 'Want a coffee while we wait?'

'No, thanks. I'd better stay within earshot. Toby's very nervous.'

Oliver disappeared into the kitchen again and Chad began to look at the paintings and photographs in the hall.

Inside the room, Kevin tried to set Toby at ease. 'No one's going to make you go back to Mrs Corrish if you're unhappy there, I promise you.'

Toby looked at him suspiciously. '*She* said you send me back. Not going.'

'Tell me, why do you keep running away?'

'To see Miss Penelope. I like to do things with her. I like to walk on the moors. I like to help in the pub. Mrs Corrish shouts if I get my shoes dirty. Shouts a lot.'

'You didn't tell me about that last time.'

Toby wriggled uncomfortably. 'She was listening. She gets mad.'

Kevin looked at him in shock. 'Mrs Corrish? But she wasn't in the room.'

'She listens on the intercom. Listens a lot. We always know.' He made a faint hissing sound. 'We can hear it.'

'I see.' Kevin was again shocked by this. 'Look, I can find you somewhere else to live, but it won't be as nice as the group home. You'll probably be with old people or in lodgings.'

Toby scowled at him. 'I've *got* somewhere to live. With Emily and Chad.'

'Do they know that you want to live there?'

'Yes. Emily said I could. I *like* the pub. It's safe there.'

It was Kevin's turn to feel uncomfortable as he wondered how to explain that Emily and Chad couldn't be considered suitable people to care for Toby, not with their own troubles unresolved. And the nephew said Emily was becoming forgetful, whatever the specialist said. Surely the nephew knew her better than someone who'd only seen her once? Dementia was such a sad condition.

Toby stood up, jigging about. 'Go to toilet.'

'Do you know where it is?'

'Yes.' He left the room before Kevin could say another word.

Toby saw Chad standing with his back to the hall and moved quietly towards the front door. He was in luck because a neighbour started mowing the lawn and the sound of that covered up the click of the door opening.

When Kevin came out to look for Toby, Chad was studying a rather lovely painting of the moors.

'Hasn't Toby finished in the toilet yet?'

Chad turned round in surprise. 'I've not seen him. I thought he was still with you.'

'No, he went to use the toilet.'

They looked at one another in dismay and Chad went to the small cloakroom near the front door. The door was half open. There was no one inside.

Kevin went into the kitchen. 'Oliver, have you seen Toby?'

'No. I thought he was with you.'

The social worker let out a grunt of annoyance. 'I think he must have done a runner. Could you check the rest of the house, please?'

A quick search showed no sign of Toby.

'He'll have gone back to The Drover's Hope,' Oliver said confidently. 'He loves it there. Why the hell don't you let him stay there with Emily?'

Kevin looked at Chad. 'There are . . . problems about that.'

'You mean someone's suggested that Emily and I are losing our wits?' Chad said at once. 'It's a lie. We are *not* suffering from dementia. I have amnesia, due to injuries, and even that is improving.' As he spoke, he saw a sudden image of Marina, her face contorted in anger as he handed her some papers, and he had to stop speaking for a moment.

Kevin didn't seem to notice his distress. 'Nonetheless, it's enough to worry the authorities. We have to be very careful where we place people.'

The image had gone. Chad forced himself to pay attention. 'Oh. So we've been judged and found guilty, have we? Even though a specialist has cleared us?'

'We can't take chances.'

'And Toby's happy with Mrs Corrish, is he? You certainly got it wrong there.'

'I'm afraid we did. I take the blame for not realizing sooner how Toby felt. I had . . . personal problems.'

'How is your partner?' Oliver asked.

'Coping. But lying down for several months isn't an easy thing to do. We won't be having any more children, if I have my way.' He ran a hand through his curly hair, making it stand out wildly. 'Um . . . so you think Toby will have gone back to the pub?'

'He usually does.'

'Does he know the way?'

'He knows this area very well. He loves the moors.'

'I think we've been underestimating him, even though we knew he was functioning at a higher level of intelligence than most people with Down syndrome.'

'He's good with people, very sensitive about their feelings.' Chad didn't mention the way Toby seemed attuned to the old house. If he'd ever believed in ghosts, he'd have believed in them at The Drover's Hope.

'Should we go after him?'

'No need. There's a short cut across the fields. I'd guess he'll be back before we can drive there. But if he doesn't want to be found, there are several places he can hide, both inside the building and on the moors nearby. I don't know them all.'

'Oh, hell! Mrs Corrish is creating an almighty stink about this already. If I lose track of him, there'll be the devil to pay from my area supervisor.' Kevin frowned. 'I can't figure out why Mrs Corrish knows so much about you people or why she's so against you.'

'I can guess,' Chad said grimly. 'Emily's nephew George is stirring up trouble everywhere and has someone in the area reporting on what his aunt is doing.'

'We'd better go back to the pub,' Oliver said.

But when they went outside, there had been an accident in the lane, a load of animal feed coming off a trailer that had lost one of its wheels. The lane was completely blocked.

Oliver reversed back into his drive. 'We could be waiting ages for them to clear that. I think we'd better walk back to the pub. As I said before, there's a short cut across the fields.'

George looked at the group of women with a smug smile. It was clear he felt things were working to his advantage, Emily thought.

'A word with you in private, Auntie dear.'

'I've nothing to say to you, George. Except that you are *not* selling my home or getting your hands on my money.'

'We really do need a quiet word.' He moved across, took her arm and dragged her away from the others. When Rachel would have gone to her help, he snapped, 'Don't even think of interfering in family matters. *You* have done enough harm already.'

Emily tried in vain to tug her arm away. 'Let go! You're hurting me.'

Liz whimpered, one hand splayed across her chest. 'Oh George, don't be so rough.'

He stopped to speak to his mother in a kindly voice. 'Sometimes you have to be firm with a person, in their own best interests, Mother. Trust me. I need to talk to my aunt privately.'

Marcia moved to bend down and take her mother-in-law's hand. 'It'll be all right. George knows what he's doing.'

'It's not—' Liz caught her son's eye and didn't finish her sentence. But she shook Marcia's hand off and moved along the sofa to sit closer to Rachel, trembling so visibly that Rachel put her arm round the older woman.

George took a deep breath. 'I'll explain it all to you later, Mother. You'll understand then that I'm doing this for the best.'

She shook her head. 'You're bullying her, George. And what Emily does is none of your business.'

'Rubbish.'

He turned to his wife. 'See that Mrs Nosey Parker doesn't follow me or poison my mother's mind against me.' He walked out, forcing Emily to move with him.

As they left the flat, she tried to sag to the ground to prevent him from dragging her, but she was so light in comparison to him that he just picked her up and slung her over his shoulder.

Ignoring her kicking and shouting, he took her into the rear bar. 'This will do as well as anywhere.'

She started to shout for help, in case Chad and Oliver were close enough to hear.

He shook her hard and set her on her feet again. 'Shut up! I'm not going to hurt you.'

'You've already hurt me.' She held out a bruised wrist.

'A tiny bruise! You did it to yourself.'

She frowned. He sounded as if he believed that. Surely he didn't really think he was helping her? No. He was just keeping up the pretence to support what he wanted: control of the money.

'Now. I think you'll agree that my mother's health is fragile and she doesn't cope easily with stress. If you don't help her, she could be in trouble.'

'I don't know what you're getting at.'

'My mother needs someone to live with her and look after her, and who better than her sister?'

'I've no intention of spending my retirement as a carer. Not even for my sister. And in that tiny house, too. No, thank you. She and I are too different in our ways. Anyway, Liz doesn't need coddling. She needs to get a life, make friends and go out more. She could do that if you let her control her own money. You keep her so short financially.'

'Times are precarious and she's not good with money. I'm making sure there's enough left to care for her as long as necessary.'

'Then *you* live with her and look after her.'

'She needs her sister, not her son, someone of her own generation.' He held up one hand. 'Let me finish.'

Emily folded her arms, wondering how he could possibly think he'd persuade her to give in.

'I already have a contract to sell this dump, signed by you before you ran away from the geriatric unit. There's a witness to your signature who is prepared to come forward: the sister from the unit. Your memory *is* faulty, and I can prove it.'

'I knew Pauline was involved in your scam. How much were you paying her to keep me doped and in that place, anyway?'

He ignored that and went on, still in the same arrogant tone. 'I even have evidence of you acting irrationally before you fell down the stairs at the hotel, driving so badly you ran right off the road.'

She frowned, not remembering any incident that could be twisted to seem like that. 'What did you arrange?'

He laughed. 'I had no need to arrange anything. The incident happened just before you stopped for the night at the hotel. One of the staff told me about it. You'd mentioned it to them.'

'Stop trying to fool me, George. I'm not as gullible as your mother.'

He shrugged. 'OK. Then let's talk frankly. Bit of luck for me, that coma. Should have made it all quite easy to arrange, once you'd been shown that you needed a quiet life from now on. But no, you had to escape and mess up the plans I'd made to look after you. And I would have looked after you, you know. I'm not heartless. Well, I know a way to make sure you won't do that again.'

'I don't understand.'

He leaned closer than she liked, almost touching her. 'Unless you do what I ask, my mother will be the one to suffer.'

She gaped at him. 'What the hell do you mean?'

'It'd be really easy to persuade people that my mother can't look after herself any longer, especially after her recent fall. I could easily persuade her that her mind is failing. She is . . . an extremely persuadable woman. If *you* aren't going to look after her, I shall have to put her into a care home. And it might not be a nice one, unless you co-operate with me.'

Emily stared at him in horror, then shook her head. She had discovered as a child that you must never give in to bullies, even when they were bigger or more powerful than you. She wasn't going to start giving in to her nephew now. 'I'm not letting you have my money, whatever you threaten.'

'What's so bad about living comfortably with my mother, anyway? At your age, a quiet life is best, much safer, especially if there turn out to be any other mental consequences of the coma. You've always been a quiet person. That's probably why you never married. It'll make very little difference to your life, really.'

He waited but she shook her head.

'And just to sugar the pill, I'll let you both live in your house. It's bigger than my mother's cottage, so there will be plenty of room for two. I can rent her house out. She won't mind where she lives as long as it's with you.'

Emily could only repeat slowly and clearly, 'No, George. I won't do it.'

'I think you will. For my mother's sake. You'll see.'

She was afraid of what he might do to her sister, more afraid, though, of letting pity for Liz ruin the rest of her life, most afraid of all of being totally in George's power. She shook her head obstinately. 'No.'

He smiled again. Was he even listening to what she was saying?

Toby arrived at The Drover's Hope out of breath from running, but stopped abruptly, ducking behind a dry stone wall, when he saw another car parked outside.

Who was here? Had they sent someone to take him away? Well, he wasn't going back. He would go into the hiding place. He could stay there for days. Even if he didn't have anything to eat.

He peered through a barred wooden gate, which was always left half open, and when they weren't looking, he slipped into the house through one of the rear doors. Miss Penelope had hidden the key. She'd told him not to tell anyone, and he hadn't. He locked the door carefully behind him and put the key in his pocket. He'd put it back in the outside hiding place later. You always had to put it back.

He was making his way towards the flat when he heard a man's voice, loud and harsh. He stopped to listen, frightened by the voice, and then he heard Emily crying out. She sounded hurt.

He didn't know what to do.

Emily began shouting for help, so Toby moved forward quietly till he got into the rear bar and could see through into the front.

A big man with a red face was holding Emily and shouting at her, shaking her, hurting her. She was trying to get away and yelling.

Toby wanted to help her – he did, he did! – but he didn't dare. The man looked nasty. Mrs Corrish got the same look on her face sometimes. She liked hurting people. This man was much bigger. Toby was frightened of him.

He shivered as he listened and watched, not understanding what the threats meant, only understanding that the man was upsetting Emily, that she had been shouting for help, was still trying to pull away.

What should he do? He couldn't help her. Couldn't fight.

Should he fetch Chad and Oliver? Could they stop the man hurting Emily? They might get hurt too. Toby didn't like people getting hurt.

He remembered another of the things Miss Penelope had taught him in case she fell or got ill. Dial 999 and ask for help.

Johnny at the group home had dialled 999 once. He wanted to see what happened. He'd got into big trouble. Mrs Corrish had hit him.

Toby didn't want to get into trouble. Then he remembered

the special phone number from when Emily was teaching it to Chad and Oliver.

He was good at remembering numbers. Even when he didn't understand them. Should he phone that one?

Emily cried out again and he knew he had to do something.

There was a phone in the pub kitchen. He could go there. What if the horrible man saw him, though? He looked round. He could bend down. They wouldn't see him. Not behind the bar.

But would the people on Emily's phone number get angry? Not if he told them the man was hurting her.

He swayed to and fro. Should he try to help Emily? She'd been kind to him.

Or should he hide in the secret place? It was safe there.

What should he *do*?

Fifteen

George heard a car draw up outside the pub and dragged Emily back into the flat.

'Who's that?' he asked.

Marcia was already at the window. 'Someone from Barton & Halling, according to the logo on the car.'

'Damnation. I told them not to come till later. Go and tell them I'm not free yet. Ask them to come back at the agreed time.' He grabbed his aunt as she tried to slip past him. 'Oh, no, you don't.'

He turned to Rachel and his mother. 'And if you two know what's good for you, you'll stay quietly on the couch and not make any noise.'

After a terrified glance at her son, Liz kept hold of Rachel's arm.

As Marcia left the room, Emily could only stand beside George, her senses alert for an opportunity. If she'd thought there was any chance of the people outside hearing her, she'd have been screaming already, but the walls were thick and the two people were some distance away.

Besides, that woman lawyer seemed to be on George's side, not hers.

All Emily could hope was that Chad and Oliver would return soon and save the situation.

George couldn't force her to do anything if she held firm against him. And she would, whatever he did to his mother.

Why was he so confident of succeeding?

That worried her. A lot.

Chad and Oliver were approaching The Drover's Hope on foot just as a large four-wheel drive pulled into the car park. There was already a strange car parked near the old pub. They stopped to check things out.

'Not that lot from Barton & Halling back stirring up trouble again,' Oliver grumbled at the sight of the logo on the doors and bonnet of the new vehicle. 'And who does the other car belong to? I'm not staying here doing nothing if the women are in danger.'

He walked across to intercept the man and woman who got out of the company vehicle. One of them was the lawyer. 'I thought we'd agreed that you people would only come here by appointment, Ms Ryling.'

'We do have an appointment,' she said with a snooty look. 'Not with you, though. We had a message from the man handling the contract exchanges to meet him here.'

'May I remind you that as Ms Mattison's lawyer, *I* am the one handling any business to do with my client and this house.'

'Actually, you're not. She's been giving you the wrong information. Perfectly understandable in the aftermath of a coma. We do understand that she's still confused and we'll treat her gently.'

'She is *not* confused.'

Ms Ryling gave him a cynical smile. 'I think her nephew would know about that better than a stranger. And, just to set the record straight, our CEO has had a handwriting expert check Miss Mattison's signature and he says it's definitely hers.'

'It can't be. She didn't sign it.'

'Her nephew has assured us that she won't deny it today, because she's starting to remember things a little more accurately now he's taking care of her properly. Comas can do strange things to people.'

What the hell had Pilby been up to now? Oliver wondered. How could the fellow hope to persuade Emily to agree to selling?

'Let's go and check that with Emily,' Chad put in quietly.

'What authority do you have to interfere in this?'

'I'm her fiancé.'

Oliver hoped he'd hidden his surprise.

There was a pregnant silence, with Ms Ryling looking suspiciously at Chad, then glancing at her watch. 'We're not going inside yet. We're a little early but as we were in the district, we decided we could walk round the outside of the buildings again, check a few things out. We don't want to disturb Miss Mattison till she's ready to see us. You go inside and sort this out with Pilby. You'll see that I'm right. Then you can leave us to complete our transaction.'

The front door opened and Marcia came out. She stopped dead when she saw Oliver and Chad, who were standing to one side, out of sight of the living room window. Then she walked across to the two people from Barton & Halling, ignoring the others.

The three of them moved apart and held a low-voiced conversation.

At one point Marcia stared at Chad in shock, then shook her head. Oliver could read her lips. She was saying it wasn't true. It had surprised him that the engagement had happened so quickly, but he wasn't surprised about Emily and Chad's feelings. It was obvious to everyone that they loved one another.

'We'll come back in an hour's time, then,' Ms Ryling told Marcia.

They got into their car and drove out of the car park and down the road.

'My husband is having an important discussion with his aunt,' Marcia said to Oliver. 'They both asked me to say they'd appreciate it if you left them to talk about this on their own. He is her nephew, after all.' She walked towards the pub without waiting for an answer.

'I don't believe that. Do you, Chad?'

'Definitely not.'

As they started to follow her, Marcia glanced over her shoulder. With a panic-stricken look, she ran up the steps and slammed the door on them.

They got to it in time to hear bolts sliding on the other side.

'What the hell has she done that for?' Oliver looked at Chad. 'She must know we're staying here.'

'Keeping us out means Pilby's up to something. I don't trust him an inch. And why hasn't Emily come out to see us herself?'

He hammered on the door, but no one came to let them in. After a couple of minutes, he gave up. 'Let's see if we can get in round the back. Even if we have to break a window. I'm sure Emily won't mind as long as we get to her.'

Toby picked up the phone in the rear kitchen. He looked at it, then put it down again. What should he do? The horrible man had taken Emily into the flat. He'd dragged her.

Chad and Oliver weren't here, so Toby had to help her.

Taking a deep breath, he dialled the number and waited. A voice told him to put the phone down and they'd ring back. It didn't shout at him, so Toby did as he was told and waited.

He watched the entrance to the kitchens. If he heard anyone coming, he'd hide. In the pantry would be best. It wasn't very safe, though.

He wanted to go to the secret room. Oh, he did. It was safe there!

The phone rang and he snatched it up. 'Yes?'

When the phone rang, George scowled at it. 'Don't answer that.'

Rachel had braced herself to run and pick it up, but it stopped after the second ring, so she sat down again.

'Must have been a wrong number,' George said. 'If it rings again, I'll answer it.' He glared at Rachel. 'If you move one inch towards it next time, you'll regret it.'

They waited but the phone didn't ring again.

'It was a wrong number then,' George said. 'Look out of the window, Marcia, and see what those two fools are doing.'

'No sign of them. They must have gone round the back.'

'They'd better not come inside.'

'They're living here,' Emily snapped. 'They have every right to come inside.'

'They're not living here any more, I promise you.'

Liz took a deep breath and pleaded in a quavering voice, 'George, *please* don't do this. I don't want you to force Emily to live with me.'

'You'll be grateful to me. And so will she once she settles down. She's been acting in a very confused manner since she came out of hospital. She *needs* my help. And you'll be able to keep an eye on her.'

'I'm not at all confused,' Emily said crisply. 'You're just trying to swindle me out of my money. As you've already swindled your mother out of hers.'

She saw a tear run down Liz's cheek, but wasn't going to back off.

George shouted, 'I have *not* swindled my mother out of anything. Her money is all there in the bank, perfectly safe.'

'She needs it to use now. You just want it to be left to you after she dies.' Emily was frightened that he was going to thump her, but though he seemed to swell up with anger, he didn't offer her any violence.

'If you say anything like that again, you'll be sorry, Auntie.'

'I shall *not* do as you demand. And I shan't stop speaking out on behalf of my sister. Whatever you do.'

George raised one half-clenched fist and took a step towards Emily.

Liz began to sob.

'You are not acting normally, Auntie,' he said. 'As Marcia will bear witness.'

Emily held her head up, her eyes challenging him. She didn't let the sigh of relief out when he moved away from her but did say, 'I'm acting so normally that I have a geriatric specialist's word for it that I'm not losing my wits. She's prepared to testify on my behalf.'

'I don't believe you. When did you see one? You haven't had time.'

She smiled. She'd caught him on the back foot there. But she still held herself ready to duck. She'd never seen anyone look so furious.

* * *

Oliver and Chad went round to the back of the barn.

'That door doesn't look very strong,' Chad said. 'I'm going to see if I can kick it in.'

He threw himself against the door, which rattled but didn't give. Nor did a second attempt prove any more effective.

'They make it seem so easy on crime shows,' he said ruefully, rubbing his shoulder.

'Let's both try together.' Oliver came to his side and they tried several times more, but the door held firm against them.

'It'll have to be a window, then,' Chad said. 'Which one do you suggest?'

'Damned if I know.'

They walked quickly along the rear of the strange assortment of outbuildings, once having to clamber over a low drystone wall. The windows had old-fashioned wooden frames, with small panes of glass, which would be much harder to break into. At last they found one which was in a very poor condition by any standards.

'That one needs replacing anyway,' Chad said.

'I'll just nip back to check whether his car is still out front,' Oliver said. 'We don't want to cause any damage unless we have to.'

He came back a couple of minutes later. 'His car is still there.'

'I'm not leaving Emily alone with him any longer than I have to, so . . .' Chad hefted the stone he'd picked up near the wall, a big, uneven chunk that had fallen off it. He hurled it into the window with all his strength, smashing several of the small panes and cracking one of the connecting struts.

It thumped to the ground inside in a shower of glass shards, but the wooden struts were still intact.

'They certainly built these houses to last,' Oliver said ruefully. 'I'm surprised no one's heard the noise.'

'If they have, I hope they won't come to investigate till we're inside.' Chad studied the ruined window. 'I think we can get in here. Some of the wood at this side is rotten. See.' He took off his jacket and used it to grip the struts and wrench them out.

He clambered up on the window sill and used a stone to knock the remaining shards of glass away from the frame. Even so, as he clambered through, he cut his hand and cursed. 'Can you get in after me? Be careful of the glass.'

Oliver clambered up on to the window sill, moving much more slowly than Chad had done.

'Catch me up.' Dropping his jacket full of splinters and wiping the cut on his shirt, Chad ran off towards the front of the house.

All his thoughts were centred on Emily. He wasn't letting that bully hurt her.

Ms Ryling sat in the car, a frown on her face. 'I've had the office making enquiries and Tapton is a well-respected lawyer round here. I should have checked that earlier, but I was too busy settling in. Talk about being thrown into the deep end. This is a devil of a thing to happen in a new job.'

Her companion frowned. 'You mean, you're not sure Pilby's telling the truth?'

'Not as sure as I was. He's very plausible, but today his wife seemed . . . a little furtive, don't you think?'

'She did look worried, I must admit.'

'But the handwriting expert told the CEO it was Emily Mattison's signature.' Ryling shook her head in bafflement as she stared at the inn. 'If this wasn't the best prospect for our new housing development, I'd be suggesting we look elsewhere for land. Family quarrels aren't only the devil for garnering bad PR, they can cost the earth in legal expenses.'

'The CEO's very set on this project. It's his final one with the company.'

Ryling rolled her eyes. 'Beware men departing the company and wanting to leave their mark.'

'Are you really going to advise the CEO to back away from it?'

Ryling paused, then shook her head. 'Not without more proof. After all, the handwriting checks out. But I'm going to scrutinize everything extremely carefully and move forward as slowly as I can.'

'Rather you than me if you have to tell the CEO to back off.'

'I'm paid to tell him when to back off. And if he doesn't like what I say and gets me fired, I can always find a new job. I only accepted this one to be near my husband's elderly parents. I'd far rather live in the south.'

* * *

Toby listened to the man on the phone. He said 'Yes' when he understood. He said 'I don't understand' sometimes. Miss Penelope had told him to say that.

The man began to speak more clearly. He didn't use long words. Toby listened carefully.

'Do you understand that, Toby? We can be there in an hour. Can you tell Emily that?'

'I don't know. Not if that man's with her. I'm frightened of him.'

'Well, do your best, lad.'

'Yes, I will. I always do my best.'

'You were right to phone us. Well done.'

As he put the phone down and stared at it, Toby heard running footsteps. He peeped out of the kitchens and saw Chad. Thank goodness!

But Chad went into the flat and then the big man started shouting again.

He was a very bad man.

Toby stayed where he was.

George swung round. 'How the hell did you get into the pub?'

Chad pushed between him and Emily, slapping the other man's hand away from her. 'Are you all right, darling? He hasn't hurt you?'

'I'm all right, much better now that you're here.' She touched his arm once, then faced her nephew.

Footsteps pounded towards them and Oliver ran into the room, puffing slightly. He stopped by the door to stare round, assessing the situation. 'Why are you keeping my client here against her will, Pilby?'

'I'm looking after my aunt's interests. After all, she signed the contract, she has money owing to her and this fellow is after it.' He jerked his head at Chad as he spoke.

Marcia called from near the window, 'The people from Barton and Halling have come back.'

Oliver immediately walked out and they could hear the bolts sliding on the front door. His voice echoed from the front bar. 'Do come in. We need to get some things clear.'

George growled something under his breath, then said to Emily, 'Remember who'll suffer if you do this.'

'Don't listen to him,' Liz quavered. 'I don't want anyone forcing you to live with me, Emily.'

Emily watched her sister press one hand to her chest, which she did when her heart was fluttering. 'You sit quietly, Liz dear. We'll work something out. Maybe you can come and live near me.'

'Easier for you two to live together,' George said. 'I have another job lined up abroad. My mother will definitely need help. It's that or put her into a care home.'

Marcia looked at him. 'You never told me that you'd got another job, George.'

'It wasn't settled. I was waiting to be sure.'

'Not the Middle East again?'

'No. Australia.' He ignored her look of astonishment and turned back to his aunt. 'So you can see why I'm anxious to get my mother settled.'

'What has persuading me to sell this place got to do with that?' Emily demanded.

He smirked. 'I don't need to do any persuading. I keep telling you, it's already sold. The CEO has had your handwriting checked by Parkers, the top experts in the country, and it's your signature all right. So there's nothing you can do about it. It's signed, sealed and almost delivered, and a good thing, too. You don't understand finance as I do.'

There was silence in the room, then Chad said quietly, 'Actually, there hasn't been time to have her signature checked. I've used Parkers myself to verify signatures on antique documents and they're always very busy. It's never taken them less than two weeks.'

Ryling muttered to her assistant. 'Would the CEO lie about this?'

The man shuffled his feet uncomfortably. 'He's . . . um, very keen for this sale to go through.'

Ryling looked across at Chad and Oliver. 'I'll check that out.'

'In the meantime,' George said smoothly, 'we'll stay here with my aunt. She needs family with her at this time. Doesn't she, Mother?'

Before Emily could speak, Liz shook her head and said firmly, 'No, George. She doesn't. Not family like you.' She sobbed and as he opened his mouth to speak, said in a rush, 'Ms Ryling, I'm afraid my son hasn't told you the truth. I overheard him talking and he wants control of my sister's money. He doesn't want her to spend it, just as he won't let me touch mine. He's waiting for us to die and leave it to him. That's all he cares about. Money. My only son.' Then she collapsed in tears again.

Emily went to sit on the arm of the couch next to her, holding her hand.

George seemed stunned by his mother's outburst. He opened and shut his mouth but didn't say anything.

Marcia was avoiding everyone's eyes.

As her son opened his mouth again, Liz said loudly, 'I've been a coward letting George take over my life like this. It's not going to continue, though. I'm sorry, George, more sorry than I can say to be at outs with you, my only son. But I'm going to find a lawyer and revoke the power of attorney. I can no longer trust you.'

'I can handle that for you, if you like, Liz,' Oliver said. 'Though only if you want me to. You mustn't feel pressured.'

'Don't be foolish, Mother. They're lying. These two hangers-on are the ones who want my aunt's money.'

Liz looked at him sadly. 'I overheard you and Marcia talking about it when you were staying with me. I *know* you've been lying, George. You don't know how much that hurts me.'

There was silence, then Ms Ryling said, 'This doesn't negate the fact that Miss Mattison may well have signed the contract while she was in hospital.'

Emily was tired of repeating herself. 'I – did – not – sign it. I'm quite sure of that. And actually, I'd never sign a contract that had me down as *Miss* Mattison. Never in a million years.'

'As if a trivial matter like that would stop you,' George said. 'You weren't yourself, Auntie dear, and—'

'Don't you call me that!' she yelled. 'You're a cheat and a liar, George, and I wish I wasn't your aunt. I never have been your *dear* aunt and I don't want to be.'

There was a sudden hammering on the front door and someone opened it, yelling, 'Emily? Emily Mattison? Are you there?'

Emily's face brightened. 'It's Leon.' She raised her voice to yell, 'I'm in here, Leon.'

A man came into the room, a man with an aura of power that was unmistakable. 'Are you all right, Emily?'

'Yes, thanks to my friends and sister. How did you know I was in trouble?'

'A young man rang us up. Someone called Toby.'

'Are you mad at me?' Toby came into the room, hesitating by the door, looking ready to run away.

'I'm pleased! You did the right thing,' Emily told him. 'You were very clever.'

He gave her one of his beaming smiles.

'Well done, Toby,' Chad said, and Oliver echoed that.

He continued to smile broadly.

The slightest compliment made him so happy, Emily thought. He was willing to help and work hard. How could anyone ill treat a young man like him?

Chad was looking uncertainly from her to her former partner, as if wondering whether there was still something between them. 'I think we should all sit down quietly with a cup of tea and we'll explain to Leon what's been going on.'

George beckoned to his wife. 'If I'm no longer wanted or trusted, there's no need for us to stay.'

Leon smiled, a tiger's expression. 'There's every need if you've been harassing Emily. Sit down, Mr Pilby, or we'll assist you into a chair.'

'You've no right to order me around and I'm definitely leaving.'

Leon sighed and nodded to a man standing by the entrance to the flat. 'Show him our credentials, James, then make sure he stays.'

The man pulled an ID card out of his pocket and showed it to George who gaped, then moved back into the room.

'I used to work for that unit, *nephew dear*.' Emily turned to Toby. 'Will you please put the kettle on and make us some tea? Are there enough beakers?'

'Use the best beakers too?'

'Yes, please.'

'*He* isn't having a good one.' Toby gestured to George.

The mood in the room suddenly lightened at the sheer outrage on George's face at being spoken to like that.

When everyone was seated, Emily explained the situation to

the newcomers, with the help of Chad. Some of it was clearly unknown to the Barton & Halling people.

Leon nodded and sat thinking for a moment. 'It seems to me the sticking point for clearing this up completely is the validity of the signature. I think Chad's right. There hasn't been time to have it checked.' He gave Chad a nod of approval. 'I know Timothy Parker quite well. I'll just give him a call and ask him. If he hasn't done it already, he'll check the signature for me straight away. We work together sometimes.'

He went out into the front bar and made a call. When he came back, he was smiling. 'They've not got round to that job. Your CEO is lying, Ms Ryling.'

'Then I'll advise him to back away from the case.'

'Best if we have it checked before you go and confront him, just to be a hundred per cent sure.' Leon looked at Emily. 'All right if everyone waits here? I doubt it'll be long before Timothy calls me back.'

'Fine by me, but it might be better if we go out into the front bar, where everyone can sit down. Rachel, do we have any biscuits to offer our guests?'

'I think so. I'll see to that and help Toby with the drinks.'

It was only half an hour before Timothy Parker called Leon back. Everyone fell silent, listening shamelessly, and this time Leon didn't attempt to keep the call private.

When he ended it, he looked across at Emily. 'Now that they've checked the signature, they're certain it isn't yours. Whoever signed it wasn't an expert forger in the tiny details that give people away.' He looked at George. 'I'd like a sample of your handwriting, sir. They may be able to find some points of comparison.'

'I refuse.'

'You can't refuse. We have the authority to search your home or business premises, if necessary, and find samples of your handwriting. If they do match, you'll be in serious trouble for forging a signature.'

Liz suddenly sobbed.

Emily closed her eyes for a moment, then sighed and whispered to Chad, 'I can't do this to her.'

'You'll let George get away with it?'

She shrugged. 'I don't really have the choice. For Liz's sake.' She turned to Leon. 'I don't want to prosecute him. For my sister's sake.'

'You should do.' He grinned suddenly. 'But you always were soft-hearted, which was why we never transferred you to Operations.'

'I never wanted to do that sort of work. I enjoyed the research side of things. You and I are very different, though we make good friends.'

He looked at Chad. 'You two seem very together. Am I right?'

'We're engaged.'

'Thought there was something. I wish you well, but I'm warning you, Chadderley, if you treat her badly or let her down, you'll have me to answer to.'

'I won't.'

Emily turned to her nephew. 'If Leon doesn't need anything else, you'd better leave now, George.'

'You should be very grateful to your aunt,' Liz put in.

'Grateful! I think she's being stupid. I was only trying to look after her money, after all.'

'And you'll no doubt continue to maintain that, whatever people say,' Emily said. 'Well, I'll look after my own money, thank you very much. And none of it will come to you when I die. I'll make sure of that tomorrow.'

He glared at her then turned away.

'Oh, and George . . .'

'Yes?'

'Don't come here again, or to my other house.'

He shrugged and turned to his mother. 'Do you need anything? We'd better leave at once, before my aunt changes her mind yet again.'

'You can stay here, Liz,' Emily said. 'Stay till you decide what you want to do. I'll get you back home when you want.'

'Thank you. I will stay.'

Marcia didn't say anything. She turned and followed George out.

Liz didn't fall about sobbing, as Emily had expected. She turned to Oliver and asked quietly, 'Since you're a lawyer, could you please act for me to get my money back and cancel the power of attorney my son holds?'

'It'll be my pleasure.'

'Thank you.' She stood up. 'I'd like to lie down for a while now, Emily, if you don't mind.'

Rachel stood up too. 'I'll find you a bedroom and settle you in, shall I, Liz? I think your sister still has some other business to sort out.'

Ms Ryling stood up, clearing her throat to get everyone's attention. 'I'll inform the Board of what's happened, but you can take it that the contract is now null and void. I'm sorry for any inconvenience caused, Ms Mattison. If you're out of pocket in any way, we'll pay your expenses, naturally.'

When they'd gone, Emily turned to Leon and held out her hand. 'Thank you.'

He clasped it in his. 'I did promise to guard your back if you ever needed help.'

She smiled wryly and let go of his hand. 'And I promised not to need it. But I did, after all. Thank you for ignoring that rash vow. It'd have taken a lot longer to settle all this without your help.'

'My pleasure. I have some other news. Chadderley, you need to get back to London and stop that ex-wife of yours from milking your business. How much of your memory have you got back now?'

'A fair amount since Marina came to visit me here. What exactly is she doing to the business?'

'What isn't she doing? Some of her deals have come to our attention from other informants. Certain antiques are not allowed to leave the country, as you know. She *will* be prosecuted about that, so I hope you're not as soft-hearted as Emily.'

Emily looked from one man to the other. 'You may know what you're talking about, but I don't.'

'Chadderley here runs a rather exclusive antiques business in London. Or he did till he disappeared suddenly.'

'I was beaten up and left for dead.'

'Yes. We know who did that and we'll be making sure they leave the country and never return. You've made a few enemies with your refusal to act outside the law, you know. Some people, both at home and abroad, will do anything to get hold of items they consider special. Unfortunately we can't prosecute the people concerned without causing a diplomatic incident.'

'So you're not exactly short of money, Chad?' Emily asked.

'No.'

'And you have a life in London.'

'I had a life there. I don't think I want to return to the pressure of it. It was my father who set up the business, who gloried in wheeling and dealing. He died last year. I've been . . . considering my options. Marina has expertise in certain areas and my father insisted she should stay in the business when our marriage broke up and—'

Leon interrupted, 'In the meantime you need to put a stop to what your wife has been doing – ASAP. After that, let my unit smooth things over. I could give you a lift to London. In fact, I'd urge you to come with me. The sooner this is sorted, the better.'

'Unfortunately, you're right. I'll go and get my things.'

Emily listened to this exchange open-mouthed. 'You're just going off and leaving me?'

Chad shook his head. 'Only temporarily, darling. I'll be back as soon as I can. But this matter could be rather urgent and I don't want my company to be prosecuted.'

'Marina will have to be removed completely from your company,' Leon warned him.

'Don't worry. She will be.'

They had left within ten minutes. Chad's final words, after kissing her, were, 'Trust me, Emily.'

She nodded, then stood by the window and watched them leave.

'I'm sure you can trust him,' Oliver said reassuringly.

'Yes, I know I can.' But she still felt upset that Chad had left so quickly.

Surely he would come back? Yes, of course he would. What was she thinking? He loved her and he was free to marry her. She had to hold on to that.

Sixteen

The weather became gloomy as the afternoon turned into evening and this didn't cheer Emily up. She paced to and fro, unable to settle to anything.

She was expecting Chad to call her when he got to London, but the phone didn't ring. Surely he had a mobile phone in his home, wherever that was?

She didn't even know where he was, let alone his phone number.

By eleven o'clock, Liz, Rachel and Oliver had gone to bed. Emily stayed up, waiting for a call. But it didn't come.

The journey to London seemed to take a long time. Chad was lost in his thoughts for most of it, as memories continued to click back into place. He rubbed his head, which was aching, wishing he'd remembered his address and phone number in time to give them to Emily. He'd had to rely on Leon taking him home.

Chad was not surprised that Marina had been pillaging the business. She'd changed so much in the past few years that he didn't recognize her as the woman he'd married and loved. These days she spent a huge amount on staying young and pursuing the much younger lovers she seemed to favour.

Beside him, Leon was working on a smartphone, concentrating so hard he didn't even turn sideways.

They stopped only once, out of need.

As they were approaching London, Leon looked up. 'Where do you want us to drop you?'

'At my home. It's in Richmond.' He gave them the address.

'Do you have a key?'

'No. But it's a luxury flat complex and the porter will be able to let me in.'

'Good.' Leon fished out a business card. 'If you need help urgently, don't hesitate to contact me. Otherwise I'll visit your business tomorrow.'

'You're very kind.'

'I don't want any diplomatic incidents and I think a lot of Emily. See that you treat her right.'

'That's the second time you've said that.'

'And I meant it both times.'

The porter on duty looked up and his face creased into a smile when he saw Chad. 'Are you all right, sir? Mrs Chadderley said you'd been seriously ill and were convalescing.'

'I'm fine, Malcolm, but I've lost my wallet and keys. Could you please let me in?'

The porter looked puzzled. 'Mrs Chadderley is there. She'll be able to let you in, surely?'

'What? She's in my flat?'

'She said you were in hospital and she needed to take things in to you, and to manage your affairs.'

'Did she now?'

'She was very convincing, sir. I'm sorry if I did the wrong thing letting her in.'

'She's always convincing when she wants something. Just let me have the key. I'd like to surprise her.'

He took the lift up to the fourth floor and opened the door as quietly as he could. Lights were showing, so Marina must still be up. He hated the idea of her taking over his flat.

As he closed the door, he heard voices coming from his bedroom, a woman's low laugh, sexy, aroused. Fury surged through him at this further violation of his private space. She could have got him out of that hospital. Instead, she had chosen to leave him there and steal his life . . . and who knew what else?

He had been about to throw her out of the flat, but instead he stayed where he was, thinking furiously.

Not something to rush into. She was clearly staying here. He could use this time to see to other things.

He left the flat as quietly as he'd entered it, asking the porter not to mention his return to his wife, pretending he was planning a big surprise for her. Well, he was. But it wouldn't be a good surprise.

He used the porter's phone to ring the security company who

dealt with his business, identifying himself by the agreed code and arranging to meet them at his office.

Once there, he went inside and asked the two security guys to wait with him.

In his office, he opened the safe and took out some cash, noting with a tight scowl that there was far less than usual. He then went into his secretary's office, where he found further surprises which made him ring her at home, waking her up.

'Petra? It's Chad.'

'Are you all right?'

He explained the situation.

'She fired me, you know. Because I questioned what she was doing. Had me escorted out of the building straight away.'

'You're reinstated as of now, if you want the job.'

'I was thinking of retiring, Chad.'

'Then would you come back for a few weeks and help me put things to rights? Please.'

'Will Marina be working with you?'

'No. She'll not even be allowed in the building again.'

'Then I'll be delighted to help you in any way I can.'

'Could you bear to come now?'

'I couldn't bear to be left out.'

By morning the two of them had pulled together enough evidence to convict Marina of fraud, so he rang Leon to ask him to be ready to deal with it.

Then he returned to the flat, accompanied by Petra, wanting to have a woman as witness, as well as the two guys from the security company.

He opened the door of the flat to find everything dark and silent. He gestured to his companions to stay quiet.

In the doorway of his bedroom he stopped to study Marina and her lover in the chill pale light of early dawn. The man looked much younger than his ex-wife. Another of her toy boys, probably. Chad wasn't concerned with him.

He roared at the top of his voice, 'Out! You, get out of my home!'

They came awake with a start. She screamed and tugged the sheet up to cover herself. The man cursed and eyed Chad apprehensively, staying at the far side of the bed as he scrambled into his clothes.

'Get the hell out of here,' he told the man, and let the security guys see him out.

Then he turned to Marina. 'You have five minutes to get dressed and ready to leave.'

She stared back at him defiantly. 'At least allow me some privacy.'

'I've seen it all before.'

When she'd finished dressing, he gestured to her to go into the living room.

'I think I'd rather go home.'

'You need to wait here for the police. Petra and I spent the night at the office and I have enough evidence to have you arrested. If it had only been theft, I might have let you off, but you left me to rot in that geriatric unit, *paid* for me to be kept quiet there, and I can't forgive that.'

Her face turned chalk white and she sat on the chair he'd indicated, as deflated as a punctured tyre.

'Marina, I'm sure things will be easier if you give me my money back,' Chad said. 'I'm presuming I can't retrieve the antiques you sold at such bargain prices, though I will check them out. Some of them are in the hands of an agency charged with preventing certain secret sales of specially listed antiques overseas.'

'But—'

He held up one hand to stop her speaking. 'Most of my memories came back quickly once I got to the gallery last night, I'm glad to say. I looked round the showroom, so I have a pretty good idea what's missing, and the accounts list the rest. And by the way, the Denassi you bought is a fake. You were cheated. You never were any good at buying paintings.'

She began to plead, 'I worked for this business too, Chad. I had a *right* to take over when you vanished. The boys couldn't have done it.'

'Were you involved in sending those men to kill me?'

'*No!*'

She stared at him in such amazed shock that he knew she hadn't done that, at least.

'You took advantage of the attack, though,' he went on grimly. 'I know about Sister Pauline's little tricks to earn extra money. The police will be arresting her, too.'

'She said you'd never regain your full senses.'

'Or hinted that she could stop me recovering fully, to keep me out of your way.'

A flush stained Marina's cheeks.

'I thought so.'

'What are you going to do?'

'It's out of my hands. You've been playing in some big leagues. I think you should come clean about everything and make a plea for leniency.' He smiled and added, 'Once everything's settled, I'm going to sell the business.'

'*Sell it?*'

'Definitely.' He didn't bother to explain. She already knew he'd had enough of a high-flying city lifestyle, had only stayed to help his ageing father.

It was mid-morning before everyone left and he slumped exhausted on his white leather sofa. One more thing to sort out, then he could sleep.

But this was the most important thing of all.

The day passed slowly and Chad didn't ring. Emily tried to fill the time, but she couldn't settle to anything.

Her friends looked at her pityingly. She didn't want their pity.

Over the midday meal, she said abruptly, 'He *will* phone. Something important must have cropped up.'

They nodded, but she wondered if they believed her.

She didn't eat much, couldn't force it down, so left them still eating and wandered out to the old barn. She felt closest of all to Chad here, because he loved the old building as much as she did.

Peace settled round her like a cloak. The birds twittered in the corner of the roof they used as an entrance.

It took her a moment or two to realize someone had joined her: Toby.

She turned to ask him to leave her alone, but he gave her one of his luminous childlike smiles and her sharp words died unspoken.

'Chad will come back, Emily. I know he will.'

'How do you know, Toby?' And how did he know what she was worrying about?

He shrugged. 'Sometimes I just know things. Miss Penelope said that was good. I don't tell people. Not unless I like them. She told me not to. She told me a lot of things.'

He patted her clumsily and repeated, 'Chad *will* come back.'

'When I'm out here in the barn, I believe he'll return to me.'

'It's nice here. You should stay. It makes you feel better.' He turned and walked out.

After that she sat for a while on an old bench in a corner, and let the peace lift her spirits.

When she felt mentally stronger, she rejoined the others.

Chad would ring as soon as he could. She felt more sure of that now.

Emily was about to go to bed early when her mobile phone rang. She snatched it up, seeing a strange number, but she knew . . . Oh, she knew before he spoke that it was him!

'I'm sorry, Emily darling. I should have rung you sooner. But I was so focused on sorting things out, and it took longer than I'd expected. Then I fell asleep sitting on the sofa, because I'd been up all night.' He explained about his ex-wife.

'So you have a big business in London?'

'Yes. Antiques.'

Her mobile started beeping. 'I can't believe it. My battery is low. I was sure I'd topped it up.'

'I'll ring again in the morning. I'm coming back in a day or two, and then I want us to get married as soon as possible.'

'Yes, please.'

She smiled as she got up to plug her mobile into the charger, feeling young and foolishly happy.

She was still smiling as she lay down and fell fast asleep.

When she awoke to a morning full of sunshine, her first thought was that Chad still loved her. They were getting married.

As soon as possible.

Oh, it was such a beautiful day!

* * *

Chad arrived three days later, driving a late model Mercedes convertible, loaded with flowers, wine and all the ingredients for a celebration.

He looked so elegant, Emily could tell at a glance that his clothes must be very expensive. She felt shy of this new Chad as she walked towards the door.

But when she saw him drop the things he was holding back on to the car seat and reach out his arms to her, she forgot everything but the need to run into his embrace and smother him with kisses.

He held her at arm's length, then pulled her close to kiss her again.

'I missed you so much,' she said.

'I missed you, too.' He began to pick up the parcels. 'Better not drink this champagne till it's calmed down from being dropped. I hope you like chocolates. And flowers.' With a bow made awkward by the need to hold the bottle safely, he offered her the most sumptuous bouquet she'd ever seen, with a broken bloom at one side.

She buried her nose in the flowers, enjoying their wonderful perfume.

'How is everyone?' he asked.

'Fine. Liz is still here. She's looking better already. She and Rachel get on like a house on fire because they both love cooking. And my sister seems to have taken Toby under her wing. She's teaching him to cook as well.'

Chad stopped to look round the outer bar, which now shone with polish. The surplus chairs had been removed, and they had made it a dining area with a table close to the window, where someone had left a laptop. The place looked lived in, if somewhat sparsely furnished.

Chad looked around. 'Where is everyone?'

'Staying tactfully out of sight.'

'If they'll just stay away a little longer, I want to ask you something.'

'Ask away.' She looked up to him, feeling bright and happy, as if the room was filled with sunlight.

'Do you still want to live here?'

She hesitated.

'The truth, mind.'

'I'd prefer to, but not at the cost of being with you.'

'I like it here, too. In recent years I've found London too busy, too dirty, just . . . too much everything. Once my father died, I started planning to move. What do you think of setting up an antiques centre here? Renting out space to other people, perhaps, and selling some of the specialist stuff I'm known for? After all, with the internet and modern technology, I can still hit the international markets. Though I don't want to work nearly as hard as I used to.'

'Will people really come all this way?'

'I think so. But it's your house, so . . .'

'I love that idea. I was going to learn about antiques when I retired. I'd even booked into a course just before my accident, but then Liz had a fall and I had to look after her.'

She hesitated. 'What about Toby? I thought of making him a flat in the rear part, maybe making two or three flats for people like him. He's brilliant at cleaning and setting things to rights, once he's got it fixed in his own mind where things go, so he could work for us. And he loves it here.'

'Good idea.'

She looked at him in wonderment. 'You're agreeing so easily?'

'Yes. I think we're on the same wavelength about a lot of things. I'm so glad we've found one another.'

She sighed. 'Too late to have children, unfortunately.'

'I'd have liked a child by you.'

'Yes. So would I.'

He gave her a quick hug, then his wistfulness faded and he smiled down at her. 'We can do a lot of other things now, though, can't we? Together.'

'Yes.' She hugged him back.

He kept his arms round her. 'No wonder your relative said you'd find hope here. Since we got here, Emily my love, I've been filled with hope, and things have started to go right again for me, so very right.'

'Let's tell them what we're going to do.'

'Yes, let's. But after that I'm going to sweep you away for a few days in a luxury hotel and enjoy your company in style. Will you come? I'm sure Liz and Rachel will look after the pub and Toby.'

'I'll come with you anywhere, Chad.'

Epilogue

Six months later

Reporters from the local newspaper and TV station turned up for the opening. Emily hadn't intended to make a fuss, but Chad said it was good publicity for their new business.

Toby got up even earlier than usual, setting out the breakfast things, making such a clatter that he woke everyone else.

'Moving in today!' he said as soon as Emily and Chad came out of the bedroom.

'Yes, you and the others are moving into the flats today.'

After breakfast he cleared up, as he always did, then went to put on his new clothes. By that time Liz, who had insisted on helping with the catering, had come down.

'Did you sleep well?' Emily asked her.

'Very well, dear.'

'You're looking good. I love that outfit.'

Liz stroked her skirt and top. 'I'd forgotten how much I loved clothes. Where's Toby?'

'Getting ready for the opening.'

'But it's not for two hours yet, surely?'

'He's too excited to wait.'

'He's a nice lad. And I'm so proud of you, Emily, for providing a home for him and the others. It must have cost you quite a bit to convert the back into flats.'

'Chad and I could well afford it and actually, the three of them make ideal employees for the simple tasks here. It turns out Robbie already knows about gardening from when his mother was alive and Nicky loves dusting and polishing. You never saw anyone as careful as she is, even if she is a bit slow.'

'Better safe than sorry with antiques.'

Emily smiled. 'She certainly loves the fine glassware.'

* * *

Two hours later, the guests had all arrived and everyone gathered in what had been the rear bar. They waited for the photographers to set up, then at a nod from Chad, the famous actress Jackie Sanders stepped forward to do the honours.

'How did you get her here?' one of the reporters whispered to Chad. 'She hardly ever does things like this.'

'She had a sister with Down syndrome, so she cares very much for anything connected to helping such people live normal lives. Sadly her sister died quite young, but Jackie is always happy to help others in her name.'

They'd warned Toby and the others about the flashing lights and reporters, but though the three of them stood close together, they didn't get upset.

Toby's expression of sheer bliss when Jackie cut the ribbon and he was waved into his own flat brought tears to Emily's eyes.

This was definitely a place of hope. She intended to keep the tradition alive.

Chad gave her a quick hug. 'Wife of mine, we need to distract the visitors and let our new tenants finish taking possession of their homes in peace.'

Emily clapped her hands together to get people's attention and called, 'We have some refreshments for you.'

'This way,' Rachel said.

Emily lingered to give Chad a big hug. 'It's going well, isn't it?'

'Of course it is.'

'Maybe we can think about helping others, as well as runing our business.'

'I hope so. Come on! I'm ravenous even if you aren't.'

Arm in arm they joined the group. Emily watched Liz chat happily to a woman she'd made friends with in the block of flats where she'd found a home.

Rachel moved over to join Oliver, love showing on both their faces.

So much happiness sparkling in the air today, Emily thought. Long may it continue.